# The Clones of Langston

The Clones of Langston



ISBN 978-0-578-07728-4

Summer Read Publishers
Box 592
Benton, AR 72018-0592

http://ClonesofLangston.com

A teen edition of this book is also available, with subdued language and reduced sexual content. Other adult themes remain unedited.

Cover design by Carol Fullerton-Samsel
Photos © 2011 Catalin Stefan, Antonis Papantoniou, and Kirsty Pargeter. Licensed through BigStock.com

# The Clones of Langston

Carol Fullerton-Samsel

## Author's Writing Awards and Credits

- ☐ Finalist, New Century Writer Awards for Novels/Novellas
- ☐ Nicholls Fellowship competition—top 15% out of 6,073 entries
- ☐ Semifinalist (x2), WriteMovies International Screenwriting Contest—top 6% out of 1,000 entries
- ☐ Semifinalist, 20/20 Screenwriting Competition
- ☐ Semifinalist, International Screenwriting Awards—top 14% out of 1,297 entries
- ☐ Semifinalist, Anything But Hollywood Screenwriting Competition
- ☐ Honorable Mention, Filmmakers Fourth Annual Screenplay Competition
- ☐ An Artist's Path: Two Years Toward Professionalism, ISBN 978-0-578-04486-6, 208 pages

## Contents

## Chapter 1 - Discovery

Twenty-year-old Camryn stood by Brian's bed. "What is it?" she said.

"I don't know," said Brian. "When I picked up my clothes it was underneath."

A translucent tongue flickered at them.

"It climbed up the wall yesterday." He pointed to the edge of the ceiling. "Way up there."

She ran a hand through her blonde hair and scrunched her nose. "But it doesn't have legs."

Brian shrugged.

"You should report it," said Camryn.

"I want to keep it. It's the only animal I've seen. Except for *Rodentiacaca*."

A strip of patterned scales wound across the shadowy floor.

"I bet somebody cloned it. They're probably looking all over for it."

"Then they'll have to keep looking."

"You should report it Brian. Besides, how are you going to feed it? You don't even know what it is."

He nodded. "It's been weeks and it hasn't eaten anything. It wouldn't even try reconstruction."

"Food isn't allowed out of the commissary. You know that."

"Then you shouldn't keep sneaking those snacks into your desk drawer."

Her mouth opened, but she decided not to answer.

"Maybe the authorities will know what to do with it."

Brian frowned. "Kill it. That's what they'll do."

They stood quietly for a time, watching the creature's thin body glide along a wall.

"Does it bite?" said Camryn

"I don't know. I hate to admit it, but I'm afraid to pick it up. I touched it though."

Her eyebrows arched.

"Just for a moment. It was firm; smooth; kind of oily."

Camryn stooped in front of the little animal. "It is pretty. Who'd have thought something like this could have lived?"

She reached a hand toward it and the creature whipped wildly. Camryn stepped back, clutching her hand to her chest. She stood frozen, watching the animal.

Its movement slowed.

"I should just let it bite me and see what happens," she said.

"Now you're being—"

The creature coiled in a corner and Camryn stooped in front of it. The little beast raised its scaly head and spread wide its mouth. It hissed.

"I don't know why I'm so afraid. I don't see any teeth."

"Just leave it be," said Brian. "If you wind up at the clinic, how will we explain it?"

She backed out of her squat. "I'll see what I can find out about— Well, whatever it is."

He took her hand and gave it a squeeze, distracting her from his find. "Just be discreet."

She smiled at him coyly. "Haven't I been discreet so far?"

## Chapter 2 - The Expert

In the lab, Camryn edged up to forty-two year old Dobie and leaned against the counter. "What are you doing?"

"Same thing as the past twenty years."

"Reading DNA sequences?"

"Um hum."

"Anything interesting?"

"Adjusting one of the technical lines. I'm supposed to make them more tractable; and yet free thinking—so they can figure out how to fix things."

"I wish we could see the finished product."

"Our job is to write the sequence, not produce it."

"But wouldn't you like to talk with them?" said Camryn. "I mean, I've talked to some of the messengers; and occasionally to the food handlers—"

"Why doesn't that surprise me?"

She smirked. "What I'm saying is, how do we know we're doing a good job?"

"As long as there are no complaints, I assume everything's fine."

"Have you ever talked to any of them? About how they feel or what they think—or if they think? Have you had an actual conversation with say a technical model—or a medical? Anyone other than a creative?"

He shook his head. "I'm afraid I'd be disappointed."

She smiled mischievously. "I hear you're quite proud of your work. Some say you keep a personalized model locked in your cubicle."

"And hopefully she'll never get out. She might report me to the authorities."

Camryn cocked her head. "I'm sure she'd realize all of your endearing qualities, and wouldn't have the heart."

"You don't have to be nice to me—just because of Brian."

She shrugged. "Brian thinks very highly of you. He admires your ingenuity."

"You mean he fears my ingenuity."

She didn't answer.

"But tell me Camryn, what do you think of me?"

Her lips pursed as she considered his question. "You pretty much keep to yourself. Spend a lot of time on the computer. But you must know more about ancient animals than anyone else in the sphere."

"You've pulled my research history? My files?"

"Nothing like that. Sometimes I see the screen from across the room. All kinds of wonderful beasts! Sometimes I want to come over for a look, but I know you don't like me much."

"I don't dislike you."

"When I'm around Brian you're polite enough. But most of the time you don't even acknowledge me."

"So did you come over here just to make me feel guilty?"

"Maybe I just wanted to say hi."

He blushed. "Okay. Hi."

"Plus, something's prying on my mind. I wanted to ask you—"

His blush deepened. His chest froze mid-breath.

"Hypothetically—"

He gave a quick nod.

"If someone happened to see something unusual—"

He began to let out a tiny bit of air.

"But didn't quite know exactly what they'd seen—"

The blush faded and he turned back to his work.

"I bet you could tell them what it was."

"So," he sighed. "What does this sequence of yours look like? The one that you saw?"

"Well, actually it's a whole series of sequences. Put together so that it's living and breathing."

His jaw dropped. "You've seen it, haven't you?"

She took a step back, her face blanching. "Seen what?"

"Whatever it is that Brian's been hiding!"

"What's Brian got to do with this?"

"I know he has *something* in his cubicle. We usually hang out there, but lately he won't let me in; always wants to meet in the commissary or the lab. Something's in there."

"Like what?"

"Well I don't know, because I haven't seen it. But you have, haven't you?"

"Sometimes Dobie you get the strangest ideas."

She turned to leave, and he put a hand on her arm. "Hypothetically—," he soothed. "What might this thing you saw look like?"

"I only saw it in passing."

"It's all right Camryn. Brian's my friend. I don't want to get him—or you—in trouble."

The rims of her eyes began to redden.

"That gross, huh? You know, with enough persistence and research you could probably find the answer yourself."

"There might not be time for that. It hasn't eaten for weeks. It's bound to die."

"Let me understand this. Brian cloned—what I presume is an animal—and he doesn't know what it eats?"

"He didn't clone it. He found it. Look. I wasn't supposed to say anything. If you're going to turn anyone in, could you just report me and leave Brian out of it?"

"And what happens when they question you? I can see you're slick at hiding your feelings."

"Just promise me."

"I'll tell you what. Come by my cubicle tonight, and we'll figure it out."

"We might need a computer though."

"Maybe, but then things will be quieter around here and there'll be fewer questions." He raised an eyebrow toward a coworker across the room. "Harmon's probably wondering why you're talking to me right now."

She met Harmon's inquiring gaze, and then lowered her eyes.

"Come on," said Dobie. "I'll tell my sexy clone to be on her best behavior."

She thought for a moment, and then nodded.

"It's a date then. Let me finish with these, and I'll see you later. And bring some of those snacks you've been stashing."

## Chapter 3 - Contraband

She stood at the door and pressed the button again.

Dobie answered, sliding the door aside manually, just wide enough to squeeze through. "Hi," he said, joining her in the corridor.

"I was beginning to think you'd changed your mind."

"No, but I think you're right. We're going to need a computer."

"I had a little trouble finding you back here, even with your directions. Why aren't you in one of the dorms like everyone else?"

"I have a bit of insomnia. This way, if I can't sleep, I'm closer to the lab—and something to do."

She nodded to a door as they passed. "Who's in that one?"

"Storage I think."

"And that one?"

"More storage?"

"Aren't you lonely back here?"

"Nah. Sheila keeps me company."

"Sheila?"

"You know. My personalized clone."

"Well in that case, it *is* best you keep to yourself. The corporation tends to frown on unauthorized clones, you know."

They entered the lab. Their hands brushed as they reached for a switch on the wall. The overhead lights flickered.

"What if someone comes in?" she asked.

"Then they'll see me working at night—as usual."

"But they'll also see *me* working at night—highly unusual."

"Yes. Well, we have all noticed your lack of enthusiasm."

Her mouth opened a bit.

"And it's curious. You seem very loyal to the corporation; yet the corporation values productivity above all else."

"Sometimes I just want to enjoy myself," said Camryn. "You know—relax and have some fun."

"Here?"

"It's just hard to get enthused about work when I'm denied the results."

"Knowledge would only interfere with productivity."

"I always fulfill my assignments. My productivity rating is actually very high."

"You needn't defend yourself. I highly admire your lack of focus."

"Could we just get to work?"

"Not so fast," he said. "I think some snacks would be in order."

"Why does everyone think I'm sneaking food?"

"Nobody opens and closes their drawer that much. Or chews thin air."

"I'll make you a deal. Let's get to work, assume I've nothing in my desk, and I won't say anything about Sheila."

"Fair enough."

"And how do you rate a computer at *your* desk?"

Dobie shrugged. He took a seat and Camryn pulled up a chair. "So," he sighed, "what does this creature of yours look like?"

"It's hard to describe."

He pushed a data pad toward her. "Draw."

She drew a circle attached to a squiggly line.

"Oh!" he said. "I can tell you what that is!"

"What?"

"Sperm!" He looked at the drawing a second time. "Yes. Definitely sperm."

"It's not!"

"Round head. Moving tail."

"The tail's really long," she said, holding her hands apart. "Like this."

"What does the head look like? Does it have a big snout? Little ears?"

"Like a circle. Maybe an oval. I didn't see any ears."

"And where are its legs?"

"It doesn't have legs either."

"Are you sure you're not describing Brian's wiggly? It can be quite a shocker the first time you see one."

Camryn reddened. She bumped a stack of yellowed papers filled with charts and formulas, and it slid off the desktop. The items fell into a loose pile on the floor and something clapped on top.

"What's this?"

"Leave it," said Dobie. "I'll get it later."

"Is it a box?" She reached down and lifted it gently with both hands. "No," she mused, "papers." A few sheets slipped from the collection. Camryn pressed the remaining sheets together to keep them in place, and then found they were attached.

"It's called a book."

"Clever the way the paper's all stuck in like that."

He reached toward it and she drew it away. "Can I take a look?"

"You probably shouldn't. It's considered contraband."

"Yes?"

"It's very old. Maybe before the time of computers. Who knows?"

"Before the corporation?"

"Could be."

She looked down at the loose pages lying about her. One had a fanciful picture of an animal with great horns.

Dobie helped her gather the strays, and then watched her face as she leafed through the book. Her mouth lipped the captions beneath each illustration. He watched the lips move.

"Where did you get it?" she asked.

"Found it."

"Found it where?"

He pointed to an animal with brown spots and a long neck. "I like that one."

"You think someone made all these animals up? I can hardly believe—"

"They're real. Or at least they used to be."

She ran a finger around the giraffe. "What are these things behind it?"

"Trees."

"They're plants?"

He nodded.

"I saw a plant once—a real one. About so big." She held up her thumb and index finger. "So we could make all of these?"

"In theory. Some of the DNA isn't in the library though. I've checked."

"How long have you had this?"

"I don't know. I thought I'd lost it. Guess I need to organize my stacks every now and then."

"Do you think our animal would be in here?"

"You can look if you want. I'll try the computer."

"This one looks like *Rodentiacaca.*"

He leaned over for a closer look. "Lemur," he read. His breath floated a strand of her hair. The warmth about her cheek seared his. Reluctantly he drew away. "So are you going to tell the authorities? About the contraband?"

She flipped to another page. "Umm huh. After I've looked at the pictures."

When she noticed his silence, she looked up. "Just kidding. I won't mention it to anyone."

"I just wondered. I heard that you reported someone once—for keeping a plant."

"Well yes, but I was only eight years old. She was my best friend."

"You turned in your best friend?"

"I was eight! I was just following the rules."

"The rules haven't changed."

"It's just a bunch of paper. I'm sure it's valuable, but I don't think there's any danger to it."

"But who knows what eons-old, DNA-altering bacteria might be lying in wait—there on those very pages?"

She rubbed her fingers together.

"Don't worry," he said. "I've had it for years and I'm still alive."

"Besides," she said, "if I report your book, you could report Brian's creature."

"I would never report a friend."

"I was eight! Nothing happened! The authorities came and gave her a scare; that's all. They tore up her plant and stomped on it, and then hugged her when she cried. She never broke the rules again."

"Or confided it to you."

"You think she had other secrets?"

"You'd never know."

"So if she had the plant, and you have this book, and Brian has his little creature, does that mean I'm the only one not breaking the rules?"

"Depends. Are we still overlooking the snacks in your desk drawer?"

"The alleged snacks."

"And the fact that you're helping Brian keep an unauthorized animal? And that you're helping me conceal a contraband book?" He gently took the book from her hands and laid it on the other side of his desk. "Your animal's not in there."

"How do you know?"

"Everything in there has legs."

## Chapter 4 - Mouse32

"Okay," Camryn mumbled to herself. "Let's get some food for Brian's snake." Her fingers tapped out a search and a menu appeared.

*Results for primordial mouse:*

1) *Mouse32: Origin of genetic predispositions*
2) *Recombinant DNA creates ultimate lab animal*
3) *Lab mouse. Variants available.*

"Let's try number three."

*Results for lab mouse variants available:*

1) *Epileptic Qualified engineers only*
2) *Diabetic Qualified engineers only*
3) *Alopecic Qualified engineers only*
4) *White Qualified engineers only*

*5) Recombinant Macaca*

*Qualified engineers only*

Camryn scanned the results, and then typed "Dictionary: Epileptic."

A small window appeared on the screen.

*One who has epilepsy, a dysfunction of the neurological system presenting as recurrent episodes of convulsive seizure or an altered state of consciousness.*

"Better go with white. At least I know what that is."

*Order placed. Confirmation number ZZ8972.*

"But what if someone asks? I was curious what they looked like?" She shook her head. "I could have searched visuals for that." She scratched her chin. "I bet a colleague that I could obtain some original mouse DNA? Which colleague? How about... I was helping my boyfriend? Definitely not."

She smiled to herself. "What am I worrying about? Brian won't say anything. Dobie's got the book, so he can't report me. What if the professor finds out? Maybe if I order a couple of common samples, it won't seem so suspicious."

"Can I borrow that computer?"

Camryn jumped at the voice.

"Mine's processing a formula," said Dobie. "And the other one's taken."

"Oh. It's you. Just placing the order."

"I thought you were upping your productivity level—afraid the corporation might discontinue your genetic code."

"I hope they do," said Camryn. "I like thinking I'm one of a kind."

"Don't we all? I just hope they don't clone another Engineer Seven-ninety-seven until I'm gone."

"No one could replace you, Dobie. Why a new clone would be all fresh and wrinkle-free. It wouldn't be the same at all."

"I'm not *that* old."

She ignored his protest and typed in the order.

"Okay. Done. It's all yours." She touched his sleeve as she rose to leave. "I appreciate your help. I hope you know that."

"It's all right," mumbled Dobie, taking her chair. "As long as *Brian's* safe and happy. That's what's *really* important."

## Chapter 5 - Corridor Thirteen

*Corridor 13. Compartment 9.*

*Vial 54/89.*

*CLASSIFIED.*

*Corridor 9. Compartment 3.*

*Vial 24/62.*

*Rodentiacaca.*

*Common name Mouse232.*

*Corridor 8. Compartment 6.*

*Vial 62/98.*

*Rodentiacaca sapient.*

*Common name Mouse232-5.*

A librarian in the archival compound received the order. His lips moved as he rehearsed it a few times.

Carrying a small box, he passed down a long tunnel and entered Corridor Eight. He retrieved a sample of mouse two-thirty-two-five and continued to Corridor Nine, where he collected the last remaining vial of two-thirty-two.

In Corridor Thirteen, he wandered the aisles, each of which was walled with environmentally-controlled compartments. Each compartment held flats of stumpy vials and cards with gelatinous smears.

He selected a vial and held it to the light, imagining what legendary animal might dwell within. Was it huge? Could a hoselike nose wrap a person and squash them lifeless? A part of him hoped so.

He placed the vial into the container, and then turned the knobs on the box to match the compartment settings.

He returned to his station and, remembering that he'd retrieved the last vial of a kind, sent notice to the head librarian.

> *Mouse232 to be sealed. See final order issued below.*

***

The head librarian read the message over her assistant's shoulder.

"Not good," said the assistant. "Nothing makes an engineer crankier than to tell them a line's run out."

The head librarian laughed. "The last time that happened, you'd have thought the waves were crashing in."

"Yeah, and we just about drowned in complaints," he said. "It's funny how one line can be used up so quickly, while others sit for decades—sometimes generations. See. Here's a request from Corridor Thirteen. No seal on that one."

"No one asks for anything that old! Make sure it's not a mistake. Send an inquiry to the originating librarian, would you?"

The assistant typed.

> *Please confirm request for vial 54/89, Corridor 13.*

They waited.

> *Confirmed. Requested by Engineer 621. See engineer for further information.*

"Should I ask what kind of DNA?" asked the assistant.

"No, because he won't know. Items in that corridor are classified."

"Wait. Another message."

> *I hope they're cloning an elephant. I'd like to see one of those.*

"What's an elephant?" said the head librarian.

The assistant shrugged, and then typed "Dictionary: Elephant."

*Herbivorous animal approximately 7 m at the shoulder and weighing approximately 5,800 kg, having a long, muscular nose used for grasping, large fanning ears, and long, outwardly pointing upper incisors used for digging and combat.*

"Don't want that thing running around!" said the assistant.

"Better notify the authorities."

"We don't know that elephant was ordered though."

"No," said the head librarian, "and it probably wasn't. But I don't mind making a little trouble for the creatives, do you? Keeps them humble."

"I guess so."

"Go ahead. Make the authorities work a little too."

The assistant typed.

*Order placed to DNA library for unknown item. Old DNA no longer used. Suspicious? Item requested by Engineer 621.*

## Chapter 6 - Trust

Camryn glanced over at Brian as he worked, pausing a moment to consider Harmon and Penny and what contraband *they* might be hiding. Her eyes moved toward Dobie. She started a bit when he smiled and nodded back.

"It should be here shortly," she thought.

She pictured the professor signing for it. "Dangerous order," the old man reprimanded, laying it on her desk.

"Professor— I could be involved with something I shouldn't be. Can we talk?"

He grunted. "You're a creative, Camryn. One of a select few. The group with the most flexible genetic arrangement. You should, after all this time, be able to think for yourself."

She shook herself from her thoughts, as a messenger entered the lab. In his hands was a small black box. Camryn watched him cross the room, and suppressed a gulp. In protest, her leg jerked spasmodically beneath her desk. She attempted to hear better than her ears might allow, catching snatches of the messenger's remarks. "Delivery for— Is it— elephant?"

The professor gave his usual grunt and dismissing nod. He set the box aside before returning to his work.

Camryn scribbled on a data pad for effect, but her eyes returned to the little box on the counter. The professor cleared away several pieces of equipment, and Camryn hoped he'd finished for the day. He retrieved more equipment from the cupboards and drawers and then, with a surprisingly agile hop, settled himself atop his lab stool.

Camryn eased out of her chair. Feeling a bit lightheaded, she reminded herself to breathe. Her fingertips dragged across the desktop as she stepped forward, and then paused at its edge.

Across the room, Dobie left his desk. He stopped a moment to speak with Harmon and then, hands tucked into lab coat, made his way toward the box. "Is this—?" He read the digital label and shook his head. "I'll take it to— Thanks."

Dobie fixed his eyes on Camryn as he handed her the container. "Your *sperm* order ma'am."

Hearing the word, Harmon glanced at them. Camryn rolled her eyes and shook her head. When Dobie was again seated, she carried the box to an open computer station.

"Now what?" she typed.

"I'll see if they'll work it in," Dobie replied.

"How long will it take?"

"Don't know. Do you know the growth rate?"

She looked over at him and shook her head.

"Don't look! Type!"

"Won't they want something in exchange?"

"Probably. They're taking a risk."

She hesitated. "Have you done this before?"

"Do you really want to know?"

"No."

"A few times, and you're right. They'll want something."

"What?" typed Camryn.

"The book."

"You gave it to me."

"I loaned it to you."

"I'm not done looking at it."

"Do you have something else then?"

"Clothes?"

"Our wardrobes are limited. Don't think so."

"Everything's limited," argued Camryn.

"Do *you* have any contraband?"

Her heart pounded at the question. She scanned the room, assuring herself that others couldn't hear her thoughts. "The corporation provides all," she typed.

There was a long pause.

"The book then," Dobie replied.

Camryn hesitated before answering. "Do you have anything?"

"I HAD the book. This is YOUR project. Remember?"

"Maybe it's already dead."

"You're giving up then?"

She looked toward Brian, who was speaking with Penny. Penny, she thought, seemed overly flirtatious.

"Okay. The book. How? When?"

"Tonight at the commissary."

"How will I know who to give everything to?" asked Camryn.

"You won't. I'll make contact."

"Then how will I know who's doing the work?"

"You won't. That's part of the deal."

She frowned at the screen. She typed something, deleted it, and then began again. "Does ANYBODY trust me? How come they trust you?"

"A) Should they?  B) I'm cute"

She felt annoyed at B; stared at A.

"Yes, they should trust me," she wanted to answer. "No," she thought. "Maybe." She wanted to be a person with books—to see the cloned mouse before it disappeared into the snake. But she worried about gaining too much knowledge—the responsibility and consequences that knowledge might bring.

"Do YOU trust me?" she typed.

The lack of response made the blood rush to her head. She typed again. "Do you trust me? Do you trust me? Do you trust me?"

An answer flashed onto the screen.

"Do you trust yourself?"

Her temples throbbed. Her chest burned with stale air. Her hand moved toward the keyboard. A finger pressed "Clear."

## Chapter 7 - The Investigation

"Do you mind if I call you Jorge?"

The old man gazed into the enforcer's brown eyes. His attention returned to the sequencing monitor. "I'd just assume you call me Professor."

"Professor then."

"You're still standing next to me. I take that you want something."

"Can we speak privately?"

The old man looked around. "Everyone's at breakfast."

"Can we go somewhere where we won't be interrupted?"

"Say what you want, and perhaps you'll finish before someone comes in."

The enforcer sighed. "It's about one of your engineers. Engineer Six-twenty-one."

"I'm afraid I'm on a single-digit basis with my colleagues."

"Female. Blonde."

"I never greet colleagues by number," the professor reiterated.

"Camryn. Her name's Camryn."

"Ah yes. One of our less gifted members to be sure."

"Less gifted?"

"Competent. Can't say much beyond that. Performs her assigned duties, but never innovates. So tell me. What did our poor Camryn do to bring the authorities upon us?"

"She placed an order for some very unusual DNA. It hasn't been requested in years, and appears to be some ancient line. We're hoping you can tell us why it would be needed."

"Is it plant DNA or animal?"

"We don't know. Since you have access to the same information as Engineer Six-twenty-one, I thought you might tell us."

"I can assure you Enforcer, that if this atypical item was ordered by Camryn, there's no need for alarm."

"What is it she's working on?"

"I have no idea."

"But you direct the lab."

"In name. My colleague Dobie does the real work. My years—they're running out. I'm beginning to wonder," he growled, ""if I'll survive to read these samples."

"But you must have some idea what your engineers are working on."

The professor sighed. "In a truly creative environment, no one rules another. We share ideas. It's an exchange. Occasionally we collaborate. I have a thought! Why don't you just ask Camryn?"

"Jorge—"

"Professor Nine-eighty-three if you don't mind."

"I'll be sure to note your lack of cooperation in my report."

"And who exactly receives your report?"

"The corporation."

"Who in particular in the corporation?"

"I give the report to my superior, who then forwards it to the appropriate department."

"And you're sure your superior forwards it?"

"It's his duty."

"And if he does forward it, how do you know the appropriate person in the appropriate department will not simply click 'File: Store'?"

"I carry out my duties and trust others to do the same. Those who are not loyal to the corporation are dealt with by the authorities."

"And who files their reports again?"

"There are others in the creative compound with access to this same information."

"True, but if you can't verify the information they supply is correct, then how do you know they're not misleading you?"

"Because they're more loyal to the corporation than Professor Nine-eighty-three!"

"Indeed. I must agree with you there. Were it up to me, the sphere would be punctured by now and we'd be swimming for our lives—or drowning in the attempt."

## Chapter 8 - The Interrogation

The room wasn't as scary as Dobie had imagined. It was, however, a lot pinker. The chairs were pink, and even the carpet had a rosy tinge. The walls were fuchsia, taking on orange and violet hues as ever-changing ceiling colors drifted overhead.

He wondered if this is what detainment might be like. Perhaps he'd been imprisoned already, things being so different. The walls in the lab were gray after all, as were the counters, cabinets, and stool coverings. "At least here," he considered, "there's some color."

He watched the door and wondered how long he'd been waiting. Gradually, his eyes returned to the ceiling. He wondered what type of trade—okay, bribe—might make a spectrolight ceiling available to the lab. He considered whether the violets might make the professor's white hair look purple.

The door slid open and Dobie jerked to attention. His heart pounded but, left ankle on right knee, he slumped into his armchair.

The enforcer took a seat on a small sofa across from him. "Unusual," Dobie thought, "for an enforcer to have brown hair and dark eyes." He wondered if the sequencing was some of his own.

The enforcer shifted a bit and squared his shoulders. Dobie considered how comical he looked, this large man in black sitting so uncomfortably upright on a tiny pink couch.

"I hope I didn't interrupt your work too much," said the enforcer.

"Any diversion is a welcome one."

"Would you like anything to eat?"

"Is the food pink too?" Dobie asked.

"Same as your own, I'm afraid."

"Oh."

"I thought," said the enforcer, "that it might be easier to bring you here, rather than speak with you in the lab."

"Exactly where is 'here'?"

"You're in the inquiry lounge."

*The inquiry lounge*. The words reminded him of a scene in a contraband detective novel. Dobie chewed on the tip of his tongue to keep from laughing.

A band of red on the ceiling passed slowly overhead, giving the enforcer's cheeks a crimson glow.

"You're smiling," said the enforcer.

"The color here— It's dizzying."

The crimson band crept down the enforcer's face to form a pink mustache. Dobie began to snicker.

The enforcer raised an eyebrow. He cast his eyes downward, and fingered a hole in his shirt.

Dobie laughed. "I'm sorry," he choked. Bits of moisture sprayed from his mouth as he attempted an apology. "I'm truly sorry."

Seeing the enforcer's confused expression, Dobie now guffawed. Tears puddled in his eyes and zigzagged down his face.

"Are you all right?"

He wheezed and sputtered, trying to catch his breath.

The enforcer was at Dobie's side. "Do you need something? Are you on medication?"

Now Dobie howled. He hanged himself over the chair arm. His face was red and drooling.

The enforcer turned his head; spoke into his lapel. "Get a doctor here now!"

Dobie's laughter slowly subsided.

"Why don't you lie on the floor," said the enforcer.

Dobie waved an open palm at him. "I'm all right."

"Hold that order," said the enforcer, again into his lapel. "I think he's coming around."

Dobie wiped his nose on the edge of his shirtsleeve. Disgust crossed the enforcer's face, nearly setting him off again. Slowly, he righted himself. Unable to speak, he pointed toward the agent's neck.

"Oh. The microphone? It's for emergencies."

"Am I being recorded?"

"We document all inquiries."

Dobie rubbed his face with his hands, trying to smooth out the smile and regain his composure. "I'm not on medication."

"Should I give you a few minutes?"

"No. I'm okay. I'm here for a reason. Better find out what it is."

The enforcer stiffly repositioned himself on the pink sofa. "Jorge—your supervisor—told me you're an exceptional engineer. He seems to hold you in very high regard."

"Are you two friends?" said Dobie.

"Acquaintances."

"You talk together a lot?"

"Just in passing."

"How many times have you passed? I haven't seen you in the lab."

"Not important," sighed the enforcer. "Some of the people in the lab say that you're very close to a particular coworker."

"I'd like to think I'm friendly with everyone."

"We're only concerned with one. Her name's Camryn."

Dobie shifted involuntarily and hesitated before replying. "Is she the redhead perhaps? I thought her name was Penny, but I guess I wasn't paying attention."

"According to our records, you've been with the same people for several years. Surely you know their names and who's who by now."

"Not as well as you do apparently."

"Your colleague Harmon says you talk with her a lot."

"Who? The redhead?"

"Camryn. A blonde. He says you've been spending a lot of time with her lately."

"Oh, her? We decided to call a truce," said Dobie. "Until recently we didn't speak. Highly unproductive."

"You didn't get along?"

"We didn't get along, or not get along. She barely knew I was alive."

"But you wanted her to?"

"I wanted us to be on speaking terms. We're in the same lab after all."

"Does she confide in you?"

"Who? Camryn? I only just got to know her."

"But you're already close."

"Not really. I think she's kind of cute, so I try to chat with her when I can. You think she's cute, don't you?"

The enforcer opened his mouth, and then closed it abruptly.

"Because I don't see that many women. She might be plain ugly for all I know. We only see the girls in our compound, and mostly the ones in our own lab."

"Have you kissed her?" asked the enforcer.

"Thought about it." His eyes sparkled. "Do you think she'd let me?"

"I wouldn't know about that."

"I know, but if you had to guess—"

The enforcer frowned. "I understand you took a box of DNA samples to her."

"When was this? I don't remember it."

"A messenger dropped them off?"

"Oh, those? I thought they were mine, but when I checked the label they weren't."

"Do you know what she's using the DNA for?"

"We're geneticists, so we use DNA all of the time. Maybe if you tell me what she's working on—"

"We don't know what she's working on. We're hoping you can tell us."

He shrugged. "We mostly work on our own projects, and with DNA somewhat frequently."

"But not from Corridor Thirteen."

Dobie coughed. "Is that something special?"

"I thought you might know," said the enforcer. "Have *you* ordered anything from Corridor Thirteen?"

"I don't think so."

"If we provide the sample number, will you look it up for us? Tell us exactly what she ordered?"

"Why don't you just ask this Camryn girl?"

"Because she's the one under investigation. It might tip her off, don't you think?"

"Why don't you ask the librarian who filled the order?"

"Corridor Thirteen is restricted. For security purposes, the librarians retrieve samples by number. They don't know what individual vials contain."

"I'm afraid I can't help you," said Dobie. "It's against the engineer's creed."

"The engineer's creed?"

"The rules the creative compound lives by—so that everyone can get along. Surely there are certain unwritten rules among your colleagues."

"So this 'creed' isn't really a set of rules."

"More like a set of expectations. According to the creed—let me see how to explain it. Now how does it go again? Oh yes. No engineer will usurp the work of another."

"I don't see how looking an item up on the computer usurps anyone's work."

"It might give me some idea as to what her project is, and she might want to keep that to herself."

"If you're so concerned about staying out of her work, then why did you just ask me what she was working on?"

"A slip. Can't help but be curious sometimes. Won't happen again."

"Professor Nine-eighty-three didn't mention this 'creed.'"

"Professor Nine—? Oh, the professor! Did he retrieve the information for you?"

The enforcer regarded him contemptuously.

"I guess not," said Dobie, "because if he had, I wouldn't be here then. Would I?"

"If you won't help me, I'm sure someone else will."

"Maybe you could ask someone in a different lab."

"We thought of that, but yours is the only one with access to older samples."

Dobie pulled his shoulders to his ears.

"But you're right," said the enforcer. "Someone else will help us. I hope you won't mind, but we'll have you stay the night. You understand that we can't have you talking to anyone else in the lab—not until we've completed our investigation."

"But—"

"And don't worry. The cell you'll be taken to won't be quite so pink."

## Chapter 9 - The Messenger

The cell was less pleasant than the inquiry lounge. Here the only bit of color was a large, brown stain on the cot's mattress. Dobie wondered whether it might be blood or excrement.

He played with the gray glob on his plate. Reconstruction was apparently the same in every compound. He took another spoonful.

Dobie thought one night had gone by, and that he might be approaching a second. It was hard to tell, with no activity or lighting change to mark the passing hours.

He laid the plate on the floor. Stretching out on twisted sheets, he forced his eyes closed. He worried that the authorities might lie. That they might tell Camryn he'd betrayed her. Maybe she'd panic and tell them about the book—or about Sheila.

The doors hissed open and Camryn entered the cell with the enforcer. Dobie smiled at her, but she ignored him, focusing instead on his captor.

"This the one who gave you the book?" said the enforcer.

"He's the one. I don't have it any more though. He slipped it to someone at the commissary."

"Do you know who?"

Dobie tried to remember if he'd confided in her.

"It was the redhead."

"From the cloning compound?"

"That's right."

"The redhead's Penny!" thought Dobie. "She's in *our* compound."

"And he gave Penny the book? To get her to clone a snake?"

"Um huh. A snake for a bear to eat."

That wasn't right! Dobie tried to talk, but his lips wouldn't open. He watched Camryn's face, but she continued to smile up at the enforcer.

The enforcer turned to go and Camryn followed.

Dobie shadowed them, hoping to squeeze through the door. The hydraulic door hissed; gripped his hand. He pulled and then yanked. It wouldn't come loose. He awoke.

The twisted sheet was looped tightly around his wrist. The plate on the floor clattered against his foot as he bolted upright, struggling against the tangle.

Through bleary eyes, Dobie saw a man standing at the door. "Come with me," said the messenger.

Dobie fingered the sheets to reassure himself he was awake. He pulled himself up from the cot. "Am I okay to go?"

"Not today. Enforcer Nine-eighty-six asked that I read the following statement to you." The messenger pulled a small data pad from his pocket. "This is to notify you that you are under investigation, and will be detained until such investigation has been completed."

"They're not investigating *me*!" argued Dobie.

The messenger motioned for him to follow.

"I was just brought here for questioning."

"I just read the statements. I don't validate them. Let's go."

"Where? The lab?"

"Detainment compound."

"Where's that? I mean, why? I haven't done anything."

"If you would just follow me."

"I want to know where I'm going."

The messenger started down the corridor. "Look," he called back. "I hear the detainment compound isn't that bad."

Dobie trotted up to him. "Compared to what?"

"The cell you were just in for one thing."

"A latrine would be better than that."

"And detainment's better a latrine, so things are looking up."

"My lab's going to worry."

"I'm sure your superior will be notified."

"Could you pass along a message?" said Dobie. "Could you just tell my boss I'm being held? See, there's this technical line I was working on. It needs to be sent out for cloning. It's important."

The messenger checked a map on his data pad. "This way please."

"We've been working on it for months," said Dobie.

He appeared not to listen.

Dobie walked a few steps behind, and then stopped altogether in protest. "So this compound— Where is it?"

"It'll take several hours to get there. It's far away from everything else of course."

"I guess that makes sense," said Dobie, coming up beside him. "I'm really not that frightening though, am I? That I need to be locked up?"

"I don't know what you did."

"That makes two of us."

"This way now."

"What are the others there for? The ones in detainment? Did they murder someone? Steal?" Dobie felt his heart pulsing in his neck. "Are they nuts?"

"My job is to drop you off. As long as you don't cause me trouble, I won't cause you trouble."

"But you've met them, haven't you?"

"Actually, you're the first one I've taken to detainment."

"Well how many are there? In the compound?"

"Guess not many if you're the first one I've taken. Most people are good citizens."

"I'm a good citizen."

"Obviously you did something."

"I'm just being held for questioning. They're investigating someone else."

The messenger shrugged.

"Really," said Dobie. "Yesterday, or at least I think it was yesterday— I know I acted kind of goofy but—"

"Oh, so you're the one they're talking about!"

"Something struck me funny. I started laughing. I'm not crazy."

"It's not my job to pass judgment. If it makes you feel any better, you seem sane enough to me. But then, I spend all of my time walking people and messages through corridors and tunnels. How sane is that?"

"How old are you?" said Dobie.

"Twenty. Why?"

"I engineered your line!"

"Now I know who to blame for my boring life."

"I'm just the engineer," said Dobie. "The corporation decides where the line's placed—what it does."

"I guess there are worse jobs. I could be in Reconstruction, making food."

"So now you can thank me."

"Who are you anyway, to create me in the first place? To say what traits I should and shouldn't have? What traits anyone should or shouldn't have?" He looked at Dobie scornfully. "You don't seem all that fabulous yourself!"

"I don't decide anything," said Dobie. "The corporation sends me guidelines. I follow them more or less."

"Looks like your line needs the work. You're the one going to detainment."

They walked for a time, the messenger exuding hostile silence.

"You must have some life beyond this," said Dobie. "You must think about other things; hopefully more pleasant things than what traits you've been denied."

"What's the point? My life is set. As long as the corporation is productive, what else matters, right?"

"Do I detect a bit of cynicism?"

"What good does thinking do if you do the same job the same way each and every day?"

"But you meet all kinds of people in your job. That must be fascinating. You've probably met every line that's ever been made."

"I meet people briefly. Most are quick to point out that their lines are considered superior to mine. I could argue the point, but figure their egotism is predetermined—preprogrammed if you will."

"I can guarantee you that it's primarily acquired."

"Anyway, why argue with them? Even if I was the smartest person in the entire sphere, I'd have to perform the same role."

"Maybe you are the smartest!"

The messenger smirked.

"I designed your line. I can tell you that it's superior to most."

"Why would you make a messenger line superior?"

"Because your line links to so many others."

A smile flickered across the messenger's face.

"Look," said Dobie. "Those in the creative compound have the most variation—the most ability to think for themselves. The most imagination."

The smile faded.

"No!" said Dobie. "I don't mean it that way! I was just about to say that our lives are dull beyond imagination. We're pressured to be productive like everyone else, but we're dying to think about anything other than work. There've been times when I've wondered if the corporation might be better off with a little less productivity and a little more play. Sometimes I wish everyone would just break out into utter, unproductive chaos!"

"With words like that, I can see why you're going to detainment."

Dobie sobered. "I was just talking. I know the corporation is important. The corporation provides all."

"Don't worry," said the messenger. "If I reported everything someone confessed—or everything I'd overheard—well it would definitely interfere with productivity."

"And we wouldn't want that."

"Of course not," said the messenger.

Dobie sighed. "I would like to get back to my cubicle, though."

"If you're as bored as you say you are, you might like detainment better."

"What do you mean?"

The messenger shrugged. "One man went there. They asked him to come back, but he never did. Never even replied to their requests. He's been there for years now. Must have liked something about it."

"How many years?"

"Fifteen. Sixteen. Maybe longer. Sometime before I started."

"But that's the exception, right? What's the average?"

"Most are there a while I suppose."

"A week?"

There was no answer.

"A month?"

There was still no answer.

"More than a month?"

"I don't know. Forever?"

Dobie mouthed the word.

"But what do I know? I mean, you're the only one I've ever taken. And remember, I've only been working five years. And they asked that one man to come back, but he didn't. And it was entirely his decision."

Dobie wasn't responding, and the messenger's voice grew shaky. "I mean, they used to send him messages. 'You're free! Meet the messenger at the door to return to your compound and assigned duties.' But nothing."

Dobie stammered. "But you would know, wouldn't you? If he died?"

"Maybe."

"Because he might have had an accident. I assume somebody checked."

"No one but detainees is allowed in. But he was a young man when he left. He's probably still alive."

"What's his name? Maybe I can find out—tell you when I'm back at the lab."

The messenger raised his eyebrows.

"I do plan to get out," said Dobie.

"I'd love to see everyone's expression if I suddenly showed up with him," said the messenger. "He's a legend!"

"Do you know his name? I'll keep a lookout."

The messenger wore a preoccupied smile.

"Never mind," Dobie sighed. "You probably don't even know it."

"It's pretty easy," said the messenger. "It's Freeman. Free man. Think you can remember that?"

"Yes," Dobie chuckled, "I do. When I get out I'll let you know."

"Yeah. When you get out."

## Chapter 10 - Detainment

The door hissed and the messenger vanished. Dobie wanted to believe the door would reopen—that the messenger would be standing there. "I'm so, so sorry. I've made a terrible mistake. You're not going to report me, are you?"

Dobie touched the doors and then pushed on them, hoping they were pressure sensitive. They weren't.

His footsteps echoed, and he realized he must be walking. At any moment, someone would step out of some unseen corridor or door to rebuke him. "You shouldn't be here! Come this way." No one did.

At the end of the corridor was another set of doors. Dobie looked behind him, reassuring himself there'd been no mistake and that he hadn't missed any options. He pushed a button on the wall and the doors hissed apart. He passed through and they closed behind him with a reverberating thud.

Dobie pressed, pushed, and rammed the doors. They wouldn't reopen. He kicked at them and cursed. He pressed his back to them, and then slid to the floor.

Before him was another empty corridor. He listened again for a friendly voice or reprimand. Except for the slight hum of the ceiling lights, there was silence. He sat for what seemed a long time, wondering whether someone might hear him if he yelled. He didn't, afraid someone might.

"What if I'm the only one here? What if there's nothing to eat? How many more corridors are there?"

He stood up and began to walk, pausing intermittently to look behind him. He came at last to a bend in the hallway. Before him was an open room, and around the bend another corridor with yet another hydraulic door.

He stood at the entrance to the room. "Hello?"

There was no answer.

"Is anyone here? What am I supposed to do now?"

The flicker of a dim computer screen beckoned him forward. Slowly, cautiously, he approached. With the edge of his forearm, he wiped a thick film of dust from the monitor. He pressed the space bar on a keyboard and the screen flashed. A list appeared.

*Message for Freeman, Technician 83205,*
*03/02/2095, Please reply*

*Message for Freeman, Technician 83205,*
*02/05/2095, Please reply*
*Message for Freeman, Technician 83205,*
*01/05/2095, Please reply*
*Message for Freeman, Technician 83205,*
*12/08/2094, Please reply . . .*

He settled into a cobwebbed office chair and scrolled down the list, hoping to see "Message for Dobie, Engineer 797" Nothing. He tapped the 'Menu' key.

1) *Send message*
2) *Educational*
3) *Calendar*
4) *Personal detainment record*

He selected number 4.

*Enter personal ID number.*

Dobie typed.

*Dobie, Engineer 797, Creative Compound*
*Deconstruct/Detain: Detain*
*Period of Detainment: Indeterminate*

*Reason for Detainment: Suspect unauthorized cloning. Suspected sabotage of cloned lines.*

"Crap!"

Returning to the menu, he chose "Send Message." Two choices appeared.

1) *Send to Enforcement Messenger*
2) *Send to Other*

"Let's try 'Other.'"

To his surprise, he accessed the mail screen he was familiar with. He typed.

*To: Jorge, Engineer 983,*
*Creative Compound*

*Copy to: Camryn, Engineer 621,*
*Creative Compound*

*Was being interrogated. Am suddenly in detainment (I think). Don't see anyone but me. Don't know if I'm coming back. The messenger who brought me didn't think so. Please take care of Sheila.*

He pressed "Send." As an afterthought, he typed a similar message to Brian. A window flashed onto the screen.

*MESSAGE NOT DELIVERED.*

*User unauthorized.*

Dobie quickly typed a second message to the professor. "Let me know if you get this." The computer flashed another notice.

*MESSAGE NOT DELIVERED.*

*User unauthorized.*

He tried a note to the messenger. "Test Test Test." This time no window popped up.

"It must have gone through."

He typed again. "Messenger. No one here. Where do I go now? What do I do? HELP. HELP. HELP. HELP."

He waited for some time, but there was no reply.

He returned to the original list of messages. The last message to Freeman was dated... "Twenty years ago!"

Dobie left the room in a stupor. He continued down the corridor and through the hydraulic doors. He winced when they hissed behind him. Turning around, he touched them. To his surprise, they reopened.

He felt suddenly giddy and pleased with himself. He stepped back and forth several times, making the door open and close. The corridor continued ahead, but he walked briskly now, a light from the end of the hallway enticing him forward.

He passed a large glass door, which leaned against the wall. Grains of dirt crunched beneath his slippers. On the cracking linoleum tile were scattered, foot-shaped tread marks.

As he progressed, the light became more intense. His eyes began to water. He held an arm across them to block it.

With the brightness came a pleasant warmth. It seared through his skin and gently caressed his bones. He wanted to bathe in it, but his eyes ached and throbbed, forcing him back.

Dobie retreated until the pain began to ease. He tried again, and once more was stopped.

Dobie sat on the floor, his back turned toward the light. He listened. Somewhere in the distance broken melodies chirped and whistled. Folding arms on knees and resting head on arms, he tried to think of what to do now.

***

Suddenly his head jerked up. It took him a moment to remember where he was and how he'd gotten there. The light in the corridor was dimmer now; the air in his nostrils heavy and damp. Dobie stood and walked slowly forward.

He held an arm before his eyes, and then found he could lower it. He passed a hanging glass door and stepped into darkness. As he kept walking, the corridor fell away around him. He stopped.

Behind him it stood intact, the last ceiling light flickering uncertainly. Ahead of him lay a field of cement blanketed by shadow. There was a large globular light in the ceiling, which went higher than any he'd seen. He stared upward, trying to determine where walls and ceiling met.

There were smaller lights in addition to the large one. "Not very useful," he thought, and then considered that they might be brighter at different times of the day. Perhaps together they'd produced the intense light encountered earlier.

He walked the barely lit field. Scattered here and there were metal poles. They towered upward and ended in a half arc.

Dobie stopped and looked behind him. In the distance, the detainment compound was a colossal, dome silhouette against a nearly black backdrop.

Across the field, Dobie made out a hulking figure bent close to the ground. A white stripe shimmered down its back. Otherwise it was blacker than the darkness. Dobie watched it waddle, trying to determine where its legs and arms started. The figure swaggered into blackness, leaving behind a pungent, musky odor.

Dobie walked the field perimeter, and then halted abruptly. Something still and towering stood just off the pavement's edge. He froze; turned and ran. His lungs burned from the unaccustomed effort. Gripping at the pain in his chest and gasping for air, he turned to face it. The figure waited.

"It knows I can't get away," he thought. Squeezing at a stab in his side, he doubled over. The great figure stood calmly poised.

"Where am I?" Dobie called out.

It didn't answer.

Dobie squinted, trying to make it out. "Is this the detainment compound? Where do I go now?"

The figure was stoic.

Dobie stepped warily toward it. Its hair tossed beneath the air ducts, creating tiny, silvery shimmers.

Reaching out an arm, Dobie touched it. There was no flesh. No encasing fabric. There was a warmth to it, but nothing moved or pulsed beneath his hand. Dobie looked up and made out the rounded mass of hair shimmering above him. "A tree?" He laughed out loud. "A tree?"

He gazed back at the dome silhouette. The huge room that had surrounded him fell from his mind. "I'm out!" His knees buckled beneath him and he collapsed to the ground.

"I'm out of the megasphere! I was sent to detainment, but instead I've escaped!"

He spread himself out on the ground, and then sprang up and ran in circles on the pavement, stumbling now and then when his toe met a crack or a stone. He ran in ever-widening circles. Laughing, screaming, shouting, he gripped at the pain in his side.

He ran back to the sphere and staggered down the corridor. He passed through the hydraulic door and flopped into the computer room's chair. He typed.

*To: Messenger.*

*If you get this, gather your things.*

His stomach growled.

*Bring food! Freedom awaits! No water surrounds the sphere. There is only openness. I'm not mad. Not crazy. Only delirious with possibilities. Take a chance! Bring others!*

## Chapter 11 - A Free Man

Dobie plodded along the tree-lined corridor. The blacktop he walked on radiated heat into his pant legs; against his torso and chin. Perspiration poured from his hairline and trickled into his eyes. His eyes burned and watered. His vision blurred. Pulling up the hem of his shirt, he blotted at his face. He turned and staggered backward.

He imagined himself sitting at the computer. "Messenger. Don't come! No food or water. Very hot. Skin is turning red. Very painful. Light here is too bright." He worried over the enthusiastic message he'd typed earlier.

Dobie sat on the ground and arched his body forward, resting elbows on knees. He lowered his head and thought about the lighted globe above him. Did it float in mid-air or was it set in a ceiling? He still wasn't sure. A few hours ago it barely washed his surroundings with light. Now it blazed. He thought of the sphere—how it had glimmered white as the globe climbed higher. Shimmering letters spelled out "American Alternative Research Corporation."

"What's *American*?" He understood *alternative*. Understood *research. Corporation* was the collective whole; the good of the people—the society.

His stomach gnawed from within. His tongue was unaccustomedly dry. It clung to the roof of his mouth. Maybe the chief enforcement officers knew best after all. The sphere had its limitations, but was decidedly safer than this. Dobie wondered if deconstruction might have been better.

He looked down the corridor. "Maybe I should have gone that way," he thought. He saw no end to the path in either direction. Only a long black strip walled with trees—the trees he'd delighted in seeing a few hours earlier.

"You don't look so good."

Dobie jerked himself upright. Part of him worried he'd imagined it—another that he hadn't.

"I'm over here," said the voice.

Off the road, under a collection of drooping tree limbs, stood a man. His face and clothes were dirt-smudged. Hair blanketed his head and shoulders. It trailed above and along his lips, and down the sides of his face. It was matted, with streaks where fingers had clawed through it.

Dobie stood and stared.

The man gripped a tree-branch club. "I can defend myself."

Dobie nodded. "I just got out of the sphere."

The man pursed his lips. "Guess you're hungry then."

At the promise of food, Dobie's eyes grew large.

"Follow me," said the man. He turned abruptly when Dobie's foot snapped a twig. "Mind you keep your distance now."

Dobie stepped back, mindful of the club.

"So," said the man as he walked, "why'd they kick ya out?"

"Is this the detainment compound?" Dobie asked.

"I'll ask the questions," growled the man. "You answer 'em." When there was no rebuttal, he continued. "So, why'd they throw ya out?"

"I was cloning things. They hadn't been authorized."

"So you must be a *creative*." He said the word with a note of disdain.

"Yes."

He didn't acknowledge the answer.

"That's right," Dobie called more loudly.

"What'd you clone?"

"I didn't do the actual cloning."

"Why ya here then?"

"I arranged for the cloning."

"Same thing ain't it? Suppose ya thought someone else would get the blame!"

Dobie was worrying over the likelihood when the man spoke again. "So what'd ya have cloned?"

Dobie cleared his parched throat. "A mouse. Well, also a bird. Lizards. Frogs. Mostly small stuff that I could hide easily."

The man snorted. "If ya want the company of birds 'n frogs, ya've found the right place. If ya were gonna get tossed out, ya might as well have cloned somethin' worthwhile."

Dobie frowned. "I've cloned people too."

The man shrugged. "Lots of people been cloned."

"My dad and me, we cloned a girl once."

"Lots of girls been cloned."

"This one was supposed to be my wife. Our genes were highly compatible. We made sure she was viable too. Dad wants a grandson you see. Not that I don't, but he insists on one not made to order."

"So you viable too?"

Dobie began to feel uncomfortable with the direction of the conversation. "I'm a throwback, I guess."

"So ya have a wife then."

"It didn't work out."

"Didn't work out? If your genes were so compatible and all—"

"We failed to consider one important variable."

"What's that?"

"That she might find someone else more attractive."

A sideward grin crossed the man's face. "That can happen when it's nature makin' the decisions. 'Specially when it's human nature." He snuffled at his own joke. "Met a man from Reconstruction once—"

"From the megasphere? How many others are there?"

The man turned and frowned. "I wasn't done with my story."

Dobie surveyed what he could see of the man's face. "Sorry."

"Anyways, like I was sayin'. This man and, I guess his wife, must-a-bin throwbacks too. They had a kid. Born; not cloned." He lowered a brow at Dobie. "Guess you creatives don't know what you're doin'."

"Maybe," said Dobie, "But don't you think it's good that the corporation doesn't control everything?"

The man snickered. "The corporation doesn't control shit!" He held up his arms. One drooped a bit from the weight of the club. "Don't control all this!"

Dobie surveyed the man and his surroundings. "The CEOs didn't—"

The man turned and tossed the tree limb to Dobie. "You think they could make this?"

Dobie fell back as he caught it. He looked at the flaking of the bark; felt the uneven distribution of weight. "No," he said. "Random genetics made this."

"Random genetics. Now don't that sound high 'n mighty? Judgin' from all the accidental births been occurin'—least when I was inside—I'd say your random genetics are gettin' the upper hand."

"I'm hoping they take over," said Dobie, tossing the tree limb back to him. "Some of us have been giving it a hand."

The man's mouth formed a red pit in his matted beard. "You mean you're goofin' up on purpose?"

"I like to think we're making improvements."

"How does the corporation feel 'bout that?"

"Until recently," said Dobie, "they seemed pretty oblivious."

"So how long you been makin' 'improvements'?"

"Here and there for about twenty years, give or take a couple years. My dad's been adding random elements a lot longer than that. The creative compound is pretty well staffed. I can't believe we're the only ones who've thought of it."

The old man shook his head and laughed. He tossed aside the tree limb and waved Dobie forward. "Come on. We gotta get ya somethin' to eat."

"And drink," said Dobie, rubbing his throat.

"And drink. You look awful!"

## Chapter 12 - The Campsite

"There's a bucket of water over there," said the man. "Help yerself."

Dobie looked at the rusty container, and then back at his host.

"Go ahead. It's clean. Just drew it up this mornin'. Thirst'll kill ya before the rust does."

Dobie cupped his hands and slurped from them.

The man winced. "Don't get my water all dirty! Here. Use this." He tossed Dobie a mug with a mostly missing handle. Dobie dipped it into the bucket, and then gulped eagerly.

After several mugfuls, he sat down on the grass and rolled the empty cup in his palms. The initials A.A.R.C. ran around the mug's body. Below the letters, in a smaller font, ran "American Alternative Research Corporation."

"That's what's printed on the sphere," said Dobie.

"That's right."

"What's *American* mean?"

"Means someone who lives in America."

Dobie frowned.

"It's where ya are now. What the U.S. was, before it became the N.A.U.—the North American Union." He tossed some twigs onto a blacked area on the ground. "Once we joined up with Canada, the Norties said calling the old U.S. *America* gave people the wrong idea. Implied they wasn't as American as we are. People try their damndest not to use the word any more, but don't offend me none. Watch it when you're talkin' to others though."

The man went to a large, weathered desk and rooted through the drawers. "Here we go." He pulled out a box of matches and a small plastic container that read *decaf* on the side. "Don't usually make coffee, but this is a special occasion."

"You live here?" said Dobie.

"Sure I live here. Why not? Have everything I need. There's a town a few kilometers out. Go there once a week. Dig around. Find all the necessities."

"Town?" Dobie tried to recall the word from books he'd read. "A place where people assemble?"

"That's right." The man poured some water into a little pot. "It'll be instant. Hope that's okay."

To Dobie, anything instantaneous sounded that much better.

"You live here by yourself?"

"Pretty much," said the man.

Dobie looked around him. "Where do you sleep?"

"Wherever I happen to be when I'm sleepy. If it rains, I just hunker down under the desk. If ya'd rather sleep indoors, you can have it tonight."

"Dictionary," thought Dobie. "Define *rain*. Define *hunker*."

"Or," said the man, "ya can sleep in there." He pointed to a large, leather-covered storage trunk beneath a tree. "Gets a little stuffy, but it's more waterproof. I broke the latch off, so ya don't have to worry about accident'ly lockin' yerself in. I use it when it gets cold."

"I don't think that's a concern," said Dobie, wiping his face on his shirtsleeve.

"T'ain't even summer yet! You're just used to air conditionin'. Anyway," said the man, "you're in luck as far as food goes. I just got back from town yesterday. Which do ya want? Got this dog chow here. Can you believe someone threw out the whole bag? Prob'ly just 'cause of the expiration date, too. Or I got some cereal." He shook the box. "Better save that for mornin'. Or I got some fruit."

"Dictionary. Define *fruit*."

"It's a little bruised and stinky, but it don't taste bad. Had some last night."

Dobie wondered how much longer it would be before the man handed him something. "I'll try some chow."

The man pouted his bottom lip. "Dog chow it is. Good fer ya anyway. This here's premium."

The man wiped out a bowl with his shirttail, and then dropped a handful of kibble into it.

Dobie fingered a piece and sniffed. "Smells like reconstruction," he thought, popping it into his mouth. He bit down on the little ball, pressing his teeth hard against it. His jaw pinched but the ball didn't crumble. He rolled it in his mouth and tried again. Finally he spit it into his hand.

The man laughed. "Ya might need to soak it a bit. Let it soften up."

Dobie added some water to the bowl. "So how many desks make a town?" he asked.

The man looked at him quizzically, and then laughed. "Well," he said, "I 'magine there's a fair number in most towns. Most are in houses or apartments though."

Dobie looked at him blankly.

"Cubicles."

"Oh."

"I just like my freedom," said the man. "Like bein' a free man. In fact, that's my name." He held out a large, calloused palm. "Freeman."

"Dobie."

"Pleased to meet ya, Dobie. Hold on. I think the water's ready." The man pulled the pot off a large stone, using a rag to grasp the handle.

"So why'd they kick *you* out?" Dobie asked.

"What do ya mean by that?"

"You're from the sphere. The messenger said they'd tried to reach you. Said you could come back."

"Oh he did!" roared the man. "I bet they want me back! Well let 'em want. I ain't ever goin'!"

Dobie watched Freeman stomp about, grunting curses and scanning the ground for additional twigs. He tossed what he found into the fire. When his demeanor calmed, Dobie broached the subject again. "So why didn't you go back?"

"I'll tell ya why! 'Freeman', they says. 'We need someone to go out 'n shut down that computer—the one in the detainment compound. Messengers keep gettin' strange mail from detainees—trying to talk 'em into sabotagin' the corporation.'

"'We need someone to go out and destroy it,' they says. But I says to myself, 'Freeman, they ain't' gonna let ya back in. No one comes back from detainment. *No one*. I don't care what they been sent there for.'

"So just to be sure I'd be invited, I rigged some of the computers in the enforcement area—a lot of 'em—so they wouldn't work right without my askin' 'em. Only thing is, once I get out here I like it a whole lot better. I don't wanna go back. They're just gonna have to do without their computers—least til someone else figures out what I did."

Dobie pushed some of the soaking slurry into his mouth. It squished through his teeth and down his throat. "A little spicier than reconstruction," he thought. "Do you have any family?" he asked.

"Just a wife," said Freeman, "and *I* didn't pick her. Well, I did, but there weren't much selection. I can tell ya that. If there had been, I'd of done a lot better."

"Any kids?"

"Nah. The corporation wasn't replacin' our kind at the time, so wasn't any bein' passed out."

"You speak very strangely for someone from the sphere. I mean A-A-R-C."

"It's pronounced AARC—like it's a word; not letters. And I used to speak more eloquently, but out here people speak all kinds a dif'rent ways. If you're gonna blend in, ya'd be 'vised to do the same." He smirked at Dobie's distressed expression. "Don't worry," he said. "It'll come nat'rally as ya get out talkin' to people. How ya speak will depend on who ya 'sociate with."

Dobie felt more and more confused. Words and ideas swam through his head. With belly satiated by bloating dog chow, his eyes now grew heavy. He lay down next to the mug of untasted coffee and closed his eyes. His rapidly changing world faded into blackness.

## Chapter 13 - Subtle Engineering

"I had an interesting visitor a few days ago."

Camryn looked up from her work and toward the professor's back. He sat at a counter, hunched over a sequencing dock. She waited, but he continued to scroll through Gs, Cs, and As on the monitor.

Her eyes swept the room behind her. No one else was there. She waited for him to turn—to show any sign of acknowledgement. "Must have imagined it," she thought.

"An enforcer."

She looked his way again. Her voice was shaky. "Did he want something? This enforcer?"

"He was curious as to why an engineer might order a particularly rare and ancient DNA sample. He wanted me to look the sample up on the computer, so they'd know what type of animal it was from."

"And what was it?"

"He asked me to look it up. I told him it wasn't worth my time."

"Has he come back?"

"Who?" said the professor, "Dobie?"

"The enforcer." She thought a moment before asking. "Dobie went somewhere?"

"The authorities took him."

"He's coming back though?" Her voice quavered. "I mean, why would they want Dobie?"

"I didn't retrieve the information they needed, so they went to someone else."

"They'll let him go though."

"They might. If he's cooperative."

Camryn felt lightheaded.

"I hate to think I'd lose him over a simple white lab mouse."

"You said you didn't know what the sample was."

"I said I didn't look it up. Didn't need to. When I was young—well before you were born—we must have gone through hundreds of samples of mouse thirty-two. Then we realized the things bred like mad. We didn't need to clone them. You know, it was our group that developed the improved line, mouse *two*-thirty-two."

"What was wrong with the old one?"

"Nothing was wrong. But we'd depleted our samples and, with so much inbreeding among the reproducing animals, the sequencing errors became more pronounced. We decided to use some samples we had left to develop an even better lab animal.

"We recombined thirty-two with some core samples of *Macaca*. *Two*-thirty-two has the rapid metabolism of a mouse, but the thought and systemic capabilities of a monkey."

"I hate to ask this, but what's *monkey*?"

"Resembles a human, but it's smaller. Hairier. In any case, we've now managed to deplete our stores of that. I finished two-thirty-two-*five* just in time. It's even closer to a human model." He winked. "Added a bit of my own DNA."

"You created the new line?"

"The corporation felt I was the only one who could develop it in time. Most of us who worked on the previous line have died. To start from scratch could have taken years."

Camryn tried to remove the stunned expression from her face.

"But what I can't understand," said the professor, "and what is truly puzzling me, is why you would want primordial mouse DNA in the first place. What could you possibly be working on that couldn't be accomplished with the better variation?"

"I wasn't sure two-thirty-two would be small enough," said Camryn.

"Small enough for what?"

"I just thought primordial mouse would work better for my particular need."

"What need?"

Her words came slowly. "For feeding a snake."

The professor worked his chin with his fingertips. "Snake?" His eyes began to dance. "A snake! One of those long, skinny-bodied creatures?"

She nodded.

"With no legs!"

She nodded again.

He clasped his hands together. "Where? Show me!"

"I—"

"Oh come dear. If I were going to turn you in, I'd have done it by now!"

"It's in Brian's—"

"Brian's involved too? I mean, I could expect it of Dobie, but you? Brian? And what if other labs are cloning such things? Can you imagine the possibilities!"

"What possibility? That the sphere could overflow with mice and snakes?"

"No! That people are beginning to think for themselves—and to do something with what they're thinking. It's taken so long. Generation upon generation of subtle engineering. But now it's happening. It's finally happening."

She nodded, feigning understanding.

"Oh enough of my babbling! I have to see it!"

## Chapter 14 - Ancient History

Camryn scrunched her nose as they entered Brian's cubicle.

"What's that odor?" said the professor. "Does Brian smell like this all of the time? I hadn't noticed."

"I don't think we should be in here," said Camryn.

"Neither do I," said a voice behind her.

"Brian!"

"We came to see your snake," said the professor.

"I'm sorry," said Camryn. "I'm not even sure how I wound up telling him."

"Where is it?" beamed the professor.

"I think there's been some mistake," said Brian.

"Don't worry son. I'm not here to pry. I just want to see a snake with my very own eyes."

"I'd rather you both leave."

"The sooner I see the snake," said the professor, "the sooner I'll leave."

"I don't have it any more."

Camryn's eyes grew wide. "Did it get out?"

"It's gone."

"Did you pass it to someone?"

"Maybe *they'd* let me see it," said the professor.

"Then *they'd* be in trouble," said Brian.

"I don't want to get anyone in trouble. I'm perfectly thrilled you had the gumption to clone it!"

Brian sneered. "I found it."

"Oh."

"See," said Camryn, "someone else must have cloned it and let it escape."

"Or," said the professor, "no one cloned it and it found its way into the compound by itself."

"From where?" asked Camryn.

"From beyond the walls of the sphere."

"It definitely crawled," she said, "and it didn't have gills."

The professor shook his head in annoyance. "Of course it crawled. But I'm forgetting. You've been indoctrinated with the ark theory."

"It's in the records," said Camryn.

"So are tales of witches and fairies if you go back far enough."

"Dictionary," thought Camryn, "define *witches.*"

"Historians have rewritten history many times. When I was your age, a different theory was popular. It said we aren't adrift at all. That our megasphere's a mere speck on an even larger one—one that floats in a sea of air."

"It's amazing what some engineers will propose for the sake of notoriety," said Brian.

"And that was only a theory," said Camryn. "It's never been proven."

"Only a theory," agreed the professor. "But there is data that lends credence to it. Of course that information is no longer available."

Brian sighed. "The records clearly state that an asteroid was about to strike earth, so the sphere was made with impenetrable walls. All the DNA samples in existence were brought inside to preserve them."

"That's right," said Camryn. "The asteroid hit the earth and caused massive earthquakes and huge fires, followed by flooding. Except for us, the world no longer exists."

"I'm aware of the story," said the professor, "but how does your snake fit into this tale? If it wasn't cloned, then where did it come from?"

"We don't know that it wasn't cloned," said Brian.

"For the sake of speculation, let's say it wasn't. Now where did it originate?"

There was no answer, so the professor continued. "It must have come from outside the sphere. From beyond the megasphere itself."

He stepped over to one of the walls. "I wonder what else might come in were we to drill here, or chip away here, or go right through the floor—"

"Stop!" said Camryn. "This is getting *way* too scary. You wouldn't really—? I mean, one leak could flood the entire compound. Maybe the whole sphere!"

"Now you've stopped speculating with me."

"It's one thing to hide a little animal that someone's cloned," said Camryn. "It's another to drown an entire colony."

"I apologize," said the professor. "I mistook you for someone with imagination. I hold now to what I told the enforcer. You're best suited to menial tasks."

Her eyes welled with tears.

"What enforcer?" growled Brian.

Camryn rested a hand on his arm and choked back a sniffle. "I told someone else about the snake—someone besides the professor."

"I think I should turn myself in," said Brian. "This whole thing is getting out of hand. There's a difference between a little harmless curiosity and—well—the kind of sedition the professor's expounding."

The professor frowned. "Is there a difference? Status quo relies on lack of curiosity. It exists on complacency."

"So you think—?" said Camryn. "You truly believe—? And you're not just saying all of this for the sake of argument—that we're *not* surrounded by water?"

A bit of warmth seeped into his gaze. "I believe that we're sometimes told things to make us feel at ease."

"Complacent," said Camryn.

"And I believe we accept these things to maintain that sense of ease."

"To stay complacent?"

"So that we won't suffer the turmoil that comes with non-complacency."

Brian bounced his head about in annoyance. "But what makes you think that there's anything but water out there? What are your facts?"

"Again, it's simply a theory proposed some years ago."

"But you believe it."

"Let's look at what we know," said the professor. "It's a given that from time to time, in the seam of a wall or a fine crack in the floor, a tiny bit of green will appear. Just a thin bit of stem or a few tiny leaves. Where do these little plants come from?"

"From seeds," said Camryn.

The men stared at her.

"That's what my teacher used to say. Seeds from the shoes of workers who originally built the sphere. She said they're tiny bits of history."

"That's what who told you?" said the professor. "Your grade school teacher?"

Camryn felt herself turning red.

"But what if they're not from dormant seed? What if these little plants are actually the outside coming in? Does anyone seek to preserve these—what did you call them? Tiny bits of history? No! They're squashed out. The holes where they appear are plugged. Why bother to seal the holes?"

Camryn rubbed her nose sheepishly and chuckled at her own words. "Because the holes are weak spots that water can weaken?"

"Or," said the professor, "are they plugged because they're tracts? Through a very thin tract, a blade of grass emerges. Widen the tract and your snake might appear. Widen it still and a man might crawl out."

"This tract could prove a gateway for fatal bacteria," said Brian. "Did you think of that?"

The professor sighed. "At least you didn't say water."

"You're saying," said Camryn, "that we're trapped in a bubble? That things are living and breathing all around us we aren't even aware of?"

The professor considered her question. "I'm certain of it."

"What difference does it make?" said Brian. "Even if there is life beyond the sphere, if we went out into it we'd die from bacterial exposure."

"Some of us would I'm sure. But I'm just as certain some of us would not."

"So you're saying we should just open her up and take our chances?"

The professor shrugged. "Or wait for the world to come in. It is coming, whether we like it or not."

Brian scowled. "But what if you're wrong professor? What if we tunnel through the walls and water comes rushing in?"

"I can assure you it won't."

"I'd rather not take that chance if you don't mind. And I'd rather you not take that chance for me."

"I won't," said the professor, "but I was hoping Dobie might."

"Dobie was trying to break through the sphere?" said Camryn.

"Not that I know of. I had hoped at some point the notion might strike him. Could take generations for someone to get the nerve, now that he's gone."

"Gone for now," said Camryn. "But he'll be back."

"What's happened to Dobie?" growled Brian.

"I've seen many people taken away," said the professor. "I've never seen anyone come back."

Camryn hesitated to ask. "You think he's dead?"

"I believe the corporation prefers the word *deconstructed*."

"What's going on?" said Brian.

"Dobie was helping me," said Camryn.

"Helping you?"

"I doubt that's why they took him," said the professor, "or not entirely. I think they were investigating you and some of his little projects came to light. He was so inquisitive. Brilliant I'd say. I'd see him work and feel as though I'd accomplished something."

Brian frowned.

"I'd hoped there'd come a time when he might lead you out of this tomb and into something better."

"If Dobie's been listening to you," said Brian, I can see why he's in trouble. How do you know that this dream world of yours is so much better anyway?"

"Oh I don't. I know that it's different—unpredictable—random. Offspring are born through their mothers' wombs. They get sick. They get well. Some of them die. The sheer uncertainty of it is exciting."

"And to get to this imaginary world, Dobie was destroying the sphere?"

"Oh I doubt that," said the professor, "but if anyone had the gumption, it would be him."

"Because the rest of us can't think for ourselves," said Brian.

"Dobie's just a bit older. He came along when the corporation was more lax in its indoctrination."

"So because we're loyal to the corporation, that makes us stupid."

"Naive. Ignorant. More difficult for you to imagine what might be. I mean, you're standing here telling me that if I punched a hole into this wall the room would fill with water!"

"I don't feel so well," said Camryn. She sat down on the edge of Brian's bed and put her head between her legs.

The professor pulled off his lab coat and wadded it into a ball. "Here," he said. "Push your face into this. Take deep breaths."

"Thanks," she burbled from the folds. "I think the smell is getting to me."

"What *is* that smell?" asked the professor.

Brian reached an arm beneath the bed and retrieved a small box. He shoved it at the professor.

The professor looked at him, and then slowly lifted the lid. A nauseating stench invaded the air.

"It's the snake you were so eager to see," said Brian. "I found it lying belly up yesterday. I didn't know what to do with it."

The professor tossed the lid onto Brian's bed. He shook the box a bit, trying to get a look at the snake from different angles.

Camryn stood up for a better look, the coat still squashed over her nose and mouth. "It was prettier when it was alive," she muffled.

"I'm open to ideas as to what to do with it," said Brian. "I'm afraid the smell might get stronger."

"Perhaps you could burn it," said the professor.

"You don't think the smell of this thing burning would attract attention?"

"The smell's going to draw attention in any case."

"I was thinking I could drop it down a latrine port," said Brian.

"Hmm. I don't know that the chemicals will break it down. They may only work on substances once reconstructed."

"But we don't know that," said Brian.

"I'm a geneticist—not a chemical engineer."

"It's the best I've come up with."

"I think I'd better leave," said Camryn, rearranging the folds of the coat over her nose.

"I'm jealous of you son," said the professor. "You saw this extraordinary little animal while it was still alive."

"If I had it to do over," said Brian, "I'd have just turned it in. Then I wouldn't be in this mess."

***

"Hey Brian! Come join us!"

Brian waved tensely and smiled as he walked by the commissary. A computer case swung at his side.

On another day, he'd have stopped to chat. Today he continued to the lavatory. A man coming out wrinkled his nose and snorted as he passed, but didn't look back.

Brian stood at a sink and ran a hand through his hair. He washed his hands thoroughly, allowing enough time for anyone in the stalls behind him to leave. No one did. He checked beneath the doors for feet. Assured that he was alone, he backed into a stall and closed the door. Laying the case on the floor, he opened it. Stench sprang at his face and filled his nostrils. He coughed.

He removed a spotlight from the case and shined it into the port. Blackness. He reached into the tissue dispenser and felt something moist and velvety. "Plenty." He pulled out several long strips and folded them into a thick, gray pad.

He stared at the little gray snake lying inside the case. Carefully he gathered it in the tissue. The snake's tail fell out and brushed his wrist, making him jump.

Holding the snake over the port, he let it drop. The tissue drifted down after it. He looked into the hole once more with the spotlight, assuring himself it couldn't be seen. He could still smell it though.

Outside the stall he heard footsteps. "Brian?"

He hesitated to answer. "Yeah?"

"What have you been eating?"

"My stomach's upset." He pressed a button on the wall that released a deodorant. "Any better?"

"I guess. We were wondering if you're coming."

Brian unzipped his pants and backed up to the port. "I'm still not feeling well," he called.

"Okay then. Let me get out of here before you blow."

Brian groaned for effect. "Better hurry."

When Brian was sure his friend was gone, he rearranged his clothes and pressed the button once more. The smell of the snake was fast in his nostrils. He wasn't sure whether the odor was on him, his satchel, or coming up from the port.

"Next time I find an animal," he thought, "I'm turning it in."

## Chapter 15 - Responsibility

Camryn scooted closer to Brian on the bed and fingered his shirtsleeve. "It's my fault. About Dobie I mean."

"How is Dobie's arrest your fault?"

"He was helping me clone a—"

"Shush. I don't want to know any more."

"He's your friend. You don't want to know what happened to him?"

Brian's face grew stern; his brow and chin set. "Dobie's done a lot of questionable things. It was only a matter of time before he was caught."

"But he was taken away because of me. Because he was helping me."

"Let me put it this way." He stood and stepped away. "If Dobie had told me straight out that he was doing anything illegal, I'd have reported him."

"Brian!"

"But he was friend enough *not* to tell me."

She studied his face, but it betrayed no emotion. "I guess your friendship meant more to him than it did to you."

"Why should I risk trouble for the likes of Dobie?"

"You risked trouble for the sake of a snake!"

"A judgment lapse."

"So you're telling me that if I did something wrong—something to help you—you'd report me too?"

"It would be my responsibility."

Her neck stiffened. "Let's see if I understand this. When you do something wrong, it's a mistake. But if someone else does something, they should be sent to detainment—or deconstructed."

"If Dobie did something wrong, he has to take responsibility for it."

"Even if he was helping me?"

Brian gave a considered nod.

"And even if he was helping you?"

"That was his decision."

"I helped you hide a snake. Was that my decision?"

"It was a choice. By rights you should have reported me. Things would have been better if you had. Then Dobie'd still be here."

Her jaw dropped. "All of this is my fault? I never asked to see the snake. You showed it to me."

"It was wrong of me. You should have contacted the authorities."

"Instead I tried to help!"

"But you knew it was wrong."

She huffed. “Are you the one who turned Dobie in?"

There was silence.

“Have you turned me in too?"

"Now you're being silly. Just for seeing a snake?"

"For not reporting you, and for cloning something for your snake to eat. Dobie and I—"

"Camryn! Stop! I mean it."

"Or what? You'll report me?" Trembling with anger, she rose from the bed. Her eyes searched the room for something to throw; something to break; something to destroy to make him as angry as she was.

At first, she wasn't aware of his hand on her shoulder. When she did feel it, she flung her arm at his face. He arched back, avoiding contact.

"To think," she said, "that anyone would go to detainment for you!" She wanted to do more—to say more. The blood pulsed in her face; neck; brain. She stormed into the empty corridor and punched a button on the wall. The door closed behind her.

Gradually her breathing slowed. She stared at the door, hoping Brian would come through.

"I'm sorry," he said.

She rested her head on his shoulder. "I'm sorry too."

But it didn't open, and he didn't come out—and the blood pounded in her head all over again.

## Chapter 16 - Release

Camryn smiled weakly as she took the box.

"Some of my special mockmeal cookies," said the cook.

Her smile brightened, and for a moment she forgot her earlier upset.

"There's also a few smushers in there. *And* a little something extra."

"What would I do without you?" said Camryn.

"Sweet talk your way into another old man's heart."

Camryn stood on tiptoe and kissed his cheek, being careful not to brush his dirty apron.

The old man blushed. "That makes it all worthwhile."

"If there's anything I can ever do for you—"

"Actually," he mused, "there just may be." He turned his opposite cheek toward her and tapped it with a finger. She laughed and gave that one a bigger kiss.

As she walked down the corridor behind the kitchen, something moved within the box. She stopped and listened, but the container went still and silent. Shaking her head at her own imagination, she tucked it beneath her arm and continued back to her cubicle.

Sitting on her bed, Camryn removed the lid with ritualistic care. She reached in, and then jumped to her feet, hands balled to chest. A tiny white animal sat facing her in the box, its own pink hands clutched to its chest. Its nose quivered and long whiskers waved back and forth.

"Oh," she moaned, catching her breath. "I forgot about you."

The mouse wiggled its nose over the lip of the container.

"Now I don't know what *you* eat!" She noticed a sprinkling of crumbs near the smushers, and her jaw dropped. "Apparently mockmeal cookies!"

She reached over the bed and lightly picked up the lid. She moved it slowly toward the mouse, which crawled away from the edge and into a corner. She pushed down firmly.

Camryn paced, and then stared at the wall. "Of course!" she said, snatching up the box.

There was a thud from inside.

"Oops. Sorry."

***

Camryn walked down the storage corridor and stopped at a door. "He probably hates being disturbed," she thought. "That's why he's back here. He was so happy about us hiding the snake." She glanced down at the box in her hands. "This should make him ecstatic. What if this isn't the right cubicle? Then what?"

She answered herself. "Then you just say, 'Wrong room. And by the way, do you know where the professor lives?'" That would be suspicious. She couldn't imagine *anyone* looking for him.

The box rattled a bit, reminding her why she was there.

"Okay. Here goes." She pressed the buzzer and waited. "Okay, no answer." She turned to trot away as the door slid open.

The professor stood rubbing his face. There was a prominent linen indention across one cheek.

"Oh! Sorry. Wrong room." She averted her eyes and turned to go. "I'm sorry."

"Wrong room? Who else lives back here?"

"Well, Dobie does."

His eyebrows arced. "I'm surprised he told someone. He told you that I live here too?"

"He said your room was storage."

"So you figured it out yourself?"

She felt flattered; then annoyed.

"Come in," he motioned.

"It's not important. I should go."

"Nonsense. You came here for a reason. Now come in."

She stepped inside his dim quarters, starting when he reached behind her. He pressed a button on the wall, and the door closed behind them.

The professor stumbled across a rug, making his way to a computer terminal. Camryn wondered how he could have his own machine. Of course Brian had a portable, and Dobie had his own in the lab. Was she the only one—?

"Professor—" she ventured.

He raised a finger to her, and then struck a few keys. "A message," he said. "There's a message from Dobie. Looks like a copy went to you too. Have you seen it?"

She shook her head. "What does it say?"

He seated himself in front of the monitor and Camryn stood behind him. They waited and the message appeared.

When Camryn read the last line, "Please take care of Sheila," she giggled.

"What's so funny?" asked the professor.

"Nothing. Private joke."

He furrowed his brows, scanning the message again. "Where?"

She pointed and he shrugged.

"He wants me to take care of Sheila. So?"

Now it was Camryn's brows that furrowed. "She's his imaginary lover."

"They're close, but not that close."

Camryn reread the message.

"He's not coming back," said the professor. "Now I know for certain."

"He says he's not sure."

"He won't be back."

"He's still alive. There's hope."

Tears collected in the old man's eyes. "I wanted to believe—" He shook his head. "I knew better."

"Can we send a reply?"

"Detainees are allowed one outgoing message; no incoming. He's gone."

A rustle from the box reminded Camryn of its contents.

The professor turned slowly toward her. "The mouse," he mumbled. "That's the mouse I suppose."

Camryn nodded and backed away as he stood up.

The old man laughed. "To think I'd lose Dobie over a stupid little mouse." He looked at Camryn. "So what are you going to do with it?"

"I don't know. I thought you might. You said you know all about them."

"So you want me in detainment too, is that it?" He chuckled at her discomfort. "It wouldn't matter," he said, patting her arm. "I'll be dead soon anyway."

Camryn's eyes began to water.

"Don't cry for me," he admonished. "I've lived a full life as it were."

She couldn't explain that the tears were from fear and embarrassment, rather than sympathy.

The professor put on his lab coat and buttoned it down. He checked his face in a mirror and rubbed at the pillow mark. With a little comb, he carefully arranged his thinning hair. He smiled at her slyly. "I have a reputation to uphold." He glanced around the room, and stepped over to a chest of drawers; picked up a sliver of metal and put it in his pocket.

The professor took the box from Camryn's hands. "Are you ready? Come on. I have an idea."

The halls were empty, most people having retired to their cubicles. They passed the lab, the dormitories, and more labs. They zigzagged through corridors Camryn had never seen. She pictured the professor collapsing as they walked, deconstructing before her. She wondered if she could find her way back on her own. "Where exactly are we?" she asked.

"At the perimeter of the creative compound." He stopped and handed the box to Camryn. "If you'd be so good as to set this down for me."

"Now what?" said Camryn, placing it on the floor.

The professor kneeled with a wobble and removed the lid. The mouse crawled onto his hand. "Tickles." He nudged it onto the floor and it scurried along the wall.

Camryn started forward to catch it, but the professor grabbed her pant leg. "Leave it."

"We can't!"

"Why not?" He offered his arm to her. "Help me up, won't you?"

"But professor—"

"Leave it be," he said, pressing his free hand to the wall to steady himself.

"Someone will find it," said Camryn.

"Good. It'll stir up a little trouble. It's what Dobie would have wanted."

"But—"

The professor walked away as Camryn collected the box. She stepped toward the mouse; then toward the professor. She repeated the dance several times before catching up with the old man.

The professor smiled mischievously. "Are those *smushers* in there?"

"Yeah. There were some mockmeal cookies too, but the mouse got 'em."

The professor reached into the box.

"The mouse probably peed on them," she thought. Before she could speak, he popped one into his mouth.

"Not as good as I remember." He chewed, and then swallowed the remnants with a forced gulp. "You're lucky that your mouse didn't gnaw through the box. They can chew through just about anything."

Camryn wondered what difference it made if they were just going to turn it loose anyway.

"We used to keep them in glass cages. They can't gnaw through glass. Why a mouse anyway?"

"What do you mean?"

"Why a mouse? A snake eats any number of things. Insects; lizards; frogs; birds. What made you choose a mouse?"

Camryn knew what an insect was, but couldn't picture *frog* or *lizard*. "Dobie said snakes eat rodents. I figured little snake, little rodent."

The professor nodded. "I suppose Dobie wouldn't have considered a bird in any case. Would have made more sense though. He's more experience with those."

Camryn spoke tentatively. "The animals that fly?"

He chuckled. "Yes. The animals that fly. Like Sheila."

Camryn grew quiet. "Are you saying that Sheila's a bird?"

"A parrot is a type of bird."

Camryn wished she had access to her computer and its dictionary.

"Have you seen her?" His eyes twinkled. "We need to get her out of Dobie's cubicle. They'll search it eventually."

"If they can find it," she thought.

"Do you want to keep her in your room?"

"Who?"

"Sheila."

Camryn was still trying to image the word *parrot*. She shook her head. "I just got rid of one problem."

"That's all right," said the professor. "I'll take her. If the authorities find her, they'll kill her."

"I guess so."

"She's really remarkable. She talks you know. Well, babbles really. A little like me, huh?" He waited for a laugh or smile, but Camryn was preoccupied.

"So did Dobie clone Sheila too?"

"More than likely."

"And do you think he's cloned other things?"

"Oh I know he has. Since he was a boy. All of his life he's been getting into mischief."

"You knew him when he was little?"

He nodded.

"But didn't he need contraband to have things cloned? We don't have the facilities at our compound." She hesitated. "At least I don't think we do."

The professor shook his head. "Used to when I was young. That stopped when some friends and I decided to clone a bear."

"Bear?"

"Impressive animal. Big. Strong. A lot stronger than you or me. Claws as long as my fingers."

"What happened?"

"Well, bears grow quite large and quite quickly it seems. It wasn't long after we'd cloned it that it was chasing us around and grabbing our legs. We thought it was funny. We wouldn't give it a mouse until in managed to tackle one of us."

Camryn tried to imagine an animal large enough to knock her down.

"It wasn't quite so big then, but just kept growing. One day, Professor Stern—do you know him? He's the one with the missing hand. Limps."

"I've seen him in the commissary."

"Well, anyway, he was feeding it one day and the bear became a little annoyed at the game. It chewed up Stern's arms and legs pretty badly. A couple of us tried to chase it off."

The professor stopped and bent over stiffly to pull up a pant leg. "This is where it got me."

Camryn stared at a long, puckered indention running down his calf.

"Lucky it didn't get the tendons. Makes me laugh every time I look at it."

Camryn gaped. "It doesn't seem funny to me."

The professor shrugged. "Happier times." He shook down his pant leg. "Exciting times."

"What happened to it?"

"The bear? Well after seeing what happened to Stern, we all tried to hide from the thing. Some made it back to their cubicles. I dragged myself behind a counter. Poor Stern was still out in the middle of things, lying still, trying not to draw the bear's attention—bleeding all over the place! The bear was pulling the lids off the mouse cages and gobbling them up. Pretty well tore up the lab in the process.

"Someone messaged the authorities. They suddenly appeared and shot it. That's when they still had some bullets left. We thought they'd kill us too. Got in lots of trouble, but as you can see I'm still here.

"After that, it was decided that one compound should order and engineer the DNA; another produce the finished product."

"What made you pick a bear?" asked Camryn.

"Heard it was big. Sounded more interesting than the little animals we'd been cloning. Rabbits, a cat—which ate one of the rabbits by the way; and some mice. And of course, once we got the bear, we cloned—and then bred—lots of extra mice." He poked out a lip. "Seems anything will eat those things."

"I want to see Sheila," Camryn declared. Then, "Does she bite?"

"Pinches. She's brought the blood maybe a couple of times. Nothing serious."

"Is she big?"

"Normal size I think. It's hard to compare. She's the only bird I've ever seen."

"I mean, is she smaller than the bear?"

"Oh yes! Much smaller."

They walked quietly a bit.

"If Dobie cloned Sheila," said Camryn, "and other things, didn't he need bribes?"

"The cloning lab's never worked cheap."

"So where does Dobie get all of his goods? His contraband?"

The professor didn't answer, but Camryn didn't notice and continued to think out loud. "For the mouse we used a book. But where does he get all this stuff? I mean, is all this stuff just floating around out there and I'm totally unaware?"

"Items have been passed back and forth for some time," said the professor. "Even in my day, one could obtain a substantial favor for a book."

"And yet I've never had anything—besides what the corporation provides. Not everyone has contraband, do they?"

"Not everyone," said the professor, "but enough."

## Chapter 17 - Sheila

As the door opened to Dobie's cubicle, they were greeted by a piercing shriek.

"Hurry! Someone might hear," said the professor.

Camryn stepped into the room and pushed the button.

"That doesn't work any more," said the professor. He stepped around her to drag the door closed, and then nodded toward the foot rail of Dobie's bed. "I'd like you to meet Sheila."

A little green bird bobbed its head. "Hehwo," it gurgled. "Hehwo."

"Hello to you too," cooed the professor. He offered the animal a pair of fingers and it climbed onto his hand.

"Hehwo."

"Sheila, I'd like you to meet Camryn."

The parrot stepped off the old man's hand and edged up his forearm.

"It's all right, Sheila. Camryn won't hurt you."

The parrot stood at the crook of his arm. It hooked its beak into the sleeve of his jacket, and climbed toward his shoulder.

"You can come closer," said the professor.

Camryn stepped cautiously toward him. The bird peeked at her from behind his ear.

He reached a hand behind his head and the parrot climbed onto it. As he lowered the hand, the parrot twisted its tail to one side and gave a little shake. A watery brown spot formed at the edge of his sleeve.

"Did it poop?" said Camryn.

"The proper term is *defecate*. But yes, that's exactly what it did."

Camryn stepped a bit closer and the bird began to flap its wings. Only its toes, wrapped tightly around the professor's knuckles, kept it from flying off.

"I don't think she likes me," said Camryn.

"She's just not used to seeing anyone but Dobie and me."

Camryn stood gazing at the bird's orange eyes. They seemed to glow, even in the low light. The dot in the middle grew large, and then barely visible.

Camryn looked over the bird to the room beyond. There were several glass boxes on a counter. "Is Dobie keeping other things?"

"Those? I think they're empty right now. But if you look around you might spot Harriet."

Camryn walked over to the cages.

"She won't be in there. She came in on her own. Comes and goes as she pleases. She might be in my cubicle right now."

"Okay," said Camryn. "What's Harriet?"

"A spider."

She shook her head.

"Tiny," said the professor. He held thumb and index finger slightly apart. "Maybe so big. Has eight legs. Likes to hang upside down from the ceiling."

Camryn's eyes scanned the ceiling tiles.

The bird shrieked and fluttered into the air. Camryn felt its feathers brush her neck, and she instinctively scrunched her shoulder. The bird's nails scraped her arm as it grasped for her sleeve. It missed and flapped to the ground.

"See. She hates me!" said Camryn.

"No," said the professor. "She was trying to land on you. I think she likes you. Come over here." He teetered into a kneeling position in front of the bird. Camryn crouched down beside him. "Hold out your hand. Like this."

The parrot backed away a few steps and cocked an eye at them.

"See," said Camryn. "Hates me."

"Talk to her."

"What should I say?"

"Doesn't matter really."

"Hi Sheila," stammered Camryn. The bird stood gaping at her, trembling slightly. "Are you Dobie's friend?"

At mention of Dobie, the parrot sidestepped back and forth. "Goud wird. Goud wird. Wuv you."

Camryn laughed. "Yes, Sheila's a good bird." She offered the back of her hand. "You want to come up?"

The parrot stretched one leg out as far as it could, and grasped the air with its toes.

The professor took Camryn's elbow and guided her hand closer. The little parrot climbed aboard. It's feet felt hot on her hand. The needle-tip claws poked her skin. "Now what?" Camryn smiled.

"Get up. Slowly."

She eased herself to her feet. The parrot danced little circles on her hand. It pooped again. The poop was hot and creamy.

"She's nervous," said the professor.

Sheila screamed and Camryn winced.

"Loud! That's why I had Dobie take this cubicle. It's relatively soundproof."

"Another reason I can't keep her."

"She better stay with me," he agreed. "I wasn't thinking when I suggested you take her. I just thought you'd enjoy her, and Dobie obviously trusted you."

"Did Dobie talk to you? About me?"

"A little. He told me he was helping you with something. Frankly it concerned me, but I'm beginning to see why he was so eager."

Camryn's cheeks and temples grew hot. "And because of me he's gone."

"No," said the professor. "It wasn't because of you. Your order, I suspect, led to a review of past DNA orders. There were a lot of suspicious requests—most placed by Dobie. He's had a veritable menagerie of animals and plants through the years."

"Still, if I hadn't ordered the mouse, they might never have noticed."

"That's a big supposition."

The parrot now sat on Camryn's shoulder. It probed the edge of her ear with its tongue. She giggled. "It doesn't pinch at all. It tickles."

"She only bites when she's angry. Come on. We'd better go."

She followed the professor into the corridor.

"On second thought, let's leave her here for now," said the professor. "I have to prepare my cubicle to accommodate her." He took the bird from Camryn's shoulder and put it back in the room.

When he stepped out, he pressed a button on the wall. The door hissed closed behind them. "Works on this side," he explained.

"Smells better out here," said Camryn.

"Nothing I can do about that. It's from Sheila being in there all of the time. Shouldn't matter though. The authorities won't know what it's from. With any luck at all, they'll stumble onto Harriet—think she's causing the smell."

"Are spiders stinky too?"

"No, but if *you* don't know that, do you think they will?"

## Chapter 18 - Mikel

His hand slipped and he tumbled through a network of bars. His shoulder banged one as he fell. On his back, lungs empty of air, Mikel gazed up at faces peering down. His lungs swelled and the faces grinned. There was laughter. Lots of it.

"Maybe you can make it to the top when you're older!" chided one boy, a little huskier and taller than Mikel.

"His palms must be sweaty!" laughed another.

A little girl climbed down from her perch. "Are you all right?"

His legs shook a bit as he stood, which brought more guffaws from above.

"You walk like a doll!"

"Yeah! Like a marionette." The boy worked a set of imaginary strings.

"Your girlfriend can make it better! Let her kiss it!"

The children made smooching sounds as Mikel marched away.

The little girl ran up behind him. "Are you okay?"

He nodded, glaring over his shoulder at the boys. They were already engaged in another sport—trying to knock one another off the jungle gym. "Fall Mikel! Fall!" they laughed.

When Mikel saw they were no longer looking at him, he rubbed his shoulder.

"They're mean!" declared the little girl.

"I'll arrest them all. You'll see."

"If you're an enforcer, I want to be one too!"

"You'll never make it! You always stay on the bottom rungs!"

Her little nostrils flared, and she stopped short behind him as he walked. "At least I don't fall and hurt myself!" She waited for him to notice she was no longer following. When he didn't, she ran to catch up. "So whatchya gonna do now?"

He shrugged his good shoulder and went into another module. Soft streaks of blue, gray, and white drifted across the spectrolight ceiling. Mikel dropped onto the green floor pad, enjoying its bounce.

The little girl sat on her knees, and then pounced on her hands.

Mikel smiled, looking away and shaking his head.

"You wanna play a game?"

"Nah." He nodded to a box behind her. "Give me those blocks."

She dragged the box toward him.

"And I'm not your boyfriend."

She didn't respond but peered into the carton. Inside, the plastic cubes rattled. Anna fell backward. She was whiter than usual; her eyes wide and glassy.

"What are you doing?" Mikel chortled.

She pointed at the box. "I think there's an animal in there."

Mikel scrambled to the box, and then cautiously peered in. "I don't see anything."

There was scraping, like fingernails across a desktop, and Mikel jumped back. He sat on his knees next to Anna. They sat listening, but heard nothing more.

"The blocks just shifted," said Mikel.

"Or the animal moved them."

Mikel smiled mischievously, and then gnashed his teeth. "The animal's going to get you!" He raised up his hands and formed claws with his fingers.

Squealing, she covered her face. Hunching her shoulders, she invited him to continue.

He snarled and jumped at her again, his foot kicking the box. This time something scrambled and scraped inside.

They ran across the room to a corner, and clutched one another.

When their breathing slowed, Mikel took a step toward the container. He glanced back at Anna. "Stay here!"

"It might eat you."

"Enforcers investigate scary things." He crept toward the box. When he was within arm's reach, he gave it a hard shove. The blocks slid and clattered as the box toppled over. There was silence.

Anna crept up behind him and peered over his shoulder at the spilled contents. Among the colorful cubes was something new. It waved at them with tiny hands. Long hairs framed a quivering pink nose.

The children stared. Red eyes glowed back at them.

Mikel eased himself into a squat. The creature twitched.

"I wonder if it eats people," said Anna.

"It might eat a finger," Mikel considered, looking at one of his own.

"I'll go get the teacher!"

"Anna! No!"

"Why not?"

"I want to look at it." He reached a hand forward to remove the surrounding blocks. The animal started, and then scrambled across the room. It seemed to glide along the edge of a wall until it huddled in a corner.

"Shut the door!" said Mikel.

"We're not supposed to!" said Anna.

"Do you want it to run out?"

"I think I should get the teacher!" She marched toward the door.

"No Anna! If you get her, I won't be your boyfriend any more."

Her march slowed. She pressed a large button with the palm of her hand, and the module door slid closed. She squatted down next to the door. "If that thing eats you, I'm outa here!"

"Great backup you are." He crouched on the floor and crept slowly toward the mouse, stopping each time it twitched or seemed ready to run. He stretched a finger toward its forehead and felt a piercing stab.

"Ouch!" A droplet of blood beaded on his finger.

"It tried to eat you!" Anna was now standing with her back pressed against the wall.

Mikel squared his shoulders and put the injured finger in his mouth. He sucked it, and then watched blood reform over the wound. "Bit me is all. I think I scared it."

"Maybe it thinks you're another animal."

"Maybe I am!" He snarled at her once more, and a broad smile crossed her face.

"Can I get the teacher now?"

"No! I want to try again."

"Does it hurt?"

Mikel nodded as he sucked on his finger. He stepped quietly toward the mouse, which was now in a different corner. "I want to touch it."

"It's gonna bite you!"

His tongue wrapped his upper lip as he crawled slowly toward the corner. He laid his palm out before the mouse. The creature took a hesitant step forward, its whiskers probing the edge of his hand.

Anna stepped away from the wall, standing on tiptoe for a better look.

The mouse stepped onto Mikel's palm and then, seeming to realize its predicament, sprang straight into the air. It scurried along the wall once more.

Mikel turned and grinned at his companion. "I did it!" He scrambled after the little creature and slowed when it seemed aware of his presence. He laid an open palm before the mouse; pressed the creature toward it with his other hand. Slowly it climbed aboard. Even more slowly, Mikel eased himself to his feet. He cupped the animal in his hands and smiled.

The creature grasped his fingertips and peered over the edge. Mikel froze, afraid it might jump. "You want to look?" he whispered to Anna.

She shook her head no, but began stepping forward. "What does it feel like?"

"Warm. Soft."

"Can I hold it?"

Mikel enjoyed the feel of it a few more moments before answering. "Okay, but be careful. Put your hands out."

Anna cupped her hands against Mikel's. Noticing the smeared blood on his fingertip she pulled suddenly back.

"What's wrong?"

"Nothing." She held out her hands uncertainly and the animal climbed onto them. She giggled and smiled.

The creature turned slowly about, and then made its way toward her wrist.

"Get it off me!" she said, holding her hands away from her.

The mouse crawled onto her arm, and her voice became frantic. "Get it off of me!"

Mikel encircled the mouse with his hands and retrieved it.

"What are you going to do with it?" said Anna.

"Keep it."

"Mommy says it's against the law to keep animals."

"So."

"They're going to send you to dentment!"

"I'll hide it."

"Where?"

"Right here." He held the mouse beneath the edge of his shirttail, and it wriggled into the warm space beneath.

"What if it eats your stomach?"

He looked at her and frowned.

"You don't know!"

"Don't tell anyone, okay?"

"Can I come see it?"

He nodded. "Sneak some food out of the commissary. I will too."

"Mommy says that's not allowed."

"Never mind. I'll take care of it."

"You're gonna get in trouble."

He didn't answer, but tried to position himself so that the moving bulge beneath his shirt would be less noticeable.

They jumped as the module doors parted. "What are you two doing in here?"

"Just playin'," said Mikel.

"The kids outside were being *loud*," said Anna.

Mikel's eyes widened, surprised at his friend's resourcefulness.

"The doors are to stay open," said the teacher. "What if someone got hurt in here? No one would realize!"

Mikel tucked his injured finger beneath one of his loosely folded arms.

"And Mikel, why are you standing like that?"

He felt the little animal pushing against his arm and the confines of his shirt. "I always stand funny."

Anna giggled.

"Go back to class. Recess is almost over." She frowned at the joyful way they ran out. "We'll be right behind you," she called.

Mikel ran into the classroom. He squirmed to keep the mouse under his shirt as he flipped up his desktop. "Take my data pad out of the case."

"Why?" said Anna.

"Just take it out!"

Anna unzipped the case and worked its contents free.

There was chatter in the corridor.

Mikel grabbed the case from her and tossed it into his desk. He shook the little animal loose from his shirt and it fell among the clutter. Mikel closed the desktop as the others filed through the door.

"Everyone be seated," said the teacher. "Settle down!"

Mikel sat stiffly, his hands folded over his data pad.

The teacher scanned the room. "You seem unusually eager Mikel."

"I like math!" he declared.

The teacher's eyes grew wide. Her lower lip puckered out. The children looked from her to Mikel, and then burst out laughing.

Mikel glared back at them. "I'm trying to do better! What's wrong with that?"

The class laughed even harder; so loudly that they didn't hear the little animal scurrying about inside Mikel's desk. The desktop vibrated beneath his arms. He wanted the others to stop laughing, but was relieved when they didn't.

"Enough! Enough!" shouted the teacher. "Settle down."

The room quieted but for an occasional snicker. The little animal quieted as well.

"These are your problems for tonight. Copy them down. Solve them. Bring them back tomorrow."

There was shuffling and clacking as the students retrieved their data pads and styluses.

Mikel realized he'd forgotten his stylus. He pushed his hand beneath the lip of the desktop. He jumped and banged his knee when his fingers encountered fur. He fumbled with the stylus, and felt the mouse trying to squeeze out next to his hand. He pushed it back with his fingertips.

The room quieted once more as the students began copying the problems from a screen. A scuffling sound emanated from Mikel's desk. He looked up just as the teacher located the source. Mikel looked down intently, and scribbled and scratched furiously at his data pad. This sent the children into another round of guffaws.

"Five minutes!" the teacher shouted, watching the clock more intently than the children.

"Three minutes!"

The rustling in Mikel's desk slowed, and with it his writing speed.

"One minute!"

Mikel looked up; tried to figure out if one figure was a five or a six.

"Time's up. Remember to press 'Save.'"

The problems disappeared.

"Ah!"

"I wasn't done"

"Can we have another minute? Ple-e-e-ase?"

"We have to move on," said the teacher.

Mikel sat back with a frown.

The math lesson seemed to drag on forever. Afterwards the teacher talked about consonants and vowels. The words meandered aimlessly through the air. Mikel stayed awake by pulling at his face with his fingertips.

The teacher looked at the clock. "Okay," she finally announced, all but bolting for the door herself, "You can go home now. Would the last one out be sure to close the door behind them. And set the lighting dial to night please."

Mikel and Anna dawdled behind the others. When the class was finally gone, Mikel slowly raised his desktop. The mouse was sleeping in a corner. It blinked at the incoming light, scurried a bit, and then froze in place.

"What are you going to do with it?" asked Anna.

Mikel scooped the little creature into his data pad case. "There," he said, pushing the tail through as he zipped it shut.

"You can't keep it in there!" She sniffed the air over his desk. "Besides. It stinks!"

Mikel waved a hand through the air. He put the mouse-filled case under his shirt, and then held his data pad in front of the bulge. "Can you see it?"

"No. But you're gonna get in trouble. You're gonna go to dentment!"

"I'm not going to de-*tain*-ment."

"If they catch you, you will!"

"My dad says hardly anyone goes there any more. He complains about it all the time."

"But some people do!"

"I guess so," said Mikel. "If they do something *really* bad."

"Do you think I'll go to dentment too?"

"Why would you go? I'm the one keeping an animal."

"I'll go with you even if they don't make me."

"I'm just gonna keep it a few days," said Mikel. "Then I'll let it go."

"But then someone mean might catch it!"

Mikel huffed. He marched for the door and waved for Anna to follow. She trotted obediently behind.

Mikel closed the door and turned the dial from day to night, wondering what difference it made if no one was there to know it was dark. He started down a corridor for home, and then realized he forgot to say goodbye to his companion. He turned around to find Anna standing somberly at the classroom door. She was watching him go.

"Come over later!" he called.

"Okay!" she beamed, and then trotted in the other direction.

## Chapter 19 - The Colony

The enforcer stood at the professor's door. "Does anyone else live back here?" he asked.

"Just me," said the professor, "and piles of old lab equipment."

"Can I come in?"

The professor nodded and stood aside. He glanced nervously at his latrine's closed door. "My best engineer is already in detainment," he quavered. "What more do you want?"

"That investigation is complete."

"You're still investigating Camryn then?"

"Also complete."

"Then why are you in my quarters annoying me?"

"One of your colleagues was good enough to assist us. In fact, he reviewed all DNA orders placed through your lab over the past several years. There've been many irregularities."

"And what's the name of this 'colleague'?"

"Not important, but what disturbs us are the irregularities in *your* orders, Professor."

"What type of 'irregularities'?"

"Why don't you tell us?"

"I don't know what you're talking about."

"At this point, anyone who doesn't cooperate will be considered a coconspirator."

The professor met his gaze. "You're different than most enforcers."

"Oh?"

"Most have gray eyes. Or blue. And blond hair."

"I didn't come here to have my faults pointed out."

"Not faults. It's because you're different that I'm going to take a chance on you."

"You're going to assist us then?"

"What I'm about to show you will assist you, or hinder you. You decide."

"I'll try to give you the benefit of the doubt—if you cooperate."

The professor lifted one end of a DNA blueprint mounted on the wall. "Help me, won't you?"

The enforcer lifted the other end, and with a nod from the old man they laid it on the bed.

The professor hobbled over to a chest of drawers, taking a moment to stroke the rustic piece of furniture. "Real wood, from what used to be a real tree—a plant. Had to make a rather daring trade for that one. Cloned something once referred to as a philodendron."

The enforcer's eyes sparkled as he took in the chest. Suddenly his expression flattened. "It's against the law to clone any unauthorized animal."

"A philodendron is a plant," said the professor.

"And any item containing genetic material must be turned over. Your chest will have to be confiscated."

"And what happens to it then?" said the professor. "Once it's 'confiscated'?"

There was no answer.

"It'll be turned over to another lab in this very compound. They'll draw DNA samples from it, and then our lab will again have access. So as you see, it's pointless to take it in the first place."

"I'll expect the individual's name you traded with."

"I failed to get it."

The enforcer nodded toward the item in question. "I'll have someone come by for it tomorrow."

"This chest has reached its destination. As I told you, genetic material ultimately goes to us. Aren't you listening?"

The professor lifted a lamp and, pulling its cord taut, held it to a chiseled area on the wall. He motioned the enforcer closer, and pointed to a piece of reconstruction resting in the crevice.

"It's also illegal to possess food outside of the commissary," said the enforcer. He fingered the reconstruction, and a searing pain on his knuckle made him pull back.

"Hurts, doesn't it?" said the professor. He gripped the enforcer's wrist and held the lamp over his finger. A tiny being, one tinier than the mind could imagine, curled tightly within a fold of skin.

"What is it?"

"I believe it's called an ant," said the professor. He pinched the insect between his fingers and rolled them together. "There. All gone."

The enforcer held the knuckle to his mouth. "You cloned *that*?"

"No!" grinned the professor. "I did not!"

The enforcer took possession of the lamp and held it to the crevice. Over the reconstruction crawled one ant. Two. As his eyes adjusted to the dim light, he made out many ants marching in a column. Some went toward the food, emerging from the blackened depths of the wall. Others marched away with tiny gray crumbs. Some spoke with acquaintances, tapping antennae before moving on.

"If you didn't clone these," said the enforcer, "where'd they come from?"

"From beyond the walls of the sphere—the very world we know!"

"There's nothing outside but water. Break the seal and it rushes in."

"No," said the professor. "If you break the seal, the world—and the beings that inhabit it—rush in. I'd also venture to say that some might rush out given the chance.

"These tiny creatures live on land. Before the megasphere there were more ants than people. They were everywhere—next to cubicles; within cubicles; even beneath them. These little beings could be carrying reconstruction beneath this very floor."

The enforcer stood still and listened. "I don't hear anything."

"Put your ear to the wall. Do you hear anything now? Feel any vibration?"

"No."

"They could be tunneling beneath us this very minute. Until the tunnels became so large they'd collapse the floor, you wouldn't even realize." The professor bent over stiffly and lifted the corner of the rug. "Actual wool from an actual sheep," he grinned. "An animal."

Beneath the rug was a slight depression in the floor. In the depression ran a crack.

"We must report this immediately!" said the enforcer. "Water will seep in."

"No water. More ants perhaps."

"For the safety of the compound—"

"The compound's safe! The sphere is safe! I understand this is difficult for you to assimilate. You were created not to question—to believe what you've been taught."

"I know the value of right and wrong—the need to protect the corporation from radicals like yourself."

"You're genetically programmed to be idealistic. Because of your appearance— Well, I'd hoped you might be different."

"I am different! More devoted than most. Able to think more clearly. That's why I was selected. Being an enforcer is an honor."

"Enforcement is your destiny. Just as it's another's to become a maintenance technician or a food handler. You have no choice."

"Others are destined for their positions. Enforcers are selected. Their devotion and honesty stand out among peers."

"You had no choice but to stand out," said the professor. "We engineered you to have the required tendencies. It's what we do here!"

"If you've engineered me so succinctly, then you won't be surprised when I report your activities."

"I suppose you can do nothing else. I frustrate myself sharing ideas with a brain incapable of free thought!"

"Does anyone else know about your *pets*?"

The professor shrugged. "I can only hope others have discovered their own." His eyes narrowed to slits. "You say you were *selected* to be an enforcer. But was there ever a time when you considered doing something else? Anything else? Ever?"

"Yes," thought the enforcer. "I wanted to be a doctor."

"Enforcement's your consuming passion. Just as it's your wife's consuming passion to be a teacher. Enforcers and teachers—always paired. One teaches the rules; the other makes sure they're followed."

The enforcer's mind raced. "I wanted to be a doctor! I remember now. I wanted to be a doctor."

The old man waved him to the door. "Go now. Let me be in peace."

The enforcer hesitated before setting down the lamp. "I'll have to report your lack of cooperation."

The professor bobbed his head in frustrated agreement and closed the door behind him.

## Chapter 20 - Doubt

The enforcer rubbed the sting on his knuckle, as he tried to think of an explanation for the ants. He held his breath and lay still on his bed, trying to detect sounds too soft to hear. He didn't hear ants, but he also didn't hear the sloshing of water.

He felt a surge of anger at the old man. He was the one who'd made him doubt. He'd arrest him first thing in the morning—should have done it already. The holes and crevices would be sealed and the sphere saved from inrushing water. But it wasn't water that trickled in. It was ants.

He got up from his bed and walked slowly along the walls of the bedroom. There were no holes or cracks here. He'd plugged the slightest hint of one as it formed. He scratched at one of the plugs, but it held fast. In his mind he saw the professor's ants. They seemed bigger now, each body segment connecting cleanly to the next. Some parts he wasn't sure of. He wished he'd studied them more closely. He'd panicked at seeing them—panicked again at remembering them. "Very unprofessional," he admonished.

He sat on the edge of the bed and stared at the floor—for the first time wondering what lay beneath. He'd never seen the water around the sphere. Nobody had—or nobody he knew. There were stories of workers repairing major imperfections outside. They'd been heroes, giving their lives for the corporation. Those who'd survived long enough to fulfill their assignments were left outside to die. Brought back in, foreign bacteria could wipe out an entire compound—the entire colony.

He lay back and worried whether ants carried bacteria. Had he been exposed? Assuredly the professor had—he'd crumbled one in his fingertips—was contaminating everything he touched. And yet he seemed healthy. Had he been watching the ants a week? More? He'd forgotten to ask.

The enforcer wondered whether he'd exposed his own family. His ear caught snatches of their conversation from the next room. "Mikel, I have to grade these essays." Their words intermixed with the professor's, making less sense as his eyes drifted closed.

## Chapter 21 - Betrayal

"Thank you for coming," said Brian, meeting Camryn at his cubicle door.

She stood tiptoe to give him a peck, but he pulled away.

"I need to talk to you, but not where everyone can hear."

Her hopes for an apology began to fade.

"You want to sit down?"

She took a seat on the end of his bed. Brian leaned against a counter. He folded his arms across his chest.

"I'm sorry about the other day," she faltered.

"I'm glad we talked. Made me redefine my priorities."

She began to feel more hopeful and smiled up at him gently.

"I'm sorry I barked at you," he said. "It was wrong of me to hide the snake in the first place—for starting this whole mess."

"You were curious."

"Look. I know you ordered ancient mouse DNA—and why. But there's no excuse for *Dobie's* actions."

"He was helping you—indirectly at least."

"I sincerely doubt that. He was helping you, and there was no reason he should have."

She smirked. "Thanks a lot."

"He should have come straight to me."

"But—"

"What I'm trying to say—and not doing a very good job of it—"

Her smile widened. "That's okay. I still love you."

Brian sighed. "You're loyal to me, and I appreciate that. It's why you're still here. I insisted on it."

"Why I'm still here? Insisted to whom?"

"The authorities. I turned myself in—told them everything. But they won't be pressing charges. It was one of my conditions. When I realized the professor was encouraging treason—"

"Trea—? He was just relaying ideas."

"Camryn. He was head of the lab, yet more than willing to overlook the snake; and Dobie's actions; and your mouse for that matter. In fact, he relished our crimes."

"He just wanted to see a snake. And if I remember right, so did you!"

"He should have set an example and turned me in. Apparently he should have turned Dobie in too—long ago."

"Dobie? What did he do?"

"Besides helping you? Apparently he's been cloning all sorts of things—for a very long time."

Camryn's jaw dropped. "Why would the authorities tell you that?"

"They didn't. I agreed to help them with an investigation. *Someone* ordered ancient mouse DNA. I discovered Dobie's antics in the process, and naturally I reported them.

"Then I discovered that the professor has been sabotaging entire lines most of his life.

"Yours, however, was only a momentary lapse in judgment," he continued. "I told them that, and assured them that you're normally very law abiding. They'll want to talk to you though. Just confirm what I say."

Camryn scowled at him.

"They're going to ask you about the mouse—if it's been cloned yet, and who's been doing the work."

"And what if I don't know who did the work?"

"Does that mean it's completed? That it's in your possession?"

"It means I didn't make the arrangements. And if I did, I'd keep it to myself."

"Get your priorities straight Camryn. The corporation relies on the loyalty of its citizens to remain maximally productive."

"Maybe I'd prefer less productivity and a little more compassion!"

"I'm going to overlook that, but next time I can't let you off so easily."

"Let me off? Who are you to—?"

"Consider it a warning."

Camryn gasped, and then laughed.

"The professor permitted all sorts of things. From now on, things will be different."

"I'm sure they will. I'm going to speak with him right now!"

"They're taking him as we speak. When they were clearing out Dobie's belongings, there was a scream from the professor's quarters. They found a parrot—a kind of bird."

"I *know* what a parrot is!"

"Dobie ordered the DNA for it years ago. The fact that it wound up with the professor implicates him as well."

Camryn marched for the door. Her nostrils flared.

"I took the liberty of cleaning out your desk. I'll overlook the reconstruction this time, but if I discover anything else from the commissary I'll be forced to report it."

"What gives you the right?"

"It's my right as director of the lab, and one that I'll assert."

"Director of—? The lousy lab! People go to detainment so Brian can be promoted?"

He reached for her, but she glowered at him so ferociously he withdrew his hand. "There's no need to be so upset," he said. "The professor knew the risks and chose to take them."

"And I know the risks! Get out of my way!"

She was already in the corridor.

## Chapter 22 - Emergency Exit

Camryn arrived at the professor's cubicle to find two enforcers leading him out.

"Be sure to record that wooden chest," one of them called out.

The professor's eyes were swollen and red; his face pale and drawn. There were finger marks in his hair where he'd clutched the sides of his head. "She's dead," he burbled. "They killed her right in front of me!"

Another enforcer came through the door behind them. A bloodied strip of green feathers dangled from his fingertips. At the end of it was a fractured beak. He shot Camryn an angry glance as he sucked a bleeding finger.

Camryn cast her eyes downward. There was blood on the man's slippers.

She watched them turn a corner, and then staggered inside the cubicle. In a stupor, she seated herself on the professor's bed. She sat dazed, and then jumped up; scanned the sheets for Harriet. Assured it was safe, she curled onto the bed in a fetal position.

A tear trickled alongside her nose, and then another. They soon dripped off her face and onto the pillow. She decided to let them.

***

Camryn stood outside the professor's quarters. Her eyes were swollen and scratchy. Smeared blood on the floor assured her it wasn't a dream.

She looked down the hall toward Dobie's cubicle, and then walked to the door he'd called "storage." On the door was an odd metal fixture—a short stick ending in a ball. In the ball was a thin hole. Camryn stroked it with a fingertip.

She thought a moment, and then marched to the professor's quarters. Stepping around the blood-stained rug, she ran a hand over the chest of drawers. She opened a drawer and rifled the professor's clothing. Beneath the folds was a piece of paper, bent in places and worn soft with wear. Something was written on it. "Mom, Dad, and Dobie."

Camryn flipped it over and smiled at the little boy in the photo. His lips were pursed together as though to hold back laughter. The man next to him smiled broadly, as though just recovering from a joke himself. A woman whispered something into the man's ear.

"Why does he have a picture of Dobie's family?" The oddness of it made her laugh. She looked at Dobie again, but her eyes drifted back to the man standing next to him. His twinkling eyes seemed familiar. "Professor?" She held the picture closer. "The professor is Dobie's dad?" She slipped the photo into her pocket, and then opened one drawer after another. Most were empty, but one held a book. She opened it carefully, and then frowned at the lack of illustrations.

She checked the latrine, wondering what it would be like to have her own. She sat on the closed port and propped her chin on her fists.

She noticed the professor's lab coat crumpled on the floor, fallen from a hook on the wall. As she lifted it by the collar, something clinked.

Camryn studied the floor, but it was bare but for a few green feathers. She searched the coat's pockets. One had a hole in it. The other held the sliver of metal.

She trotted down the corridor and inserted the key. She waited, but the door did not slide open. She tried to pull the key out, but it held fast.

Pressing a hand against the door, she rattled the key with the other. It popped out and the door swung open with a bang. Camryn landed on the floor.

She climbed to her feet uncertainly; swung the door back and forth. The palm of her hand patted the wall and found a dial. The lights inside grew bright.

"Contraband!" She was surrounded by contraband!

There were wooden chairs piled high upon desktops, stacks of books, and reams of paper. She tore a yellow wrapper and fanned the blank sheets. "These must be worth a fortune!"

She opened the doors of a cabinet. Within were old computer parts and gadgets Camryn had never seen before. There was a trash basket, but the lid had a switch and a series of round, toothed blades.

There was an electrical cord ending in a plastic box. The box was sealed but for a deep, round hole and a small drawer filled with squiggly shavings. She peered into the hole, but didn't see anything.

There was an envelope filled with round, stretchy bands.

Across the room, she saw a large picture leaning face-forward into a desk. She pulled it out and met the gaze of three bearded men. They sat atop large, long-legged animals. "Wow!"

She removed a large blue and brown ball from a bookcase. There were words printed across it in different sizes. She didn't recognize most of them, but when she spotted the word ocean, her face lit up. "The world before the asteroid? I think it is." She rolled the ball playfully across the floor.

On another shelf was a clear, plastic container filled with oblong metal spirals. She shook it, and one of the spirals fell out. She squatted on the floor to find it, and peered beneath the bookcase. She didn't find the paper clip, but instead a faint sliver of light.

Camryn pushed against the side of the bookcase, gently at first and then more forcefully. It shifted. She leaned her back into it and pressed hard with her legs. It moved. Behind it, recessed into the wall, was a half-sized orange door marked "Emergency Exit Only."

Camryn yanked on the door handle, and then tried pushing it down. There was a loud clank and the door eased open.

Her eyes burned and watered at the intense light. As she scrambled away from it, the picture in her pocket fell out and onto the floor. She rubbed her eyes with the butts of her hands. "Please don't be blind." The film of water cleared, but things seemed darker now. Tiny sparkles of white and yellow flashed before her eyes. Gradually, things took on their earlier appearance.

Once more, she crawled toward the escape hatch. The light seemed less intense now.

She held her hand out the door. It looked white with a greenish cast. "Gross." She held out her other hand for comparison. It looked the same.

Camryn crawled through the little door. Her fingers felt something cool and stringy between them. A row of tiny plants poked through crack-ridden concrete. Long strands of green, toppling over a cement pad, brushed her arms and shoulders. Standing on her knees, she peered over the tall grass.

She tried to remember what Dobie had called the plants in the distance. "Trews? Trells? No, tryes," she decided.

A series of shadows flitted across her face. Little black figures rolled across a gray, never-ending ceiling.

She looked over her shoulder at the towering structure behind her. "The megasphere? The outside of the megasphere?" Camryn backed through the tall grass, taking pleasure in the way it hissed and rustled around her. She stared at the towering dome.

Her heart bolted. She looked about her for water. There wasn't any. "The professor was right! I have to tell—" But she couldn't think of anyone. She began to wonder if everyone else knew already. Maybe it was like the contraband, the knowledge passing back and forth around her.

The trees whispered to one another. Something else chattered. Melodies whistled back and forth. There was a soft buzzing, and smells that tickled the deepest recesses of her nose.

"I've been exposed!" The realization popped into her head. "I've been exposed to foreign bacteria!"

"Maybe if I shower in the professor's latrine, before going back to the lab—"

She argued with herself. "Then the enforcers will be exposed when they collect his chest."

"Good!"

"You don't mean that!"

She frowned in protest. Still, it presented a dilemma.

"I'm already exposed," she reasoned. "I might as well explore a little."

She pushed her way through the field, looking over her shoulder from time to time to make sure she could still see the megasphere behind her.

As the grass became shorter, one of the black forms flitted out of the sky and landed in front of her. It wasn't black at all, but a pale gray. It lifted its tail and cocked a shiny yellow eye at her. Stretching its wings wide, it picked something off the ground and then jumped into the air.

Camryn kept walking and found herself standing on a faded yellow line on a long strip of pavement. There was no end to the corridor in either direction. Alongside the pavement was a large, metal object. Camryn went over for a better look. It sat on four black wheels. Camryn marveled at their size. One wasn't round like the others, but squashed flat.

Glass windows went all the way around. She cupped her hands to the sides of her face and looked inside. There were two seats in one end; an upholstered bench behind those. "Some kind of portable cubicle?"

In another window was a statue of a little animal. She leaned onto the cubicle for a better look, and the animal bobbed its head.

She tested a door handle. It lifted, but didn't open. She tried the others, but the result was the same.

There were voices in the distance. She scrambled down an embankment and flattened herself against it, peering over the edge. A man and woman approached the cubicle. The man carried a small red box. The woman wore a type of gown and carried a pair of pointed slippers. Camryn tried to glimpse her feet, to see how they were shaped.

"I don't know why we had to come all the way out here anyway."

"Hardly anyone's seen it," said the man.

"Hardly anyone's seen a rabid dog, but no one complains about that! Besides, there's nothin' to see. Ya can't even go inside."

"That's the excitin' part! No one *knows* what's inside."

The woman snorted. "What's inside most old buildin's?"

"Just think," said the man. "There might be a whole mess of people in there—like a whole other country. Workin'; just goin' about their business. Not even knowin' we're here. They were actually clonin' people in there."

"No one believes that any more. 'Cept you. B'sides, I think they'd of starved by now!"

"No, 'cause they figured out a way to recycle food over and over again."

"Are you sayin' they ate their crap?"

"Basic'ly. Course they changed it to somethin' else first."

The woman raised one lip.

"They even recycled dead bodies."

Camryn shook her head sharply, trying to loosen the thought.

Carrying the red box, the man walked around the side of the car and moaned. "I can't believe this!"

The woman joined him and took in the flat. "Maybe you can get one of the clone people to change it."

"I know how to change a tire! But let me switch out this batt'ry first." He lifted the car hood.

"Good, 'cause I'm not walkin' all the way back there again. I don't know why he couldn't give us a lift anyway."

"The man has a business to run."

"Way out here? Guess he can't risk missing his twice-a-year customer. That bat'ry there's prob'ly twenty years old."

"Then it's better quality than we're used to."

The woman fingered a key pad on one of the doors. "What's that number again?"

"Nine-nine. Nine-nine."

She opened the door and sat on an upholstered seat. Pulling a folded paper from a little compartment, she began to fan herself.

"You could make yerself useful and see how to get us outa here. Pop the trunk, will ya?"

"Yeah, yeah."

"And punch the tire release—left front."

He closed the car hood and went to the trunk. With a humph, he pulled out a large plastic cooler and the spare beneath it.

The woman spread the paper on the pavement and kneeled over it. "This poor dress ain't ever gonna be the same."

The man used a metal device to raise the front end of the car, while the woman studied the paper. When she was finished, she laid it on the roof, patting it with her hand.

"That was fast!" said the man.

"Ain't rocket science," she said. "We just go back the way we came; dead end onto ten; then left."

She walked over to the cooler and lifted the lid. "Ya want one?" she called.

"Yeah. I'll be done in a minute."

There was a snap and a hiss as the woman pulled the tabs from two cylinders. She set them on top of the closed cooler, and then returned to the open car door. She leaned in and fumbled about. "You got any tissues in here?"

"Don't think so."

The woman backed out. Shrugging, she wiped her nose on the back of her hand, and then wiped her hand on her hip. "Ain't ever gonna be the same," she mumbled.

"Did you say somethin'?"

"Nothin'. Your drink's on the cooler."

The man rolled the flat to the back of the car, and they stood drinking their sodas.

"Ready?" said the man, tossing his empty can into the trunk. He loaded the jack, the flattened tire, and the cooler.

The woman tossed her can onto the ground and climbed into the car.

The car screeched and rumbled as it turned about on the pavement. As it pulled away, the paper fluttered from the roof.

Camryn climbed to her feet. Her hands were cool and moist, and black granules clung to her palms. She rubbed them together. The granules scratched pleasantly before falling away. She lifted her hands to her face and smelled them. "Like the dormitory showers."

She sneezed at the acrid odor hovering over the pavement. Picking up the fallen paper and imitating the woman, she spread it on the ground and knelt beside it. "Some kind of map."

There were lines and names beyond belief. She scanned the paper for *sphere*. "How about *dome*?" Finally she found it. "Johnson's Soccer Dome. I'm probably here."

Some areas of the map were purple; others blue, yellow, or green. She looked at the trees around her. "Except that isn't in a green section." She carefully folded the map, and then smiled. "I own a piece of contraband!" She tucked it under her arm.

She went over to the soda can and picked it up. It was cool to the touch, and little droplets of water smeared beneath her fingertips.

She sniffed at the hole and her nose tickled. She gazed into it and saw liquid. Tilting the can back and forth, she watched the liquid move. She poured a little on her arm. It was brown and made tiny bubbles that clung to the hairs. She licked it, but tasted only her own salt.

Camryn held the hole to her lips and tilted her head back. A quick gush went into her mouth, and a trickle zigzagged down her chin. The bubbles burst, nipping her tongue and crawling into her nose. She opened her mouth and let the liquid spill out.

She moved her tongue in and out of her mouth and scraped it against her teeth. There was a bitter aftertaste, but also a sweet one that made her want more. She took another mouthful, this time daring to swallow. She swallowed again and again, liking the sensation more with each gulp. She shook the last few drops onto her tongue, and then debated whether she should keep the can, since it could be valuable.

She wondered how long she'd been outside; whether it was better to stay or go back.

The little door looked less inviting now, but her stomach gurgled and groaned. "Okay, okay!" She turned for one last look, and then returned to the megasphere.

## Chapter 23 - V. mysterii

Brian was coming her way. "Camryn?"

She glanced up from her data pad, as though she'd just noticed.

"I was worried about you."

She hoped her eyes were no longer puffy. "You did what you had to do."

"I know you and the professor were friends."

She tried to make her voice steadier than it was. "I didn't know him that well."

She scribbled some figures, thinking she'd correct the errors later. She looked up from the pad and met his gaze. "Besides, I thought other people were my friends. Turned out they weren't."

There was silence.

"I'm starting to realize that's just how things are. I was naive to think otherwise."

His eyes studied her as she continued to work. "I'm sure the professor meant well, but he was dangerous. He misled us all."

"I must admit that if anyone would know about misleading someone, it would be you."

He frowned, and she scribbled more numbers.

"You were late coming in this morning," said Brian.

"I just needed some time."

"Still we have a lot of work to do. It's important that the lab regain any productivity lost under the professor."

Her nostrils flared, but her voice remained steady. "Don't worry. I'll do my utmost to make the professor's loss come to some purpose." His expression made her aware of her ambiguous tone.

"I'll give you some leeway today, but from now on—"

She smiled at him coolly. "The corporation's provided for me. Now I'll provide for the corporation."

He shifted uncomfortably.

Penny came up behind him and stroked his back. "Might I get your assistance?"

"Sure," said Brian.

She looked at Camryn. "We missed you earlier."

"Thanks. That's what Brian just said. In fact, he suggested I join you tonight in the commissary."

Penny locked her eyes to Brian's. He shook his head.

"Just kidding," said Camryn. "I'm well aware of how much I'm missed."

Brian and Penny exchanged glances as Camryn continued to enter numbers. She looked up at them as though just realizing they were still there. "I'm okay. Really. I understand how things are."

"I'm sorry," said Brian.

Penny frowned; then rubbed his shoulder and smiled. "So are you going to help me?"

Camryn kneaded the back of her neck as they strolled away. It seemed harder to breathe. The sides of her nose felt swollen. Her head felt puffy between her eyes. "Probably from crying," she thought.

She looked across the room to see Brian and Penny teasing one another. With a frown, she erased the contents of her data pad. "Okay Camryn. Let's see if we can get it right this time."

***

Camryn looked at the clock. Several hours had passed and Brian and Penny were still working—and flirting—across the room. Intermittently, they looked over at Camryn.

"Now what?" she thought.

"Excuse me," said Brian, as he approached her desk. "Is it my imagination, or are you red?"

Camryn looked up and smirked. She wondered what the punch line was.

"I don't know how else to put it," he said. "You look red. Your face is red. So are your arms."

Huffing a bit, she held her arms in front of her. They were a brilliant pink. She rubbed them with her hands. They stung, and then seared. "Must be allergic to something." She wondered if foreign bacteria did this to a person's skin.

"Your voice sounds strange too."

She didn't tell him that her throat scratched and burned; that speaking to him now was unbearably painful.

"I think you should see a doctor."

"I feel okay," she lied.

"Really Camryn, you look just awful."

"I appreciate the compliment, but I'm sure it's nothing."

"I'm not playing games with you. I'm ordering you to the clinic. I've already messaged them. They're expecting you."

"You have no right—"

"I have the authority."

Their eyes locked.

"Okay," said Camryn. "I'm going."

She wondered if the doctor would be able to tell she'd been outside. She worried that everyone she touched might have their flesh eaten raw too. What if the bacteria multiplied? What if it couldn't be stopped? What if it ate right down to her bones?

In the clinic it was cool, but Camryn began to sweat. She tugged at her shirt collar. As quickly as it started, the sweating stopped. She shivered.

"I'm sorry I've kept you so long," said the doctor.

Camryn bobbed her head impatiently.

"I think we have two separate problems here. The erythema appears to be some type of burn." He took her arm in his hands. It was now crimson. "If you look here, you can see some blistering. Have you been using any type of burner? A laser perhaps? Any type of heat source? Radiation?"

Camryn shook her head.

"I've never seen anything like this."

"Maybe it's an allergy," she suggested.

"Not to your clothing. It only occurs where your clothing ends." He pulled her skin taut as he examined it. "Does it hurt?"

"Yes," she said, removing his hand.

"I'm going to give you a topical for the burn. Rub it on the affected areas, and try not to get it in your eyes. The other problem has me stumped. I've spent the past hour researching your symptoms. Your throat is irritated. You're having trouble aerating your lungs. You have a low-grade fever."

"My head hurts from listening to you," Camryn thought.

"The only thing I've come up with is a virus."

"Virus? Is that a bacterium?"

He angled his head at her. "Have you been exposed to bacteria? Something different than you'd normally encounter?"

"No. Well, I work with DNA samples. I know some strains carry remnants."

"No, a virus is entirely different. And it's completely alien to the corporation—a primitive type of illness we don't get here. Until now."

"So am I going to get better?" said Camryn.

"Well, that depends. It would seem most viruses cause only mild symptoms."

"This doesn't feel very mild."

"Others are deadly."

"I'm going to die?"

"Or get better fairly quickly. I'd like to be more definitive, but—"

"So I'm fine or I'm dead?"

"Or something in between. We'll keep you over night just to make sure there are no complications."

"Complications?"

"The thing I don't understand is, according to my reading, most viruses are spread through contact with an infected individual. It's breathed out or coughed—lands on vectors which are then handled by additional victims."

Camryn didn't care for the word *victim* either.

"Has anyone in your lab been complaining? Saying they don't feel well?"

"Not to me," said Camryn. She decided not to tell him about the map she'd handled, or the can she drank from.

The doctor stood rubbing his chin.

"Could an animal carry a virus?" Camryn asked, trying to redirect his focus.

The doctor raised an eyebrow.

"Because Brian found a snake—this animal with no legs. He said he touched it, and I touched him. I just wondered."

"And Brian's been sick?"

"I don't know, but now that I am—"

"Where did Brian get this snake?"

"No one knows. It just showed up."

"Interesting," said the doctor. "I'll see what I can find out."

Camryn was quarantined in an empty module. Each time she reclined she found she couldn't breathe. She discovered lying on her side caused one nostril to clear. She teetered on the edge of the sagging mattress; later awoke in the sunken middle, gagging and gasping for breath.

Mouth hanging open, she sat slump-shouldered on the edge of the bed. "I wish I'd deconstruct now and be done with it."

***

Shortly after Camryn left the lab, Brian began to feel achy. His head hurt and his throat felt raw. Within a few hours, others in the lab began to complain and squabble among themselves. One group, ordered to the clinic, stopped by the commissary on its way.

A few hours later, food handlers were hacking and sneezing over commissary trays. A shipment arrived from Reconstruction, and someone used the deliveryman's stylus to sign for it. The deliveryman completed his route, collecting more signatures with his virus-laden pen.

A group of enforcers arrived at the professor's cubicle to carry away his belongings. One stopped by the lab to ask more questions. At the end of the day, the men returned to their quarters feeling surlier than usual.

Their teacher wives didn't feel well when they returned to their classrooms, and the children they taught carried their own coughs and stuffy heads back to their parents.

Before long, everyone in the sphere was hacking, sneezing, and walking about with air-dried mouths.

Productivity in the megasphere came to an unheard-of standstill. The chief enforcement officers were very understanding, or perhaps became infected themselves. In spite of a virtual work stoppage, there were no reprimands or directives issued. Individual supervisors were left to determine who was able to work, and to what degree they should be prodded.

As the virus spread, Camryn watched uneasily, fearing someone might die from the illness she'd carried in. There was not a single fatality, however.

People enthusiastically related their individual experiences with the illness, embellishing their own tales to supersede those of their neighbors. And in spite of the fact that no treatment was offered, the doctor wrote a paper for the historical record: *Virus mysterii: Plague or Engineering Error?*

## Chapter 24 - Hullabaloo

Dobie pushed more pretzel nuggets into his mouth, and then coughed and sputtered as he chewed.

Freeman looked at his face and chuckled. "Still gaggin' on that stuff? Takes some gettin' used to I guess. They like things salty here."

"And things that crunch," garbled Dobie. An avalanche of crumbling bits rumbled between his teeth. He swallowed the gravelly wad and it clumped in his throat. He swallowed harder to push it along.

"What makes you stay out here?" said Dobie. "It can't be the food."

"Well for one thing, I don't have to see my wife."

"Is she that bad?"

"Not really. With someone else she'd be fine. Guess you and your DNA lab screwed up. Technicians and nurses supposed to be compatible."

"We have nothing to do with who marries whom. In theory, if no one's able to breed, it shouldn't matter in the long run. Those determinations were made long ago, by the chief enforcement officers."

"Have ya ever met one? A CEO? Hey, did ya ever clone one?"

"Never met one. Never cloned one. Now that you mention it, I've never even seen a blueprint."

"Hmm," said Freeman. "Maybe they *did* come from out here—outside the sphere."

Dobie mulled the possibility for several moments, and then spoke again. "I know you're from AARC. I'm from AARC. Are there any non-AARCs?"

"Most people ain't from AARC," said Freeman. "And if you're smart, ya won't be volunteerin' that you are. Not everyone likes the idea of clones wanderin' around. First ones to come out created quite a hullabaloo."

"Hullabaloo?"

"A to-do. A stir. A stink. Some thought they should go to jail—same thing as detainment. Funny now that I think about it. Corporation's settin' em free. Country's lockin' 'em up."

"Did they do something wrong?"

"Nope. Nothin'. People just supposed they must of been bad to get tossed out in the first place. Some non-AARCs thought that wasn't right.

"The press—they're people who tell others what's goin' on—decided they'd show everyone there was nothin' to fear. 'Cept when no one was afraid any more, there weren't any more story. So then they said AARC was dang'rous after all. They set up reporters and cameras right outside the sphere. That way, soon as someone came out, they could warn everyone."

"And TV is—"

"Way a broadcastin' pictures and stories to millions of people at a time."

"Millions?"

Freeman nodded. "You and me, we're just a piss in the forest. AARC's just a tiny dot on the planet. There are millions of people. Maybe billions! Or is it trillions? I can never remember."

Dobie's eyes glazed. His face drained of color.

"Don't worry. They're scattered all o'er. Ya don't have to meet 'em all at once. Anyway, what was I talkin' 'bout?"

Dobie blinked away the imaginary hoards. "The people at AARC. Pictures being broadcast."

"That's right. Anyway, the press sat outside AARC a couple years. The people that come out tell everyone about life inside. There's a terrible stink! Some says the AARC people in jail should be turned loose. Others say they're cannibals, so they must be murderers. Others say they ain't people at all—just manufactured goods to be destroyed.

"Some wants to tear AARC down and set everyone free. Others worry the people inside would bring terrible diseases out with 'em. Some say non-AARCs would take terrible diseases in. A few say AARC should be considered a separate country and we should 'stablish diplomatic relations."

"I'm not sure I know what *country* means."

"Let's see. How can I explain it? A big, *big* group of people who all does things a certain way on a certain piece of ground."

"So what happened?"

"Nothin'! That's what happened. The press bombarded the people with so many stories about AARC that no one cared any more. Other stories came along that were new—sounded more int'restin'. A few people did keep thinkin' about the people inside. They set up groups to help anyone comin' out to accamate. Then the gover'ment stepped in and gave 'em money to keep goin'."

Dobie rubbed his face. "Gover'ment?"

"What runs the country. The corporation of America. Oops. Don't tell anyone I said that word. Corporation of the *Union* now.

"'Ventu'ly the politicians—the chief enforcement officers here—decided AARC was a dead issue. They couldn't get any more votes by mentionin' it any more. So they cut off most of the fundin' to the accamation stations."

Dobie looked tired. "And *fundin'* is—?"

"Money. Credits. Kind of a theoretical barter system with no basis in reality."

Dobie twisted his brows.

"Ne'er mind. Gets complicated."

"These people," said Dobie, "the ones that help. Are there any left?"

"They're around."

"Any I can get to?"

The man shook his head. "You're just tradin' one corporation for another."

"You said there were millions of people?"

"Umm huh."

"Well do most of them live in town—or do most live like you?"

"Like me? Nothin' wrong with the way I live. Livin' in town there's all kinds of rules. Live out here, ya keep your freedom. Now town folk can help. I grantchya that. Winter would be mighty hard without 'em. Mighty hard.

"That's a time when it gets really cold. I mean *really* cold. Sometimes down to freezin'. We're lucky here though. Here we don't get snow."

"But what about—?"

"Ne'er mind. Like I was sayin', town folk can help, but you don't wanna live with 'em."

"But if I did, how would I find the ones that can help?"

Freeman sighed. "The way you came? Keep goin' 'bout eight kilometers. Bit of a walk, but you can do it if you're a mind to."

"I'm going to try," said Dobie.

Freeman frowned and shook his head. "Let me check my closet." He walked over to a tarp-covered pile. "Here. take this if you're goin'." He tossed Dobie a floppy, wide-brimmed hat.

Dobie pushed a finger through a hole along the seam before trying it on.

"It'll make the light more tol'rable for ya out on the road. Ya can take these too," he said, bringing Dobie a pair of blackened goggles. "Ne'er use 'em myself."

"Thanks," said Dobie, pushing the sunglasses onto his face. He lifted his chin to peer beneath the hat brim.

"If anyone asks if they can give ya ride, say no—though with that getup ya shouldn't have to worry. Hitchhikin' can be dang'rous."

Dobie rubbed the sunburn on his hands. Here, he thought, doing nothing could be dangerous. He didn't ask what *hitchhikin'* meant.

"'Remember now. Eight kilometers. You'll come to a gas station. Don't ask me why they still call 'em that. More and more of 'em don't even sell gas. Be a man there tendin' the place. He's the one to talk to."

Dobie stood up and smiled. "I'm off then."

"If ya find ya don't like it, you're welcome back," Freeman called after him.

## Chapter 25 - Reunion

"Messenger," typed Dobie. "Freeman's alive. Still likes it better here. If you haven't left, don't. Not sure how safe it is. Very different. Will come back to let you know. Dobie." He hit "Send."

He sat back in the chair staring idly through his sunglasses and playing with the brim of his hat. Slow, cautious footsteps echoed in the corridor outside. Dobie stood up. Through the doorway he saw a tottering figure.

Dobie pulled the sunglasses down his nose; peered over them. "Professor? Dad? Dad!"

The figure froze and squinted at the open door. "Who is that? Dobie? Is that Dobie!"

"Dad!"

They met at the door and clung to one another. The professor began to sob.

"Ah, don't cry Dad."

"I thought I'd never see you again!"

"So you should be smiling."

The old man chuckled and choked. He looked his son up and down. "Is that standard detainment wear?"

"Oh—the goggles?" He pulled them off.

"And that thing on your head." His face grew serious. "Sheila's dead Son. I'm sorry. There was nothing I could do."

It took him a moment to register the name. Life in the sphere seemed a long-ago memory.

"The authorities. They killed her."

But Dobie couldn't stop grinning.

"How bad is it? The detainment compound?"

Dobie chuckled. "There *is* no compound."

The professor raised his hands and stumbled about in a circle. "This is it?"

"No Dad," Dobie laughed, "there's a little more." He took the old man by the arm and guided him down the corridor. As they neared the end of it, the light became brighter. The professor blinked, and then blinked again. Water welled in his eyes, and he covered them with his hands.

"Here," said Dobie, placing the sunglasses gently over the old man's ears. "Any better?"

The professor didn't answer.

"Dad. Open your eyes."

"They are open." He grabbed at the lenses and pulled them down. Squinting, he pushed them back up. "We're out?" he whispered. He looked up at his son. "We're out?"

"We're out Dad."

The old man walked into the caressing light. "Feels good," he said, holding his arms out wide.

"At first," said Dobie, rubbing the peeling skin from his arms.

"I want to go out there," said the professor, pointing to the green beyond. "Can we go out there?"

"We have to," said Dobie. "There's someone who can help us, but it'll take a while to get there."

"Did they tell you this? They didn't tell me this."

"Freeman told me. He's from AARC too. That's what they call the corporation out here."

"There are others?"

"I've only seen one, but he says there are millions—maybe billions or trillions. Only a few are from the corporation though."

The professor clasped his hands together. "Do you realize what this means?"

Dobie shook his head.

"You could marry someone viable! These others, they're not cloned are they?"

"Apparently not."

"Then you could marry one! I could have grandchildren! Honest-to-goodness, uncloned grandchildren!"

Dobie laughed. "Right now we have other things to worry about." He offered the old man his arm.

"Too bad things didn't work out with Camryn," said the professor. "She should be out here with you—making babies."

Dobie blushed.

"Making grandchildren."

"You said Camryn's DNA wasn't worth the vial it took to hold it."

"Did I say that? Well maybe I did. I was a bit harsh perhaps."

"You hate her."

"But I don't! I think I expected her to be more like you. Of course, she didn't have such free-thinking parents as you did."

"Very disadvantaged."

"Very."

Dobie shook his head, and they started across the parking lot.

## Chapter 26 - The Arrangement

"Why pink?" asked Camryn.

The enforcer frowned at the glowing walls around them. "It's supposed to make suspects more receptive to questioning."

"Doesn't telling me that defeat the purpose?"

He shrugged. "I don't think it makes much difference. If anything it's distracting."

"Overwhelming even."

The enforcer grew serious. "We found the mouse you cloned."

"I thought Brian explained that."

"He did, but I needed a reason to bring you here. I informed him the mouse had found its way into another compound."

"Oh?"

"I assume it escaped from you, the way it escaped my son."

"Your son has it?"

"Did. It chewed through the data pad case he brought it home in. I woke up one night—found it sitting on my lips."

Camryn giggled.

"It could have bitten me. It bit him."

Camryn choked back a laugh. "Is he okay?"

"Just a cut."

"But if you know how it escaped, then why am I here?"

He leaned toward her, meeting her gaze. "I want to know what's outside the megasphere."

Camryn fumbled with the key in her coat pocket, reassuring herself it was still there. "Everyone says water."

"*You* didn't drown."

"Because I've never been out."

"Next to the professor's cubicle is a module filled with contraband, and an escape hatch of some kind. You, Camryn, have been through the escape hatch."

Her eyes wandered the room.

"No one's watching if that's what you're thinking. And the recorder has a glitch in it." He gave a half-smile. "Happened just before I came in." He leaned toward her. "I just want to know what's on the other side."

"If there's this door," said Camryn, "an escape hatch as you call it, then you know what's there."

He looked down and shook his head. "I don't. I was afraid to open it. A part of me still believes I could drown the compound—everyone in the sphere. Your professor, he put these ideas in my head. He said there was something beyond the walls. Something besides water."

"Is that why you sent him to detainment? Because of his 'ideas'?"

"I had nothing to do with that. He was swept up in the investigation. But I think he must be right. I look at you now. You've been outside. Obviously you didn't drown. I just want to know what's out there."

"How would I even know about this 'escape hatch'?"

"Now that's what I can't figure out. Unless the professor or your friend Dobie showed you. I found a picture of them inside the module. But what I do know is that there's this door, and you've been through it. Because somehow you got an illness—one that doesn't exist any more, but is acquired through someone who's affected. It's the only thing that makes sense."

"I got it from Brian's snake."

"I talked to the doctor. Brian was the first to contact the snake, but you were the first to get sick."

"Maybe the doctor remembers wrong."

"I checked the records. You were the first."

"So what happens if our conversation ends here?" said Camryn. "Do I go to detainment too?" She grew short of breath. "If I can't give you the answer you want, am I deconstructed?"

The enforcer chuckled. "I'll tell you a secret Camryn. No one is deconstructed."

"Ever?"

"Not by the authorities. Not for offenses."

"So I can go back to the lab?"

"Not necessarily. Perhaps you released the mouse purposefully—to undermine productivity. That's a very serious offense, punishable by detainment."

Her mind raced, trying to decide what to do.

"Is it better outside? Better than the megasphere?" asked the enforcer.

"Different," she mumbled. "I was only out a short time."

"Are there people? Other people?"

She nodded.

"Tell me this," said the enforcer. "Knowing how ill you became—how sick we all became—would you go out again?"

She imagined herself spending life in detainment. "If you'll let me, I'll go right now." She rolled the key between her fingers and it raised a question. "How did *you* get into the storage module?"

"The question is, how did you? My rank allows me a pass key or code to every room in the sphere. At least that's what I've been told. I haven't tried every door of course." He sucked air into his lungs, and then let it out. "I want to go out," he announced. "Camryn, let's go out!"

"But if you have a key you don't need me."

"But I do, and I'll make you a proposition. Your record is cleared but, in exchange, you accompany me out. And you make me a promise. If I'm killed or injured, you come back into the sphere and tell my wife. She has to know I didn't desert her."

He paced the room. "I can only hope there's a better place to raise my son. Where a woman isn't sterilized if she's lucky enough to bear a child. Where the corporation doesn't determine who should be granted offspring and what job they can perform!"

He seemed to forget she was there. "Can you imagine the possibilities! We were lucky, Nora and I. She actually became pregnant. We had Mikel before anyone realized we were both viable. He's creative too! I bet he could be an engineer just like you—if the corporation permitted such a thing. Maybe outside he can be whatever he wants. Maybe I can be a doctor!"

"So I'm not going to detainment?"

"You should," he said sternly. "I should too," he laughed. "So what difference does it make to the corporation—whether we leave on our own or disappear into detainment? They're rid of us either way."

"But what about your family? Are you just going to leave them here?"

The enforcer grew somber. "I don't want them involved. Not until I've seen it." He grinned. "I can't wait to see it!"

## Chapter 27 - The First Night

"So where are we?" said the enforcer. "Do you know?" He set down a bulging pillowcase and sat on the ground beside her.

Camryn ran her hand over the map. "I thought we might be here, but that can't be. The woman said this corridor connects to 'ten.'" She zigzagged a finger around Johnson's Soccer Dome. "None of these lines cross a ten."

"Any ideas then?"

"The people I saw walked from that direction, but they left the opposite way."

"If they walked from there," said the enforcer, "that may be the source of the virus."

"Good point," said Camryn. "I'd rather not experience that again." She folded the map and shoved it into her own pillowcase. She fumbled through the sack and pulled out a mockmeal cookie.

"You better save those for later. We don't know what's edible out here."

"The people I saw looked healthy enough. They must be eating something." She bit into the cookie with exaggerated relish, and then giggled at the enforcer's frown.

***

Camryn's feet hurt from walking. She plopped down on the pavement and eased back on her elbows. The sky was streaked orange and violet. It reminded her of the inquiry lounge. "How long do you think we've been out?"

The enforcer eased himself onto the pavement next to her. "Still kind of hot," he complained, rubbing his palms on his pant legs. He pulled something from his pocket. "We've been out six, maybe seven hours."

"Hey! Is that a watch? Even the enforcers have contraband?"

He climbed to his feet and squinted. "What's that?"

In the distance, approaching rapidly, were two beams of light.

Camryn sat up for a better look. There was a loud honking noise. "Get out of the road!" someone yelled. "Get out of the way!"

The enforcer pulled Camryn to her feet. They scrambled aside as the conveyance sped by. One of the boys inside leaned out a window, his red hair whipping in the wind. He held out his arm and pushed up a finger.

Camryn and the enforcer stood dazed, watching the conveyance disappear in the distance.

"Glad it didn't go over us," said Camryn, peeling her partially flattened pillowcase from the road.

"Anything left?"

She peered inside and shook the contents. "Some of its okay. The rest—" She pulled out a handful of crumbs and brushed them away on her pant leg.

"Better stay off the pavement," he said, stepping onto the grassy shoulder. "At least we know there are people where we're headed."

"I hope they're friendlier than that!"

"Maybe standing in the corridor's illegal here."

"Or maybe those things don't stop once they get going."

"In that case," he said, "they just saved our lives."

They walked alongside the roadway, stumbling here and there on the occasional rut.

"Look!" said Camryn, clutching his arm.

Ahead were several large black birds. They squawked at one another and danced up and down.

"You think they're dangerous?" said the enforcer.

Camryn considered Sheila. "I don't think so."

They approached slowly, hoping for a better look. The birds flew into the trees and cawed at them from above.

On the berm was a squished mass of fur. Camryn squatted in front of it and poked it with a stick. "You think that's what happens if a conveyance goes over you?" She could smell the blood, and parts of the carcass still looked slippery. "Look at its teeth. They're like little knives."

"Maybe they eat raw flesh here."

She wrinkled her nose. "That's gross."

"I think that's what the birds were doing. They were poking at it."

"I'm poking at it and I'm not eating it."

"One flew off with something in its mouth," said the enforcer.

"Help yourself if you like. I'll pass."

They continued walking and the light in the sky dimmed. Soon they were engulfed in blackness.

"What do we do now?" said Camryn.

"Sleep." He lay down in the grass.

"You think it's their night cycle?"

"It's dark isn't it?"

"Aren't you hungry?" said Camryn. "You've hardly had anything."

"I think we should conserve what we have—just in case."

Camryn lay down in the dampness and listened to the night. There was a melodic clicking and chirping, and something buzzed by her ear. There was a hoo-hooing from above.

She dozed off, but her eyes opened to rustling in the plants around her. Something chortled and growled. There was a chortle and growl in reply. Camryn sat upright and the noises stopped. There was louder rustling; then silence. The only thing Camryn heard was the enforcer's deep, irregular breathing.

She reached into her pillowcase and fingered through it. She retrieved a dented gnaw bar, and sat chewing and listening.

## Chapter 28 - Langston

Camryn and the enforcer stood on a thin strip of white cement, wondering whether they'd be greeted or chased. Except for a small, bug-eyed dog growling in front of them, no one seemed inclined to do either.

"Come on Casey," someone called.

The dog snorted; then bounded off.

On either side of them were buildings of varying heights and colors. Some displayed contraband behind large glass windows. There were signs above doorways and pasted on walls. Camryn pronounced the foreign words as best she could. They took in everything—rain gutters and candy wrappers; clouds reflecting in window panes.

Most of the people wore blue pants. Some had protruding pieces of cloth on their heads. One young man had green hair. It stuck out of his head in spikes.

"Recessive gene?" thought Camryn.

They stood on a corner watching a light suspended over the roadway. When the light glowed green, conveyances moved forward. When it glowed red they stopped.

"Ya lost?" A gaunt man with thinning white hair sat on a storefront bench. "Ya seem lost."

Camryn considered whether they could be lost if they didn't know where they were going.

"No," she said.

"Yes," said the enforcer.

"Well are ya lost or aren't ya?"

"Where are we exactly?" said the enforcer.

"Corner of Fifth and Main."

"This place," said Camryn. "Does it have a name?"

"What place ya talkin' about?" The man looked over his shoulder. "Ya mean the store? It's Grisham's." He regarded Camryn. "You visitin' Ella Myers? Ya look a little like Ella Myers."

Camryn and the enforcer exchanged a puzzled glance. He nodded yes while she shook her head no.

"Maybe they put up with this crap where you come from. Don't set well 'round here." He rocked forward and removed himself from the bench. "You can find yerself someone else to jerk on."

"Wait," said Camryn. "Can you tell us where we can get a drink?"

The old man stood stoop-shouldered in front of them. "Little early, ain't it?"

"Is there a correct time to drink?"

"There a correct time to drink?" he mimicked. "You're a real piece a work you are."

"I'm sorry," said Camryn. "I'm thirsty. *Really* thirsty."

"Gettin' the DT's huh? I know how that is. See that little red-brick place o'er there? That's Smitty's. They'll fix ya up. Ya'd do best to lay off the stuff. Take it from one who's been there."

"Thanks," said Camryn. She wondered how bad the water could be.

***

"What'll it be?" said the bartender.

Camryn and the enforcer looked at each other and shrugged.

"Ladies first," said the bartender. "What do you want miss?"

"Water," said Camryn.

"Tea toter, huh? And how about you?"

"Water too."

"Tourists," snarled the bartender, contemptuously eyeing the bulging pillowcases. "Let me guess. You want to use the facilities too."

"Facilities?" said the enforcer.

"Bathroom. Powder room."

They stared at him blankly.

"El baño. Bulkhead. Latrine."

"You have a latrine!" said Camryn.

"Look," said the bartender. "This ain't no rest stop. If you want to use the facilities—the latrine—you'll have to have something besides water. We have beer on tap or you can have imported."

"I guess I'm imported," said the enforcer.

"Guess I'm imported too," said Camryn.

"Bathroom's over there," said the bartender. "Through that door."

Camryn headed for the latrine.

The bartender pulled three frosty bottles from an ice chest and popped the caps. "So where you from?"

"Down the corridor," said the enforcer.

"Down the—? Oh, Dondicord. Surprised I haven't seen you before. Most Dondies do their shopping here in Langston." He nodded toward the bathroom door. "You bring the missus over did ya?"

"We're not married."

"Ah. Must be your niece then."

"No."

"Here's to two dirty old men," said the bartender. He pressed a bottle to his lips and took several swallows. "Don't tell the boss," he said with a satisfied sigh.

The enforcer copied the bartender. The coldness felt good in his mouth, but the taste was so bitter he grimaced. "This is imported?"

The bartender shrugged. "Personally I think domestic's just as good."

"Really. Just as good?"

Camryn joined them at the bar. The enforcer held the bottle to his lips and gave her a sideward glance. He gulped down the rest of his bottle, forced a smile, and then sighed like the bartender.

Camryn put a bottle to her lips and swallowed. Yellow liquid spurted from her mouth and foam coursed down the sides of her chin.

The enforcer chuckled.

The bartender snickered as he took the bottle from her. "Before you have anything more," he said, "I'll need to see some I.D." He grabbed a handful of ice from the chest and dropped it into a glass. He added some water from a spigot.

Camryn gazed at the condensing glass in her hands. She sipped cautiously, and then drank with relish.

The enforcer smirked.

"You want another one?" said the bartender.

Camryn nodded an enthusiastic yes. The enforcer shook his head and nearly fell over.

"You all right?" asked Camryn.

"Now I know why the old man said dehydration was better." He stumbled to a table and slumped into a chair.

"Lightweight?" said the bartender. "Or did he have a few before he got here?"

"He hasn't had anything to drink for nearly twenty-four hours."

"A whole day, huh? Is that some kind of record?"

Camryn understood the man was making a point, but couldn't figure out what it was.

"It'll be seven even for the beers."

Camryn hesitated. "Seven even?" She wasn't sure what an *even* was, but she was positive she didn't have seven.

"Three-fifty each."

Camryn stared at him blankly, and then joined her companion.

The enforcer's arms were folded on the tabletop. His head was buried in his arms. Camryn shook his shoulder. Out of the corner of her eye, she saw the bartender talking into some type of receiver. She shook the enforcer again. There was a snuffle, and then heavy irregular breathing. Camryn rooted through his pockets, and then stepped back to the bar.

"You said we were supposed to give you seven even," she said.

"That's right."

"I'm fairly certain we don't have any *evens*."

"That supposed to make me laugh?"

She wondered why it would. "Will you take this instead?" She laid the enforcer's watch on the bar.

"This ain't no pawn shop. We take credit cards, traveler's checks, N.A.U. debit cards, or good ol' cash—at least until the twenty-seventh of next month."

Camryn blushed. She was sure she didn't have any *cashes* either.

"What's the problem?" came a voice.

Camryn looked over at a pink-faced man in a blue shirt. On his chest he wore a shiny piece of metal.

"These two. They're the problem." The bartender nodded at the bottles. "Him, he gets drunk on two—I mean three—beers."

The officer tilted the bottle Camryn had tasted. "This one still looks full."

"Two then. But they've all been opened and someone's going to pay for them. She says they don't have any credits."

The officer walked over to the enforcer and Camryn tagged along.

The bartender slipped the watch off the counter and into his pocket.

"Sir. Sir," said the officer.

The enforcer raised his head and squinted. His forehead was splotched red where it had rested on his arms.

"Bartender there says you've had too much to drink. Can you stand?" He tugged at the enforcer's arm. "What's your name sir?"

"Enforcer Nine-eighty-six."

"Enforcer—? I need a name. What's your name sir?"

The enforcer thought hard a moment. "John."

"John what?"

He nodded an affirmation. "John."

The man sighed and looked at Camryn. "What's your name?"

She winced, certain that her answer wasn't right either. "Camryn?"

"Have you been drinking too?"

She nodded sheepishly.

"I'm going to have to take your friend here in."

"In where?"

"To my office, Ma'am—the Main Street Historical Station. You and your friend from around these parts?"

"He said they were from Dondicord," interjected the bartender.

Camryn wondered why the enforcer would say that.

"How much do they owe?" said the officer.

"Seven even," Camryn volunteered.

"Ten-fifty," said the bartender, gathering up the three bottles. "Three at three-fifty each."

"Do you have anywhere to stay tonight?" asked the officer.

Camryn shook her head. "Last night we slept next to the pavement. I can sleep there again."

"There's an extra room in back," said the bartender. "She can take that."

"You're better off with us," said the officer. He helped the enforcer toward the door.

"Missy!" called the bartender. He leaned over the counter and nodded at the pillowcases. "Don't forget your luggage."

## Chapter 29 - Pie

"He'll be okay," said the officer, closing a heavy door with a little window cut into it. "Just needs to sleep it off." He reached for one of the pillowcases. "Mind if I have a look?"

Camryn shook her head.

"No you don't mind, or no don't look through it?"

"You can look."

The officer emptied the contents of the pillowcase onto his desk. Except that some were square and others round, the items appeared very similar. "What's this?" he said, holding a crumbling block in his hands.

"Casserole," said Camryn.

The officer raised an eyebrow. He sniffed it. "Sure it's not an illegal substance?"

"It's not illegal where I come from. Except we're not supposed to take it outside the—"

"And what about these?" He pushed a couple of gray disks about with a finger.

"Mockmeal cookies."

"Please don't tell me you baked these."

"Oh no. I don't cook. You can have one if you like."

The officer took a bite and his mouth turned sharply downwards. Leaning over a waste can, he spit out the pieces. "Where did you get these?"

"A friend made them for me."

"If someone made me these, I wouldn't consider them a friend." He nodded toward the other pillowcase. "More food?"

She nodded.

"If this is what you're eating, you've got to be hungry. Why don't we call over to the diner and have something sent over?"

Camryn's stomach growled enthusiastically.

"What do you like?"

"What do they eat here?"

"Pretty much the same thing as in Dondicord. Is that where you're really from?"

Camryn shook her head.

"I didn't think so. What about your companion?"

"He's not from there either."

"Tell you what," said the officer. "Your friend's going to be sleeping for a couple of hours. Why don't we just walk over to the diner. My treat."

"Treat?"

"I'll pay for the food."

***

Some of the food on the menu looked familiar, but most of it Camryn hadn't heard of.

The waitress smiled broadly at the officer. "What'll it be?"

"Who's cooking?" he asked.

"Erv's on."

"I'll have the fried chicken then. No one makes chicken like Erv."

"Anything to drink?"

"Water's fine."

The waitress's smile vanished. "And you?"

"I guess I'll have chicken too," said Camryn.

"To drink."

"Not beer!"

"We don't serve beer here. You can have coffee, lemonade, tea, soda, diet soda, or milk."

"Am I allowed to have water too?"

"Of course you're allowed to have water too." She sneered at the officer. "Your date here's a bit of a smart aleck." She walked away scribbling something on a green pad.

"So where are you from, if not from Dondicord?"

"Johnson's Soccer Dome?"

He looked at her doubtfully. "Are you going to tell me or not?"

She sighed. "I'm not sure where we're from."

"What do you mean you're not sure?"

"I mean, I can get back there, but I don't know what you call it here."

"Are you from a different country?"

The conversation she'd heard between the man and woman popped into her head. Her face brightened. "Yes. A whole other country."

"Apparently they speak English there."

"There are other languages?"

"Look," said the officer, "Don't let the fair skin and freckles fool you. My grandma's pure Mexican, and this isn't the good ol' U.S.A. any more. Sixty percent of the N.A.U. is Hispanic. People might as well face the fact that Spanish is here to stay."

She faltered. "Where I'm from, there's nothing but English."

"No other languages at all?"

"Everyone talks the same."

"And what's the name of this country—where no foreigners live?"

"Here's your chicken." The waitress eased a plate in front of the officer and gave him a wink. "I told Erv to throw on an extra piece."

He patted his belly. "Maybe you should tell him to take off a piece instead."

"Oh you! You're the handsomest man in the county."

The waitress let Camryn's plate settle with a clatter. Water sloshed from a glass and onto her food. Once she was out of earshot, Camryn leaned across the table. "I don't think she likes me."

"I think she's jealous," he said.

The officer unrolled his silverware from a paper napkin and Camryn did the same.

"Hey! I bet I know what country you're from!"

"You do?" said Camryn.

"Iceland! I read somewhere that hardly anyone moves there and hardly anyone leaves." He thought for a moment. "Do they speak English in Iceland?"

Camryn wasn't sure but nodded yes.

The aroma of chicken wafted across the table and her mouth watered. "This is the best thing I've ever smelled!"

"They do have good fried chicken." He bit into a piece and the breaded skin crackled.

Camryn picked up a similar piece and imitated him. Her mouth watered profusely now and she burbled between bites. "This is the best thing I've ever eaten!"

The officer chuckled.

"Do you have chicken all of the time?" said Camryn.

"Occasionally we have other things."

"I'd eat this every day!"

"Then you'd be fat like me."

Camryn looked at him and took smaller bites. As she chewed, she examined the chicken cradled between her fingertips. She shifted one finger to give it a poke. "This looks like— Is this a bone?"

"Yeah it's a bone. So?"

Camryn threw the chicken onto her plate. She pressed a napkin to her lips and blinked hard at the table.

"Are you all right? Is something stuck in your throat?"

"Is chicken an animal?"

The officer stared at her.

"You eat flesh?"

"Most people aren't vegetarian. Are animals sacred in Iceland?"

"We don't have animals," said Camryn.

"None?"

"It's illegal."

"I knew dogs were once illegal in China. I didn't know that about Iceland though."

Camryn balled her hands in her lap and stared at the plate.

"Aren't you going to eat it?"

"I'm sorry," she said. "I'll just wait and have some mockmeal cookies."

"You'd rather eat those gray things? Do you eat those every day?"

"Oh no," said Camryn. "Only on special occasions. Unless you have a friend who'll make them for you like I do."

"I can see why you came to the Union. If you're not going to eat your meal, at least let me get you some pie."

"Pie?"

"It's sort of like cookies, only fluffier."

"Any muscle tissue in it? Blood?"

The officer pushed away his plate. "Suddenly this isn't looking so good to me either." He called over to the counter. "Tammy, could we have two slices of chocolate pie?"

The waitress nodded and brought two plates to the table. She placed one gently in front of the officer. "Yours is on me tonight."

Camryn's was served with a slip of green paper.

She watched the waitress go, and then reached for the slip.

"I'll get that!" said the officer, snatching it up.

Camryn poked at the pie with her fork.

"I think it's safe to eat," he said.

"No muscle tissue?"

"Maybe an egg or some milk. I think I can safely say that no animal died in the making of this pie."

She was already on her third forkful. "This is what your cookies taste like!"

"Pretty much."

"With cookies like these, who needs chicken?"

"I don't think it would be good to only eat pie and cookies."

Camryn gave him a concerned look. "It's bad to eat?"

"A little won't hurt you."

She nodded, too busy enjoying her dessert to take in anything else.

"Your husband," said the officer. "He from Iceland too?"

Camryn scraped her plate. "I'm not his wife. His wife's back home."

"Guess they're more liberal in Iceland."

Camryn looked at him quizzically.

"I mean, if I had a wife, I don't think she'd like my going off to another country with a beautiful young woman."

"She doesn't know where we are."

"He deserted her?"

"He's going back for her—if he likes it here."

"Then what happens to you?"

"I don't think I can go back."

"Afraid his wife will come after you?"

"Figure sooner or later I'll wind up in detainment."

"Is that like jail? Adultery's punishable in Iceland?"

"For hoarding food."

The officer grew silent. "I'm sorry," he said. "I didn't realize."

Camryn shrugged. "I think I'd rather stay here." She leaned forward and whispered. "Can I have more pie?"

## Chapter 30 - Realization

"Okay," said the officer. "I talked to Mom. You can stay with her tonight. She can't wait to meet someone from Iceland."

"What about—?" Camryn tried to remember the enforcer's name. "What about Jim?"

"I thought his name was John."

"John," said Camryn.

"So is it Jim or is it John? Or is that his real name at all?"

"It's John I guess."

"You're traveling with him—but you don't know his name?"

"I didn't ask."

"How about your name? Do you know what your name is?"

"Camryn."

"Okay, at least you're consistent there. Camryn what?"

"I'm not sure what you mean."

"I'm Mark Saxton. The cook at the diner is Erv Allgood. You know. Your last name—your surname."

"Sometimes they call me Engineer Six-twenty-one. Is that what you mean?"

"Engineer Six-twenty-one? As opposed to nine-sixty-two? As opposed to eight-seventy-six? That doesn't even make sense." He nodded toward the windowed door. "Is he afraid his wife will find out? Is that the problem?"

Camryn could tell Mark Saxton was becoming agitated, but wasn't sure how to respond. "He told her he's on an investigation."

"An investigation? Into what? What exactly does John do?"

"He's an enforcer."

"An enforcer?" Mark sat thinking. "An investigator? A police officer like me?"

Camryn's face lit up. "You're an enforcer?"

"What did you think I was?"

"I thought you ran the drinking place."

"You thought I was the owner, or a bouncer?"

Camryn wasn't sure whether to nod yes or no. "Is a bouncer a bad thing?"

"No, but I think I'm a little more helpful, don't you. I mean a bouncer would have thrown you into the street."

"I'm glad we didn't run into one of those."

"Anyway. You said you wanted to stay in the Union?"

"I don't want to go back where I came from."

"Tell you what I'll do. By morning, let's see if we can come up with a last name. Then we'll make a few calls. Do you have a work visa?"

Camryn stared at him blankly.

"Guess not. Maybe we can do that then. Get you a work visa. What kind of work do you do in Iceland?"

"I'm an engineer."

"Of course. Engineer two-twenty-one. Or was it fifteen-forty-two?" He sighed at her lack of response. "What kind of engineer are you? Structural? Civil?"

"I'm a geneticist."

"A geneticist, without a work visa, who sleeps alongside the road with a married man. And what made you come here? To this country?"

"I found a door."

"I think you mean, you saw an opportunity."

Camryn nodded. "The door gave me an opportunity."

Mark shook his head. "You said you stole food. Is that the only thing you're in trouble for?"

She shook her head. "I cloned something I wasn't supposed to."

"Okay. I'll play along. So what did you clone? A three-legged dog? A two-headed cat?"

"A mouse. I cloned it to feed a snake."

"Seems like the long way around for snake food. Why couldn't this snake just eat a mouse from a pet store, or one that was trapped?"

"There are no mice where I come from."

"No mice. None?" He reached toward the phone. "I need to call the farm bureau on this one. They'll want to talk to you." He waited for a response, but Camryn gazed at him emptily. "How does John fit into all of this?"

"He's the one who arrested me," said Camryn.

"He arrested you?"

"For cloning a mouse—and because he wanted out of the sphere."

"Sphere?" Mark shook his head. "So, am I to understand cloning's illegal in Iceland?"

"Cloning animals or plants is. We're only allowed to clone those workers specified by the corporation."

"The corporation? The sphere? Are you talking about the megasphere? AARC? American Alternative Research Corporation? Are you telling me you're a clone?"

Camryn hesitated. "Aren't you?"

He blinked at her.

"Can I ask you something?" said Camryn.

"Sure," he mumbled.

"Are you viable? John seems to think people here might have children on their own."

His face slowly reddened as he puzzled her words. His eyes began to bulge. "Oh I'm *vi*-able! The whole town's viable! As far as I know, the whole country's viable!"

Her eyes filmed with water. "Is it bad to be cloned?"

"Oh, I didn't mean— It's just that I've never met anyone— Well, from AARC. Sometimes Granddad told me tales when we drove past there—the sphere. Said he met a man from AARC once—one that was cloned.

"This man, he slipped out of the sphere. But everyone badgered him so much he went back in. A little while later, the folks inside tossed him back out. I thought it was a fairy tale."

"What happened to him?"

"I don't know. I was a kid. I thought it was make-believe. But now—" He looked at her and smiled. "It would make sense—"

"So what do I do now?"

## Chapter 31 - Janitors Know Everything

"Oh Mark!" scoffed the woman. "These people are no more clones than Drover was a Sasquatch!"

"Drover was our Saint Bernard," Mark explained.

Camryn and John exchanged glances and shrugged.

The woman took a seat at the kitchen table. "Your granddaddy was obsessed with AARC. It's practically all he thought about. He'd make up stories in his head, then like 'em so much he'd believe 'em."

"But Mom, I've been thinking. Remember back when I was little? Dad brought home that man? The one you didn't like very much?"

"That could be anyone in his family. You're probably thinking of Uncle Donald."

"Not Uncle Donald. Dad brought home this man. I think they talked about clones. Stayed here a while."

"Oh! You're thinking of that vagrant Dad took in. The one who runs the gas station out near the sphere. Tom? Tim? I don't remember. Something like that."

"Not Tom. This man was tall; lanky. Used to play basketball with me. Young guy."

"Tom was young once. That's him. He found out your granddaddy was interested in AARC. So he starts saying he's a clone—telling all kinds of tall tales. In AARC they did this. In AARC they did that. Your granddaddy came over nearly every day. Just about drove me nuts! He worked there a while you know."

"Who?"

"Your granddaddy. He worked for AARC. That's what got him on the whole kick. I think someone there played a joke on him. He used to say janitors knew everything going on at a place. People leave memos on their desks. Leave their computer screens on. Don't think anything about the person emptying the trash."

"And someone played a joke?"

"He said he read these memos—all about how they cloned the perfect waitress, or the perfect plumber. Some kind of perfect someone. He said they were working on the perfect soldier—special order from the government."

"Maybe Granddad was telling the truth."

"Oh Mark! Are you still watching those old space reruns? The whole town was laughing at him! No one took him seriously at all, until that vagrant came along. Then your granddaddy, he started telling everyone about the clone at his son's house. Before long this place was swarming with reporters. Granddaddy was here all the time. He'd sit next to 'Tom the Clone' during interviews, beaming from all the attention."

"Do you remember what they said?"

"Oh I don't know. When they got talking silliness, I'd find something else to do. In fact, mostly when your granddaddy came over I'd find something else to do."

"I'm just trying to follow through on a case, Mom. Think. Don't you remember anything?"

She pursed her lips and shook her head. "I can just see it happening all over." She nodded toward Camryn and John. "These people look at you and see free room and board—courtesy of me I might add. They'll tell you whatever you want to hear. And I'm going to be stuck here. Stuck with people blasting spotlights through the curtains and shoving microphones in my face—asking me all about clones and what planet they're from."

"They're clones Mom, not aliens."

"They're cons is what they are." She pursed her lips. "This is so much silliness."

"You're probably right," he said, squatting next to her. "But if you can remember anything, I could really use your help."

The corner of her mouth twisted as she scratched at a thumbnail.

"Helping people's my job, Mom. I give everyone the benefit of the doubt. You know, innocent until proven guilty?"

She looked at her hands a moment, and then patted her son's cheek. "You're such a good policeman. This town is lucky to have you. Let me see. Your granddaddy. He used to keep a scrapbook—all kinds of clippings about AARC."

"Do you know where it is?"

"Your daddy boxed up Granddaddy's things after he passed on. Stuck 'em in the attic. Might be up there. Go look if you're a mind to."

"Thanks Mom," he said, motioning John and Camryn to follow.

The old woman called behind them. "Don't break anything."

***

Camryn reached into another box of contraband. She kept a little pile to one side—items that might make interesting souvenirs or trading items. She found a hard, short-handled ladle attached to a wide, stretchy band. "What's this?"

Mark looked over and snickered. "You don't want that. Trust me."

"What is it?"

"It's a cup."

John looked up from a yellowed magazine. He gazed at the object a moment and then burst into laughter.

"What?"

Mark shook his head and continued rooting through a stack of papers.

Camryn frowned at them; returned the ladle to the box.

"I think we might as well give up," said Mark. "It's not here." He looked around at the clutter. "Mom's going to kill me. This place is a mess!"

"Can I take some of these things with me?" said Camryn.

"They're really not mine to give," said Mark.

She pouted, and reluctantly put away her collection.

"I think our best bet is to talk to Tom in the morning—right after breakfast."

"I need to go home," said John. "I've been gone from the sphere for two days. My wife must be going nuts. I've never been gone that long for any investigation."

Camryn hesitated. "Are you coming back?"

"With my family definitely. Without them—" He shrugged.

## Chapter 32 - Tom the Clone

A man squinted from his folding chair, and then rambled toward them. "Mark! By golly! I haven't seen you since you were yea high!"

"I'm surprised you recognize me!"

"Course I recognize you! Saw your picture in the paper not long ago. Said you graduated from some police academy."

"That's right!" He drew in his chin and tapped on his badge.

"Looks real! Not like the plastic one you used to wear."

Mark smiled and rubbed his nose sheepishly.

"This the missus?"

Camryn blushed.

"Nah. Not yet anyway." He gave Camryn a wink and then blushed himself.

"So whatcya doin' out here? Not that I mind the company mind you."

"Actually, Tom, I'm here on official business."

"If it's about Suttons' old cow, I didn't have anything to do with that. It was wanderin' around loose and some guy from Hobbs ran into it."

"I hadn't heard about that."

"Well if it comes up, it wasn't me."

"It was this other fellow, from Hobbs."

"That's right. Wrote down the license number if you want it."

"Maybe later. Could we speak privately?"

"Can't get more private than this. No one ever comes out. Don't even stock candy or gum any more."

Tom led them behind the building to a weatherworn picnic table.

"So," said Tom. "What can I do for ya?"

"I don't know exactly how to say this," said Mark. "It's going to sound— well, it's going to sound crazy."

"Crazier than tendin' a gas station nobody visits?"

"A little."

Camryn watched Mark as he spoke. She liked the way the corners of his mouth crinkled when he smiled. She liked his freckles too. She'd never known anyone with spots on their face.

"I got to talking with Mom—" said Mark.

"Just don't tell her you were talkin' to me!" said Tom. "Woman hates me!"

"Hate's a strong word."

"Last I saw her, she gathered up all my stuff—well, your dad's stuff really. He's the one who gave it to me. Anyway, she gathered everything up and threw it all over the yard."

"I hadn't heard about that."

"It was a long time ago, but still— You know what I think? I think she was jealous because Bill—your Dad—talked more to me than he did to her."

"Look Tom. I can't believe I'm saying this, but Mom says— Well, she says you claim to be a clone."

"Don't *claim* anything. I am a clone—if you're inquirin' that is.

"Most people don't ask any more. They're afraid I'll bore 'em with details about AARC. Seems I'm some kind of lunatic now. Government says AARC never cloned anyone, so that's that. Suddenly I don't know nothin' about nothin'."

"I'm a clone too," said Camryn.

"Are you now?"

Mark nodded. "I stumbled into Camryn here. She didn't seem to fit in. At first I thought she was from Iceland."

"Why would ya think that?" said Tom.

Mark half-smiled and shook his head. "We started talking and she mentioned the sphere. I didn't know what to think. Still don't know what to think."

"What'd you do in the sphere?"

"I'm an engineer," said Camryn. "DNA lab. Creative compound."

Tom puckered his lips and glowered at the trees around them.

"What did you do?" she said.

"If it weren't for the likes of you, there wouldn't be all those people trapped in there! You shouldn't be makin' more when there's nowhere for 'em to go!"

Camryn stammered. "Orders come in. We fill them. I have a very high productivity rating."

Tom rolled his eyes. "You should slow production! Stop it! Let everyone die out!"

"We all have roles to perform. Some are technicians. Some are teachers—"

"And some do reconstruction." His eyes became slits. "Do you have any idea what we do in there? In Reconstruction?"

She shook her head.

"You were supposed to design us so we wouldn't care! How can you not care when you dismember your own father!"

"I thought the mortuary—"

"The mortuary crosses 'em out of the database. That's all! Then they go straight to us."

"What are you two talking about?"

"I don't understand," said Tom, "why I'm suddenly supposed to help the very people that stuck me there in the first place! Seems like it's gettin' to be my regular job!"

"I didn't 'stick' anybody," said Camryn. "Orders came in and we filled them. That's all! It's the same for everyone. You followed orders, didn't you? If Reconstruction didn't feed everyone, they'd die out soon enough!"

"Just let everyone starve?"

"No! Just keep feeding them reconstruction so they can stay locked in the sphere—with nothing to entertain their minds but production goals!"

"Sounds like production goals were mighty important to you!"

"Can someone clue me in?" said Mark.

Camryn sighed. "The food we ate in the sphere?"

"Like you had in the pillowcases?"

She nodded. "Reconstruction makes that. I think it's made of fecal material. And corpses."

Tom nodded an affirmation.

"Fecal ma—?" Corps—?" His gasped like a fish. "I ate some of that!"

Tom glared at him, and then burst into laughter.

Camryn laughed too. "Actually," she said, "you spit most of it out."

"It's not funny!"

Tom doubled over and rolled off his bench. "If you could see your face!"

Camryn's face reddened as she tried to hold back. Her laughter broke through in wheezing giggles.

Tears squeezed from their eyes and down their faces.

Mark stared at them incredulously.

Gradually their laughter subsided. Tom controlled his guffaws, though now and then a snicker slipped through. "Consider yourself part of the club," he said, dragging himself back onto the bench. "An honorary member of AARC."

## Chapter 33 - Aarcania

Mark's pickup pulled behind Tom's, and Mark and Camryn climbed out.

From the veranda of an old farm house a man waved to them. As he sauntered toward them he extended a hand. "You must be Camryn! I'm Doctor Kantz."

"More's on the way," said Tom. "Some guy went back for his wife and kid."

"I didn't even know this place was out here," said Mark.

"That's the whole idea. Easier to keep a low profile when there aren't spectators passing through."

"The house is great," said Mark.

"Don't be too impressed," said Kantz. "Most of it's rebuilt. Not much of the original structure left."

"If you don't need anything else—" said Tom.

"No," said Dr. Kantz. "And I hate to rush you off, but I have a therapy group in ten minutes." He looked at his watch. "Make that seven."

"I said I was goin'," Tom grumbled. He called back without turning around. "I'll bring some groceries by later."

"Okay. Just leave them in the kitchen if I'm not around."

"Don't worry," Tom muttered, "I'll be sure to put them away." He turned the key in the ignition and the engine rumbled. There were snaps and pops as the tires turned on the gravel drive.

Dr. Kantz motioned toward the house as he smiled at Camryn. "If you'd like to come in, the session will be a great opportunity for you to meet everyone."

"Mind if I join you?" said Mark.

"Sorry officer. Aarcanians only. Might be hard for everyone to express their feelings with an outsider present."

"Aren't you an outsider?"

"Yes, but someone has to get the ball rolling now, don't they?"

"I'm not just dumping her here."

"You're not dumping her. Here we can help her."

"We?"

"Okay, I can help her. We're a little understaffed right now, but hopefully that'll change with new residents coming in."

Camryn looked to Mark. "I don't want you to go."

Kantz gave them a fatherly smile. "Look. No outsiders are supposed to know Aarcania—the halfway house—even exists."

"But now someone does, so the damage is done," argued Mark.

"It's just that the more you see—the more you hear—the more likely you are to slip. It's nothing against you personally."

Camryn's eyes grew large and glassy. "I'll leave with you. Don't leave me here, okay?"

"You could stay at Mom's," said Mark. "She might not like the idea, but if you don't mention AARC too much—"

"Hold on a minute," said Kantz. "Look officer. I'm not saying you can't see Camryn. Of course you can."

"I just can't visit the place she lives."

"I'm going with you," said Camryn.

"Wait!" pleaded Kantz. "Once acclimated, you can go wherever you want."

"She can do that now," said Mark. "Come on Camryn."

"Okay, okay! An exception. Considering you're an officer of the law— And against my better judgment— And provided you keep in mind the confidential nature of the facility— You're welcome to visit."

"How about tomorrow? Can I come by then?"

Kantz nodded slowly. "Sure."

"And the day after that?"

Camryn beamed up at him.

"Whenever you like. Of course, if we're in session, you'll have to wait til we're done."

"Fair enough."

"And no mention of Aarcania to anyone—not your wife; your mom; your little dog."

"I'm not married," said Mark, "but I get the idea." He looked down at Camryn. "Do you want to stay? The alternative is Mother."

"There are others here? From the sphere?" she asked.

"Two right now," said Kantz. "Then tonight that man and his family, right?"

"That's the plan," said Mark.

"His name's John," said Camryn. "We left the megasphere together."

"Then there'll be a friendly face to greet him when he arrives. If you stay that is."

She looked up at Mark. "You'll come see me?"

"Unless they throw up a barbed-wire fence and turn out a pack of Rottweilers."

"This isn't a prison," said Kantz. "It's a halfway house—an opportunity for her to acclimate."

"It's up to you," said Mark.

Camryn sighed. "I'll stay. At least for now."

## Chapter 34 - The Session

Kantz folded his arms, listening to the concerns of his group of two.

"I don't think we understand the point of these meetings," said Dobie.

Kantz rubbed his chin. "I think you'll find they help you make the transition—from one lifestyle to another. The people who've made the adjustment—the ones who've assimilated in the past—found support groups very helpful."

"There's no 'assimilation' to be made," said the professor. "Nothing to transition to. You won't let us go anywhere!"

"And I'm not sure I would call two people a group," said Dobie.

"Besides," said the professor, "Dobie and I, we talk all the time. Why do we have to do it in front of you?"

"It's my responsibility to make sure you're prepared to go it on your own," said Kantz. "But I can't help if I don't know what you're thinking."

"I'm thinking these meetings are pointless!" growled the professor.

"This is only your fourth one," said Kantz. "Don't you think it's a little premature—?"

The professor glared at the walls around him.

"What about you Dobie?"

Dobie lifted his eyes from the floor and glanced from one man to the other.

"There!" said the professor. "He wasn't even listening! Pretty smart on his part if you ask me."

"I didn't," said Kantz. "How about it Dobie? Maybe you'd like to share what you were thinking."

"I was wondering if that spot on the floor was an insect."

"Ha! Good boy Dobie!"

"And about what made those smudges over there."

"Okay," said Kantz. "The walls need painting. Do you have any larger concerns?"

Dobie stared ahead, nodding his head absently.

"Is there anything keeping you awake at night?"

"There is one thing. I've been wondering if it might be feasible to rescue the others."

"Loved ones? Someone you left behind?"

"No. Dad here's my family. I mean everyone else. Every person in the megasphere. I keep thinking, What would be the best way to get them out?"

"Hmm. Sounds like you miss your old life and now want it to come to you."

"It's not that. I just don't think the sphere's sustainable—not indefinitely anyway."

Kantz paused before responding. "Oftentimes when we leave a place, we like to feel it can't go on without us."

The professor huffed. "You're interpreting—not listening. We've been watching your TV, and reading the books downstairs. It seems to us that the sphere's supported from without, rather than from within."

"I don't understand," said Kantz.

"For instance," said Dobie, "how is this house powered? The lights in the house specifically? What makes them illuminate?"

"Electricity. But there's electricity in the sphere."

"But how does it get there?"

"Well, most buildings are powered by electromagnetic waves, targeted to a routing box. From there the waves are altered and redirected to receivers within various appliances.

"Of course, here in the boonies, we're still a little behind the times. Electrical cables run to the house underground. The current is channeled to appliances and lights through wires."

"Do cables run to the megasphere?" said Dobie.

"I imagine. It was built a long time ago."

"What happens when those cables deteriorate?"

"Electrical cables have a very long lifespan."

"But eventually they deconstruct."

"What he's saying," said the professor, "is at some point a factor from without will be deadly to those within."

"Unless they're removed from the sphere beforehand," said Dobie.

"Okay," said Kantz. "Let's say we bring everyone out. Then what?"

"You understand the environment. Perhaps you could devise a protocol."

"I believe that would conflict with the interests of my employers," said Kantz. "But say we devised this rescue. How many are in AARC, do you know?"

"A couple thousand?" said Dobie.

"Or more," said the professor.

"Or less," said Dobie. "We don't really know. There's a network of messengers, enforcers, technicians—maybe a few others—that cross compounds. Most people stay in their own. They live there and deconstruct there."

"And how many compounds are there?"

Dobie and the professor shrugged.

Hands folded on stomach, Kantz leaned back in his chair. "It seems to me that this may be a way of alleviating feelings of guilt."

The professor huffed. "Dobie's done nothing to feel guilty about. Neither have I for that matter."

"What I'm saying is, you left AARC—and you're happy about it. But now you feel guilty for being the lucky ones who escaped."

"I do feel guilty," admitted Dobie, "And lucky. But nobody in the sphere knows there's a choice—an opportunity for something better."

"Assuming there's more to the world than this," the professor grumbled.

"I need to let them know," said Dobie. "To give them that choice."

Kantz leaned forward, resting his weight on his elbows. "I don't understand why you feel responsible for everyone in AARC. I'm sure that those inside—given the opportunity—would stay. They're content with their lives. You've designed them that way."

"But I haven't," Dobie confessed. "The people I cloned weren't sequenced to order. I wanted them to be like me—to have hopes and aspirations. I added generous amounts of variable DNA to each and every person I engineered. There are those in the sphere who, given a choice, would be capable of making their own decisions—performing well beyond the scope of their assignments."

Kantz mumbled to himself. "And 'in the image of God he created him.'"

"I believe," said Dobie, "that unless people think, things can never improve. If everyone performs only the same role over and over—throughout eternity—then the status quo may be preserved, but there can be no development—no inspiration."

"It's not his fault," said the professor, "I raised him to think. I showed him the work I'd done."

"How long has this been going on?" said Kantz.

"My dad taught me," said the professor. "My friends taught their sons."

Kantz spoke more to himself than his group. "I'm sure the Bioengineering Council doesn't realize. They consider everyone in AARC to be—well, certainly not free thinking." He seemed suddenly aware of their presence. "I'll report what you've told me, but for now let's get back to helping you."

"Report!" said the professor. "You mean everything we blabber to you, you blabber to someone else?"

Kantz smirked. "Something like that. But the others in AARC aren't your concern. Your focus should be learning the culture—adapting and assimilating."

There was a tap on the door.

"That must be our new member! Please, come in."

The door eased open and Dobie sprang to his feet.

"Dobie!" Camryn squealed. "I can't believe it!"

They embraced, looked at one another, and then embraced again. Her feet swung off the ground.

"Welcome to the detainment center," said the professor.

"This isn't a jail!" growled Kantz.

"We're not allowed to go anywhere—"

Kantz ignored the invitation to argue. "Apparently you know one another."

"We work together!" Camryn beamed.

"I declare this session over!" said the professor.

Dobie took her hand. "Come on. I'll show you the lake!"

"Wait!" shouted Kantz.

"Hurry!" said Dobie. "Before he gets going again."

She laughed, her eyes flashing mischievously.

"We'll be back before dark," said Dobie, rushing her out of the room and toward the stair.

Kantz started for the door.

"I'm not feeling very well!" groaned the professor.

The doctor furrowed his brows at the old man, and then followed the others through.

The professor raised his voice. "Not very well at all! I believe I need medical assistance!"

Kantz reappeared in the doorway.

The professor clapped a hand to his chest and doubled over. "An old man like me can't stand such excitement."

Kantz folded his arms and frowned.

The professor gave him a sideward glance, and slowly straightened himself. "Leave them be. They're young. And I'd like to have grandchildren some day."

Kantz sighed and took a seat. "So how do you know one another?"

"Dobie and I cloned her. He was past twenty. No one in the lab seemed to suit him. We decided to clone someone compatible—someone who could give us children."

"Us?" Kantz snickered.

"Yes us! And it looks as though fate's helping us along, wouldn't you say?"

## Chapter 35 - The Confession

"It's just around the bend," said Dobie. "So much water you can't believe it!"

His face glowed with excitement. He was much more handsome than she'd remembered.

He lifted her up and perched her atop a fallen tree. A hand to her waist, he steadied her. "See it?"

She didn't answer.

"Amazing, isn't it?"

"Are you sure that's water?"

He laughed. "Yes I'm sure."

"Have you touched it?"

"Yeah."

"But it's blue."

"It only looks blue. If you scoop it into your hands, it's clear."

"How can it be blue then?"

"I don't know. I only just got here myself."

"How *did* you get here?" said Camryn. "Did you escape?"

"I got here the same way you did."

"I came through a door."

"I know—through an opening in the detainment wing."

Camryn looked down at him and shook her head. "In the storage module. It's where you've been getting your contraband, isn't it?" She teetered as she fingered her pants pocket. "But now, *I* have the key!"

"I'll take that."

"Oh no you won't."

"Dad'll have a fit if he finds out you have it."

"Maybe he's the one who gave it to me."

"Did he? Give it to you?"

"Let's just say I managed to find it before the authorities did. Besides, I'm angry with you!"

"For what?"

"You had plenty of things to trade, but you made me give up the book."

"It was *my* book," said Dobie. "But you're right. It was mean—and purely an act of jealousy. I was mad at you for caring so much for Brian."

"Makes *me* mad now," said Camryn. "Can you believe he turned me in? And the professor?"

"Nah!"

Camryn detected a note of pleasure in his voice.

"So that's how you wound up in detainment?" said Dobie.

"I didn't go to detainment. I came out through a door in the storage module. The one near your cubicle."

"There's no door—"

"Behind the bookcase."

"You're telling me that all this time—all of my life—there's been a way out of the sphere? Right next door?"

"If you didn't know about it, then how did *you* get here?"

"I was sent to detainment. *This* is detainment."

Her jaw dropped. "And here I was worried about you!"

"You were? Worrying about me?"

"A little."

He smiled at the childlike way she hopped from the log.

"Now I'm glad John made me leave the sphere again. I don't know if I'd have left on my own. He insisted really."

"John? Well I guess it makes sense someone would scoop you up. Dad told me about you and Brian."

"Brain took over as lab director, did you know that? A reward for reporting the professor."

"I have a confession," said Dobie. "I haven't liked Brian for some time."

"I thought you were friends."

"Habitual acquaintances maybe. I've known him for years. For a while he was the only guy in the lab."

"But you talked all the time," said Camryn.

"Not about anything important. I was staying close to him, hoping to get closer to you."

Her eyes studied his. A hint of a smile tugged at the corners of her mouth.

Dobie tossed some leaves with the tip of his shoe. "I think I just embarrassed myself. I mean, I'm nearly twice your age."

"Yes," smirked Camryn, "but you act only half of it."

"In any case, I'll be glad to meet him."

"Maybe you can become 'habitual acquaintances.'"

"Please, I feel silly enough. So what's he like? Your new *dream* man?"

"Very serious of course."

"Of course."

"And very devoted to his family. His wife and son. He went back for them."

"So you're not—?"

"Are you kidding? He's nearly twice my age!" She stood on tiptoe and eased her mouth close to his. "Now I have a confession for you," said Camryn.

Dobie pulled back his chin, as he watched her lips approach. They pressed lightly to his.

She cocked her head at his reaction. "I hope you don't mind."

"No no. Not at all."

She tried again, and then smiled. "You kiss pretty well for an old guy."

"It really happened then? I was thinking I'd imagined it."

"Of course it happened. How could I resist?"

His face grew suddenly somber. "There's something you should know—before things go any farther."

"Fortunately I know of your criminal past."

"It's something else. You see, the professor and I—"

"Are father and son?"

"How do you know that?"

"It's obvious, isn't it?"

"Does everyone in the lab know?"

"Does it matter? I don't plan on going back, do you?"

"But how—?" he floundered. "We've always kept it secret. Kept things in the lab on a professional level." He hesitated a moment. "There's still something I need to tell you. It's about us—you and me."

"I don't know that one kiss makes an 'us.'"

"Could you just listen please?"

"Sorry."

"You may not be able to help yourself—in being attracted to me."

She chuckled. "Your ego's healthy enough."

"Well I do have this amazing personality."

"And the most adorable father!"

"I think I'm jealous!"

"Well I do find older men attractive."

He smiled awkwardly. "There's still something you have to know. Dad and I? We cloned you."

"A little weird, but I suppose someone had to. Guess that's why I turned out so great."

"We cloned you for me specifically."

"So you're saying we're meant for each other?"

"Literally. We took it upon ourselves to design a woman—that's you—who would be compatible with me."

"So I like you because I have to?"

"Because it's natural for you to be drawn to me."

"There's that healthy ego again."

"I don't know what we were thinking."

"You don't like the results?" said Camryn.

"Yes. No. I mean, we didn't have the right—"

"So when you cloned me, you said, 'I want this absolutely adorable, gorgeous young woman—without a thought of her own.'"

"You have a very sound and varied genetic make-up. You're really quite capable."

"Ignoring for the moment your condescending tone, if my genes are so randomized, and I'm so capable, then how could my behavior be so predictable?"

He rubbed a fingertip across his lips. "Definitely not predictable—but tending toward a certain direction."

"So let me see. You designed me to find that lock of hair—the one that keeps falling in your eyes—absolutely irresistible."

He swept back his hair with his hand.

"And that twinkle in your eye simply dazzling. I suppose you planned that too."

"Now you're just being silly."

"I just think it's very presumptuous of you to assume—"

"I thought you should know. That's all. I shouldn't have said anything."

"I have just one question for you," said Camryn.

"Okay—"

"Do you mind terribly if I like you anyway? Because if I'm no challenge for you—"

"I should have kept my mouth shut. But you were bound to find out."

"So did you clone any others? Just in case I didn't work out?"

He shook his head.

"Mighty sure of yourself, weren't you?"

"At the time. But now I stand here looking at you, and I'm not sure of anything."

## Chapter 36 - A New Life

"John!" As she uncurled herself from the sofa, her foot knocked a stack of data pads to the floor. "I thought something happened to you!"

He drew her into his arms and breathed the scent of her hair.

She pulled away sharply. "Where have you been!"

Her eyes seemed puffier than usual. "Have you been—?"

"A little. Of course I've been crying! My husband disappears with barely a word!"

"I told you. I was on an investigation."

"For nearly three days? Without so much as a message?"

"The case was involved."

"You weren't on investigation. Someone messaged here—asking where you were."

"Who? What did you tell them?"

"One of your colleagues."

"What did you say, Nora? It's important."

"Don't worry. I covered for you. I said you'd be in to explain things as soon as you were able."

"That's all?"

"What was I supposed to say? I didn't know where you were. I thought you were with them—at least until they said otherwise. Then they messaged again, saying some woman you'd questioned was missing too. You were gone. She was gone. I was starting to think—"

He stroked her arms gently, and then enfolded her in his. "There's only one woman for me. You know that."

She pulled a hand to her face to wipe it free of tears.

"I would cut off my arm before I'd hurt you."

"Which one?" She made a hatchet motion, and then her flickering smile vanished. "You better have a good explanation! I've been going crazy worrying about you."

"It was better if you didn't know—in case someone asked. Where's Mikel?"

"Over at Anna's."

"I need to talk to you Nora."

Her eyes watered once more. "Here it comes. I knew something was wrong."

"We need to make a decision, and we need to make it tonight."

"I don't want separate cubicles."

"What? Neither do I. I want you with me. Always. No matter what."

She smiled at him weakly. "I just don't understand how you could leave like that."

"I know you're hurt. You have every right to be."

"You lied to me!" She began sobbing again.

"Nora. What if I told you there's another place to live? A whole other way to live? Would you go with me—if I asked?"

"Go where? What are you talking about?"

"I know how crazy this sounds—believe me I do. But I've been outside the megasphere."

Her tears stopped. She blinked at him through swollen eyelids. "You could have drowned!"

"No, that's just it. I couldn't have. Water doesn't surround us."

"Of course it does!"

"Life surrounds us. All kinds of life. Plants. Animals—"

"Animals? You could have been killed!"

He held out his arms to her. "No bites. See. Well, except for that one." He pointed to a little red dot. "Doesn't hurt. Just itches a little."

She looked at him skeptically; then scowled. "You must think I'm stupid!"

"I know how it sounds—"

"You must think I'm some kind of nincompoop!"

"I wouldn't have believed it if I hadn't seen it myself. But there's a door. You just step right through—well actually crawl right through. But it takes you out of the megasphere into a whole other world."

"You look flushed," said Nora. "Maybe you're sick."

"Flushed? Oh, that's sunburn! The light outside is so bright it singes your skin."

Her eyes widened.

"Just a little—and only at first. Then it goes away."

"I still don't understand John. You say there's this door. It doesn't take three days to step out a door and come back."

"I didn't just step out. I went exploring. I thought this new place might be an option for us. I wanted to make sure before taking you and Mikel."

"Me and Mikel?"

"I wanted to make sure it was safe for all of us."

"You expect me to believe—? To just—? To go some place you've only been a few days?"

He nodded.

"Just go there and hope for the best?"

"Why not Nora?"

"Is it that much better, this other place? Are you sure there isn't water?"

John sighed. "There's no water, Nora. And I don't know if it's better. It's different. So different I can't begin to tell you. It's a chance for something better than what we have now."

"Just crawl through a hole and leave everything we know? Are there even other people out there? Are they friendly? What about these animals? How many are we talking?"

"It seems fairly safe Nora."

"What's wrong with staying here? We can't just leave!"

"Why can't we?"

"It's not allowed for one thing. Does anyone else know where you've been?"

"You're the only one I've told. I didn't want anyone stopping us."

"But we have so much John. You want to leave it all behind?"

"What do we have? I'm an enforcer because that's what I was bred to do."

"You were selected. Not many are!"

"I was bred; just as you were bred to be a teacher."

"I like my work! I thought you liked yours."

"It's all right I guess, but how would I know? Did I ever have a choice? A chance to try something different? And you. Do you like your work that much? You sit here night after night, grading essays for other peoples' children."

"We have a great cubicle John. Most people don't."

"Nora, people out there have cubicles five times the size of this one."

She looked at him disbelievingly.

"With their own latrines."

"We have our own latrine."

"But here it's the exception. Out there it's the norm."

They stared into one another's eyes.

"Sooner or later," he said, "someone else is going to discover the way out. The doorway could be sealed. We have to decide, and we have to decide now."

"I have to think about it John."

"Tonight may be our only chance. Tomorrow I'll be back at work. There'll be questions to answer. If they find out where I've been, I'll be detained indefinitely."

Nora shook her head. "I can't believe this is happening."

"I want to go Nora. I want it more than anything. But more than that, I want to be with you. If you say stay, I'll stay too—explain things away as best I can."

"But you wouldn't be happy staying. That's what you're saying."

"I'll tell you something Nora. I've never been happy here. You're the only thing that's made it bearable, and you're the only thing I won't give up. If you say stay, we stay together."

## Chapter 37 - Watch for Sale

The man took a swallow of beer. "Let me see that." He took the watch and inspected it.

"So what do you think Lou?" said the bartender, "You know all about antiques and stuff. Is it worth anything?"

"Where'd you say you got it?"

"Customer gave it to me."

"It's in awfully good condition. Could be a reproduction. But if it's authentic it's worth a lot."

"How much?"

"Aren't you interested in the story behind it? The history?"

The bartender shrugged. "Stories I have plenty of. Money's something else."

"The thing is, there were only a couple thousand of these ever made. See the AARC logo on the face? The company gave all of its employees a commemorative watch to celebrate its reorganization. This one looks like it wasn't even worn."

"Still works too."

"Back's soldered shut. Probably is authentic. See, about the time these watches were made, a battery came out with a two-hundred-year life span. No real need for the back to open. By the time it stops working, it's too banged up to wear."

"A two-hundred-year battery! That would be great!"

"It is great, unless you're a battery or watch manufacturer and no one needs replacements. The government still uses 'em though."

"So if it's real—has the zillion-year battery and all—what's it worth?"

"A collectible's worth what someone will pay. How much you want for it?"

The bartender retrieved the watch. "That must mean it's worth keeping."

"I'll give you a hundred credits."

"Nah." He slipped it onto his wrist.

"Well how much do you want?"

"How much is it worth?"

"Would you take two hundred?"

"How about that," said the bartender. "It's already doubled in value."

"Okay," said Lou. "Last offer. I'll give you a thousand credits—but that's it."

The bartender's jaw dropped. "A thousand credits?"

"I'll go over to the bank right now and arrange it."

"I better hang onto it."

Lou took a swig of beer. "What about the man who supposedly *gave* it to you?"

"I don't know if I care for the implication, Lou."

"Ever see him before?"

"Said his name was John. That's all I know. He was with a girl. She was pretty too. Real looker. Kept ogling me if you know what I mean."

"I've seen the ladies give you the eye." He took a long swallow of beer and licked his lips. "Just before they give you the finger."

The bartender scowled. "You want another one?"

Lou pushed aside his empty mug. "No thanks. This man and woman—were they kind of unusual?"

"The man got drunk real easy."

"My ex used to get drunk easy. That's how we wound up together. Anything else?"

"They had pillowcases. Were using them as suitcases I think."

"Think they were clones? You know—from the sphere?"

"Clones? Right! Or swamp people maybe. Or aliens."

"No really. You think they might have been?"

"So you think AARC is filled with clones—filled so full they're spilling out."

"It's possible. They clone hearts for transplants don't they? They regrow teeth right in our jaws. They clone blood for transfusions. Why not the whole person?"

"It's illegal for one thing."

"Illegal's for you and me. Not for the government. Making nerve gas is illegal. Doesn't mean it isn't made. Making virulent's illegal. Doesn't mean that isn't made either. Heck. *Stealing's* illegal, but it doesn't mean—"

"Now there you go again Lou!"

"Okay, okay. Alls I'm saying is, what's so impossible about it? If Phoenix Biodevelopment had taken off, cloning people would be commonplace."

"Phoenix Bio—?"

"Biodevelopment. It's what AARC used to be called."

"No one believes those clone stories any more," said the bartender. "Besides, why would anyone want to clone a person? My niece just had twins and she's only sixteen! You don't think we reproduce fast enough? Jeez! We have to clone 'em now?"

"Couples shuttle all over the world adopting babies. You don't think they'd settle for a cloned one, right here in the N.A.U.?"

"I guess. But I read somewhere that there's all kinds of problems when they clone a whole person."

"Maybe that's what they want us to think. We only worry about things we feel threatened by."

"Why would I feel threatened by someone made in a test tube?"

"Well let's say they made the perfect bartender. One that could remember everyone's name and every drink recipe. Someone who would always stay in a good mood. Whose legs never got tired. Who had an aversion to alcohol."

"You're walking on thin ground now."

"Let's say you and this clone apply for the same bartending job. Who do you think they're going to hire?"

"I can't see the government cloning bartenders."

"But you get the idea."

"Yeah, but I just don't see it happening."

"What if they could clone the perfect politician? The perfect dictator for a regime change? Oh, never mind. Look. Don't tell anyone, okay?"

"What, that you're whacked?"

"About what I said about AARC, okay? You're right. They'll think I'm loony."

The bartender rolled his eyes.

"Okay, I'm a bit of an AARC buff. I've read all about it, and I just can't help but wonder if everything the government says is true. Remember back when? You couldn't pick up a news scroller without reading all about AARC and the clones inside. Then suddenly nothing. Government says it's all a hoax. Look here." He pulled a bit of yellowed paper from his pocket. "I found this over at Millie's. It was in one of the used books."

"You mean you *stole* something?"

"No. I gave her a credit for the book, but what I really wanted was this article. Read this part here."

> *The Federal Government has concluded its decade-long investigation into American Alternative Research Corporation (AARC). According to Robert Ranstall, Director of the U.S. Bioengineering Council, no living entities have been discovered residing in the AARC megasphere "cloned or otherwise." All surviving documentation, including records housed within the megasphere and those reconstructed with Deshred® software, have been reviewed. Said Ranstall, "Some animals and plants were engineered. However, it appears that AARC was not in the business of cloning people."*

*Irregularities were discovered in the corporation's accounting methods, from which heirs of the AARC fortune have continued to benefit. A settlement has been reached with Gerald Preston Jr., son of former co-owner and CEO Gerald Preston Sr., which will release all heirs from prosecution and further costly investigation. In exchange, the government will acquire and maintain the AARC megasphere. According to Ranstall, "This state-of-the-art facility will be maintained in a state of readiness as a biological research center in the event of another biological attack."*

*A scientific team will be assembled to enter the megasphere for routine maintenance. The team will re-evaluate available equipment and make recommendations for upgrades. It has yet to be determined which department will fund the facility.*

The bartender passed the article back to Lou. "Says the government shut it down."

"No. It says the government owns AARC. And now we'll never know what's inside."

"Of course they don't want people seeing what's in there. It's top secret."

Lou pulled a few bills from his wallet. "How can it be top secret if what it's being used for is right here in black and white?"

"So how much do you think the watch is worth?"

"Like I said. Whatever someone will pay for it. Maybe you can find another AARC fan that'll pay more."

"If I can't, you still want it?"

"Nope," said Lou. "Laugh at me all you want. I'll laugh every time I see you wearing that watch, knowing you'd rather have the thousand credits."

## Chapter 38 - The Scrapbook

Lou opened the door to his pickup. A small car had parked next to him, so backing out would be easy. Langston was a small town, but all of neighboring Dondicord and Hobbs seemed to be here on Friday nights.

He climbed into the cab and gazed down Main Street. An old neon sign poked out from a red-brick building—"Police." Lou wondered how much it would cost to buy the sign from the town.

A driver cruising for a parking space beeped at him as he sat. "Are ya leavin' or aren't ya?" hollered the driver.

"Aren't," Lou hollered back. He climbed out and headed toward the police station.

On the door, a little blue sign dangled from a bit of string. "Out on Call." A little white clock with adjustable hands read three o'clock. Traffic was getting heavy. It had to be at least seven.

Lou tested the door. It opened with a squeak, and then smacked closed behind him. "Anyone here?"

He sat down in a wooden chair, his heel ticking nervously against the floor. He got up and knocked on a heavy wooden door that read "Restroom" in black-and-gold peel-and-stick letters. "Mark? You in there?" He listened for water before testing the knob.

He went over to the door with the little window. Surrounding his face with his hands, he peered through the glass. He could only see one of the cells behind it.

He turned the knob, but it didn't open. He fingered the keypad next to the it. "Maybe he keeps the code in his desk."

He sat down. After watching the front door a moment, he pulled out a drawer. He checked another. "To think after all these years, the only thing keeping me from seeing a clone might be that damned door."

There was a squeak and a smack and Lou jumped.

"Mind if I ask what you're doing?" said Mark.

"Hey! I was just looking for a pen. Was going to leave you a note." He shut the drawer and scrambled away from the desk.

"What was it going to say?"

"What was what going to say?"

"The note."

"Oh nothing really."

Mark considered him a moment. "You hoping to get a permit so you can park in front of your shop? You'll have to see the town council about that."

"No. Well, that would be nice. Hey, I heard you had some trouble yesterday."

"Trouble? Oh, the deal with Suttons' cow?"

"Not Frannie I hope."

Mark shrugged. "A cow's a cow."

"Not to him. He just worships that heifer—ever since she won that ribbon at the fair. No, I was talking about the other trouble. I was just over at Smitty's. The new guy said he had a run-in with a couple of customers yesterday."

"Seemed fine last I saw him."

"Says a couple of Dondies stiffed him for some beers."

"Oh that! Some guy just got a little tipsy. Happens to the best of us."

"Not to me. I never drink. Never have."

"Well it happens to most of us then."

"Must have been a big call you were on. Sign says you planned to be back at two."

"Three," said Mark.

"What time is it now? Seven? Seven-thirty?"

Mark frowned.

"Just thought you might be interested. The new guy at Smitty's stole the man's watch—the one who got drunk."

"Did he tell you that?"

"Didn't have to. He tried to sell it to me."

"People sell you all kinds of things, don't they? Doesn't mean they're stolen."

"Not many people have a watch like this one. There's no way *he* came across it honestly."

"Maybe it was his great-great granddad's or something."

"This one had an AARC logo. It's the same kind they gave their employees."

"They used to sell replicas of those things over at the gift shop," said Mark. "Way back when I was a kid. Right next to the jack-a-lope display."

"I'm a professional Mark. I know an authentic AARC watch when I see one."

"I've been through your store Lou. The sign says 'antiques', but I see an awful lot of 'Made in Iraq' labels."

"Sign says 'Antiques and Collectibles.' A collectible is anything someone puts on a shelf."

Mark hit a few buttons on his cell phone while Lou settled himself on the edge of the desk.

"Busy," said Mark. "Can I help you with something else Lou?"

"I thought I might help you. With the clones."

Mark studied his face. "When did you see Donnelson? Was it at the bar? Do I have to lock you up too?"

"I'm not drunk. I only had one beer."

"I thought you never drank."

"Well, almost never. I only had one."

"Fellow in here the other night only had two."

"Don't you think that's odd? A grown man getting drunk on just a couple of beers?"

Mark pressed the buttons on the phone again and pretended to listen.

Lou walked over to a bulletin board and pretended to examine the wanted posters.

Mark sighed and put the phone in his pocket.

"I think you can take this one down," said Lou. "I'm pretty sure they got him. Saw it on the news."

"Why did you say you were here?"

"I thought you might need some help—with the clones."

"That's right. Someone had one too many and now he's a clone. Guess we're all clones then."

"Then there's the watch. That's a dead give-away. But you don't have to worry. I won't tell anyone."

"About the clones?"

"Yeah." He looked at Mark beseechingly. "I'd give just about anything to talk to one."

"Are you offering me a bribe Lou?"

"Would it work?"

Mark smirked.

"It's just that I've been following AARC for years. It was your dad who got me hooked. We got to talking at Smitty's one day. It was a breakfast place back then—The Blue Hen. I told him I'd collected a few AARC trinkets, and he said to show up at his house the next day. He was having this big garage sale and was getting rid of all his AARC memorabilia. Said his marriage would break up if he didn't.

"His wife hated hearing about AARC, and about clones. He said alls they did was fight and he was—" Lou suddenly realized it was the man's son he was speaking to. He stopped talking.

"It's all right. I know about Mom not liking it and all."

"Well anyway, I got most of his stuff. There was this data pad with the AARC logo on it. I know you can get data pads at the convenience store now, but back then they weren't as common."

"I prefer pen and paper myself."

"Best thing your dad gave me though was his scrapbook. He and his dad had collected just about every article ever written on AARC. Least it seems that way. There's even transcripts of TV reports. If you read the book from beginning to end, it gives you the whole story."

"You have the scrapbook?"

"Still add to it when I can. AARC stories are few and far between any more though." He slipped the article from his pocket and handed it to Mark. "Found this one tucked away in a used book."

Mark leaned forward, stroking the edge of his ear as he read. He glanced up at Lou. "Do you think I could look your scrapbook over some time?"

"Sure. I mean, I'm willing to help you if you're willing to help me. Just make a clone available! Just for an hour! Maybe two. Just so I know in my heart I've talked to one. I swear I won't tell anyone."

"Now Lou, it says right here in black and white that no clones were ever made."

"You haven't read the rest of the articles."

"I'd love to set you up with a clone, but even if that fellow was a clone—"

"Or the girl!"

"Or the girl—even if she was a clone—I couldn't set you up with either of them."

"Just tell me where they are. I'll introduce myself. Your name won't be mentioned. I swear."

"They left," said Mark. "The man just stayed overnight to sleep it off."

"And the girl?"

"She's left town. I know that for sure."

"Did someone give her a lift? Do you remember who?"

Mark shrugged.

"Look Mark. Do me a favor, all right? Keep this conversation between us."

"Oh believe me, I will. I'd still like to see that scrapbook though. Mom told me Granddad kept one, but I wasn't able to find it with his belongings."

"I don't know Mark. I'd like to hang onto it."

"You can keep it. I just want to borrow it. I just don't remember much about Dad, and I'd like to see what he was interested in."

"Sure. Tell you what. I'll run home and get it now."

## Chapter 39 - American Alternative Research Corporation

A bird zipped through the veranda.

"Did you see that?" said Camryn. "It flew right by us!" She turned her attention back to the scrapbook and flipped through a few more pages.

Mark joined her on the porch swing. "I've spent the past few days going through it. I'd have come over sooner, but I thought it was important to understand all of this." He hesitated. "I should have phoned."

She nodded, and closed the book. "There's a lot of information here."

"You want the condensed version?"

"It would be easier."

"Camryn! Look!" Mikel did a flop-sided cartwheel on the lawn.

She smiled back at him and waved.

"Okay," said Mark, "the short version then. You see, AARC started out as Phoenix Biodevelopment Company. They stored the DNA of children, spouses, parents— The gist is, when a loved one died, they could in a sense be resurrected.

"Phoenix built a huge, sprawling complex to serve as a cloning center, and to house peoples' relatives until they were developed enough to leave with their families. It was this complex that eventually became the megasphere.

"Trouble is, most people were more than willing to see their loved ones depart. They hardly wanted to see their parents or grandparents resurrected younger and hardier than they were. I mean, who wants to be responsible for raising their own parents, right?

"Since no one wanted their loved ones cloned, Phoenix became a different type of DNA storage bank. It stored the cells of a person's body parts. That way, in an emergency, a heart, stomach, liver, whatever, could be quickly grown for transplant.

"But technology made the new business obsolete almost before it began. Some other company started harvesting stem cells; then injecting them into damaged organs. With a little guidance, a heart would simply repair in place. A leg would simply regrow. The CEO—chief executive officer—"

Camryn frowned. "Chief *enforcement* officer."

"Same thing more or less, but here it's chief executive officer."

"Has it always been?"

Mark nodded. "Anyway, where was I?"

"Somebody was growing hearts."

"That's right. Phoenix was on the verge of bankruptcy."

Camryn shook her head.

"Means a business isn't allowed to keep going—unless it's a really big business. Then it's allowed to go in and out of bankruptcy for years on end, never really dissolving.

"Anyhow, the CEO of Phoenix and the CEO of another company decided to merge their businesses. The other company wasn't on such firm ground either, but its CEO knew someone in Congress. Thanks to this connection, the government gave the new company—now American Alternative Research Corporation—all kinds of tax breaks to stay afloat. In fact, the feds gave it huge refunds, even though the company barely paid taxes to begin with.

"AARC was going to acquire samples of every known DNA combination from every known animal and plant species. Quite an ambitious undertaking, but the environmentalists—"

Camryn frowned. "Enviro-mentlist? I don't know what that means."

"Or *taxes*," she thought. "Or *Congress*."

"Environmentalists are people who like trees and animals."

"Some don't?"

"Most people are wishy-washy on trees, but there are some who hate animals—especially cats and snakes. Never mind. That's a whole other conversation."

"But you'll explain it some time?"

"Sure. Where was I?"

"How can people not like all this?"

"I remember. The environmentalists were thrilled. No plants or animals would become extinct again."

"So you're saying some plants and animals aren't around any more?"

"Quite a few. Dinosaurs. Dodo birds. Elephants— Anyway, farm groups liked the idea of AARC too. The recombinant possibilities were endless. Farms are companies that grow plants and animals to eat."

"I can't believe you eat flesh here."

"Beef tastes pretty good though, doesn't it?"

"I guess, but every time I look at it I just see muscle. And ham! Every time I look at that I see human skin—*sunburned* human skin. All those pores! I can almost see the hair sticking out."

"Kind of squeamish for someone who eats corpses."

"At least they don't look like corpses."

"Let me see. Oh yeah, I remember. AARC kept plugging along, but still wasn't making it. Yet they kept building—adding onto the complex. They weren't making any money, but kept using their government refunds to maintain an air of prosperity.

"By now the place was huge—largest structure in the state; second largest in the country. This is when it was nicknamed the megasphere.

"It cost a lot of money to run, and hardly any was coming in. Plus the CEOs were shifting funds into their own accounts—enough to build dozens of mansions between them. A mansion is a really big house. Maybe twenty times the size of this one."

"The CEOs had several cubicles each?"

"That's right."

"Isn't it hard to live in more than one?"

"Not if you have a jet to shuttle back and forth in."

Camryn didn't ask.

"To keep the company afloat, the CEOs suggested AARC lay off—not pay—get rid of—a bunch of their employees. Problem is, if anything they needed more employees to maintain the facility, not less. The only way the CEOs were going to keep their jobs was to somehow make the place work—or at least appear to work.

"This is when someone got the idea to clone all but the lowest-paid employees, instead of hiring them. There'd be no benefits to pay—"

"Camryn! Look!"

"That's great Mikel!" she waved.

Mark sat quietly and frowned. Camryn caught his expression out of the corner of her eye and held back a laugh. "I'm sorry."

"That's okay. But you see, if they cloned the workers, they could engineer each one so that they'd gravitate toward one job or another. Plus there'd be no pesky lawsuits if someone got injured. With no relatives around, who knows or cares, right? And if someone didn't do their job properly, they'd be discreetly killed, and a better model designed to replace them.

"AARC made sure all non-clones signed confidentiality agreements, so the public wouldn't find out they were manufacturing people—and killing them of course. Who knows what silly group might complain about innocent people being killed?

"With tons of unpaid workers being fed on cheap, surplus food from an AARC subsidiary, the company was suddenly in the black. Then some of the scientists working for the company broke the confidentiality agreement. They told a reporter that AARC was cloning human beings. They didn't mention the executions though, not altogether sure if products could be murdered. They didn't want to be thought of as accomplices.

"The public complained a little about the cloning, but not enough to offset the requests from even larger companies. They wanted AARC to clone workers for them too. Since most of the congressmen had been CEOs themselves, they thought clones and the money they'd save were simply good business, and they didn't mind ignoring a few picket lines and editorials if it added to their bank accounts. So Congress pushed legislation through to legitimize AARC's endeavors.

"Things haven't changed much with the N.A.U. now, have they?"

Camryn's eyes were fixed on Mikel.

"I can stop for a while," said Mark.

"Oh no. Go on."

"If you're sure—"

"I'm sure. That's great Mikel!"

"Okay, but only if you're sure. The congressmen and even Georgia Bush-Clinton—she was president then—thought cloned workers would increase profits for themselves and their friends. But then they started wondering. What if they could clone the perfect soldier? One who'd follow orders, fight bravely, and have no family to accept a body bag? What if foreign leaders could be replaced by clones with democratic leanings, or with socialistic, depending on what was needed.

"AARC began receiving government contracts. Its CEOs bought enough lobbyists—"

Camryn gave an annoyed sigh.

"People who convince congressmen to vote their way on important issues."

"I kind of get it."

"Well they bought enough lobbyists that AARC now controlled the very congressmen who'd kept them in business in the first place. Even when they failed to produce the perfect soldier—"

He stopped talking, and it took a moment for Camryn to notice. "What? I'm listening."

"I was just thinking. What if they did clone the perfect soldier and we never noticed? I mean, without crying families back home, who'd know? Anyhow, where was I? Oh yeah. Lobbyists. AARC convinced the government to continue its cloning contracts, and to keep handing out tax refunds. They even had Congress enact a law so that companies AARC did business with couldn't sue them.

"It took time—a lot of time—but gradually the public became angry. Congressmen began to lose votes in spite of increasing campaign funds. Some senators said they were outraged that human cloning was taking place at all—even more outraged that it was government-sponsored."

"I thought you said they were the ones helping AARC."

"They were, but now they weren't. Kind of funny, huh? So the government starts taxing AARC and changes its position on lawsuits. Several larger businesses filed breach of contract suits against AARC, saying the workers they'd received from them were inferior. AARC couldn't afford as many lawyers as the companies suing them, so they went out of business.

"The CEOs were arrested and charged with murder for those they'd killed. The CEOs argued that a clone was a product and as such couldn't be murdered. Congress and the courts debated the point back and forth and got nowhere, so they charged them with money laundering instead.

"The CEOs, presidents, vice presidents—all the top guys—posted bail and stayed out of jail until their trials, which never materialized. When the story was old news and hardly anyone remembered their names, they moved to other parts of the world—with the government's help of course. Various deals were made and the government ultimately assumed possession of the megasphere.

"After more debate, it was decided that the clones in AARC were products after all, and as such didn't have the rights of citizens. They'd be left diligently performing their duties until their food stores ran out."

"They left them to starve?" said Camryn.

"I know it's awful. They said most of the clones would die before starving, having been designed with exceptionally short life spans."

"So that makes it right?"

"No. It's not! I'm just telling you what happened."

"Are these people still around?"

"Some are living in other places. Remember?"

"Didn't anyone speak out? Say it was wrong?"

"There was one reporter. He wrote article after article on the history of the sphere, the people inside, and the government's plans for them. He was very persistent, so the company he worked for fired him. You see, the companies that create the news are big businesses, too. They're always hoping Congress will aid them the way it did AARC.

"And the public was divided on whether or not to help the clones. Some said, 'If the clones won't defend themselves, why should we fight for them?' In fact, the clones didn't seem to realize the CEOs were gone—or the managers. No one was running the place and the people just kept working.

"My guess is that they were glad enough to be left alone. I mean, unless you're brown-nosing for a promotion, who wants to attract the boss's attention, right?

"With time, most people figured the clones had passed on, either starving or dying off naturally. The fervor and interest died down. When a long, long time had passed, we were told the whole thing was a hoax. No clones ever existed."

"But they do! You know they do!"

"Yes. I'm talking to one."

Camryn sat thinking. "The people in AARC. Are they safe now? From these crustmen?"

"Crust—? Oh—congressmen! AARC's still owned by the government, but they've left it alone for years now."

"What if they stop leaving it alone? What if they come back?"

"Camryn, I just don't know. Until a few days ago, I thought AARC was a hoax too."

## Chapter 40 - Union Rights

Dobie sat on a metal folding chair, his arms slung around the back of it. John sat across from him shaking his head. Nora frowned at the floor, her arms folded in front of her. Camryn's face was squished against her fist. The professor amused himself watching the others.

"Before we begin," said Kantz, "I think we need to reiterate that everyone needs to participate in our discussions. Unless I can report some progress there'll be—"

"Inadequate funding and discontinuation of the program," chimed Dobie and Nora.

"Very funny."

"Apparently," said Nora, "funding is the biggest concern in this world of yours."

"No," said Dobie, "according to the news, there's one other thing."

"In-creased pro-duc-tivity," they all chanted.

"People," said Kantz, "We're getting way off course here. It's important to familiarize yourself with your new environment before you begin to assimilate."

"How are we supposed to familiarize ourselves with the environment," said Nora, "when you won't let us experience it?"

"You have full access to scrollers; television; the library. You're all learning, but you're hardly ready to go it on your own."

The professor furrowed his brows. "According to the television, people come to the N.A.U. with all different backgrounds. Isn't that correct?"

"Well, yes."

"From entirely different ways of life. They aren't able to speak English *or* Spanish. They don't understand the customs. Many have little or no credits. Yet somehow they survive. They get by."

"True but—"

"Why do you find it so difficult to believe that we could get by too?"

"A lot of those people have relatives and friends to help them," said Kantz.

The professor sighed. "Still, it stands to reason that if one were to go back far enough, there'd be one or two arriving without family or friends to depend on. Ones who'd arrived by themselves and survived on their own."

"That may be. But many of those individuals didn't survive," said Kantz.

"But obviously many did, or there'd be no family and friends to greet others now."

"Just how long do you plan to keep us here?" said John. "I didn't bring my family out the sphere so we could be locked up someplace else. I want to go out and investigate. It's my right."

Kantz raised his brows. "Your right? According to the government, you have no rights."

"Why don't you just call it what it is?" said Nora. "It's just another corporation—just like the one we left. Keep your mouth shut, do as you're told, and don't cause any trouble."

"No!" said John. "It's in their constitution. It says anyone born in the Union has the same rights as everyone else."

Kantz huffed. "According to the government—"

"The corporation," said Nora.

"According to the government, you were not born. You were cloned. You're a product, and an embarrassing one at that."

John frowned. "The constitution says all persons born in the N.A.U. cannot be deprived of life or liberty."

"And I'm reminding you that you weren't born in the N.A.U. You were cloned in the sphere."

"Mikel was born. No one cloned him," said John.

"Dobie was born too," said the professor. "A lot of people in the megasphere were."

"Can we get back to topic?" said Kantz.

"We are on topic," said Nora. "Are you saying John that Mikel can leave?"

"Surely you don't want him out on his own!" said Kantz.

"He could go to school," said Nora.

"From what I understand of their law, he's required to," said John.

"Can Dobie leave too?" asked the professor.

"Anyone born in the Union has the same rights," John assured.

"I'm not leaving you Dad," said Dobie.

Camryn released a held breath.

"But this is your chance," said the professor. "Take it! Go! Live! Have children! Lots of them!"

Kantz got up as they debated among themselves. He walked over to his desk and extended every drawer. One after another, he slammed each one as hard as he could. One drawer ricocheted out, spilling its contents onto the floor. The group sat blinking at him.

"Now that I have your attention! I understand how frustrating it must be to go from one confined space to another. However, the world out there is a whole lot more complicated than it is here. Tell me. Would any of you know what to do if you were injured? Anyone?"

"Go to a doctor?" said Camryn. She winced, sure that her answer was wrong.

"Go to a doctor. Yes! But would he see you? No! He wouldn't. And why not? Because you don't have a citizenship chip, now do you? You don't even know what universal health coverage is!"

There was a long period of silence while the doctor reassembled his desk. When he seemed nearly finished, Camryn spoke up quietly. "I think we just don't understand what you want from us. What you expect."

Kantz sat on the desk and folded his arms. "What do I want of you? Okay. I'm going to level with you. I want to help you. I honestly do. But yes, whether you want to hear it or not, to do that I need funding. And to do that—to keep this facility open—I have to be able to justify it."

Camryn raised her hand a bit. "How did you justify it before we got here?"

"The truth is, it's been hard—very hard. You're the first people to come out of AARC in nearly a decade. We weren't sure anyone was left. We thought you might have starved after all."

"It's amazing we didn't," she laughed. "Let's hear it for pie!"

"Waffles!" said Dobie.

"Beef!" said John.

Kantz raised a hand to quiet them. "Look. The government knows people were cloned in the sphere, but they'd just assume that no one else did. They've been telling people for years that you're a fad—a hoax—something amusing from the past. Like hoola hoops or nose rings. The thing is, all of you present a huge problem." He pointed a finger toward the window. "There are people out there who'd have all clones destroyed."

"Deconstructed," John clarified.

"If that's the term you prefer. Then there are others who'd be more than willing to assist you, mostly for the attention you'd bring them. Same thing that happens when the media exploits some poor animal they've managed to piece together—say a dog with two legs, one eye, and a burned-off ear. Everyone wants to adopt that particular dog. Yet twenty or thirty healthy animals are euthanized every day right up the road in Dawson. In our world, clones are the one-eyed dogs with attention-getting stories. Trouble is, once the attention fades the help disappears with it.

"I've read the articles in your scrapbook—the one you've been passing around. Do you think the government wants to remind everyone of what they were up to? Sure, everyone would be fine with cloned soldiers giving their lives for this or that political purpose. But they wouldn't be too keen on being replaced themselves—with clones that wouldn't complain or demand living wages. Ones they could feed shit to—literally."

The group listened sullenly.

"What was your original question? Oh yeah. Funding. The fact is, the last extension Aarcania received was for a two-year period, and that's almost up. If I can't show it's doing some good for all of you—that it's had some success in making you less conspicuous to society—this is the last year it'll operate. Anyone else coming out of AARC will go it alone."

"Except now they have us," said Camryn. "Their family and friends."

"And many of those inside are capable of making their own decisions," said Dobie. "We made them want more. Now we have the chance to give it to them. It's our responsibility to make them aware they have choices."

"I agree," said John. "Besides, I took an oath to protect the corporation, and as it stands now it'll either dwindle away or eventually be destroyed by outside forces."

Nora released a hissing sigh. "John, you were never an enforcer by choice. You're under no obligation—"

"I took an oath, Nora, and I intend to honor it."

## Chapter 41 - Foraging

The adults were arguing again. Mikel could hear them upstairs. He went outside and sat on the porch step. He could still hear them. He ran into the front yard, to the silence of the tire swing.

Mikel saddled the tire and leaned back into it. He steered an imaginary car, kicking his legs to make the swing drive along. He wished Anna was here. By now she was probably friends with Zeke. "What a snot!"

The tire twirled as he kicked. From the yard, he could just make out the topmost arch of the sphere.

"Anna, try this!" He held out his hand, pretending to give her a 'chocklet' chip cookie. Her eyes grew big. Pupils dilated with excitement. She licked away a bit of chocolate clinging to the side of her mouth and smiled. He smiled back, and then frowned when he remembered no one was there.

He climbed out of the tire and hopped to the ground. He looked at the house, and then back toward the sphere. A few puddles in the gravel driveway enticed him their way.

Mikel resisted and started for the house. He walked; then trotted; then bounded up the steps, stopping to listen as he opened the storm door. The grown-ups were still "discussing things," although their voices were calmer now. He ran into the kitchen. There were dishes in the sink from an earlier argument. His mom said she only intended to mother Mikel. The professor said he would not be treated as a common lab tech.

He pulled a plastic container from the pantry. There were still five cookies left. He ran to the fridge. No, not soda. He'd be walking; maybe running; hopefully splashing. Soda would spray all over.

He grabbed a bottle of water, and then darted through the screen door. It smacked shut, and Mikel paused. Maybe someone noticed. Maybe someone would stop him. No one did.

He ran down the driveway toward the dirt road, allowing his feet to find the puddles as they went.

***

Mikel's growling stomach reminded him of dinner. He could almost smell the meat roasting in the oven. He bet they were having mashed potatoes. He liked those.

The road wasn't dirt any more but hard and black. The dome of the megasphere was larger now, but still seemed far away.

A car raced by and an older boy with red hair leaned out a window. He threw a black bag in Mikel's direction. "Boo hoo! Go tell your mommy!" The bag burst and trash clanked and tumbled in the explosion. It sprawled across the pavement and onto Mikel's feet.

A man with wild, unkempt hair and a torn shirt stepped out from the tree line. His eyes seemed to glow as he regarded Mikel. He grunted an acknowledgment, and then went from one piece of garbage to another, examining cans for contents and unfolding bits of paper. From time to time he snorted at Mikel. With each snort, Mikel backed up a step. He snorted several times in succession. "Ha!"

Mikel stood wide-eyed.

"Whatchya starin' at?"

The hair on Mikel's neck stood upright.

"Well?"

"Nothin'."

"Don't boys know any answer 'sides nothin'?"

Mikel staggered backward.

"You afraid of me?"

Mikel froze, and then grabbed up the container and bottle he'd dropped among the trash.

"Takin' the good stuff fer yerself huh?"

"These are mine!" The determination in his own voice surprised him.

"Looks like you're set then," said the man. "You from around here?" He leaned over and picked up something flat and black.

"Uh huh."

The man fingered a space on the comb that once held teeth. He dragged what remained through his beard, and then winced when it snagged. "Where ya from?" he said, putting the comb in his shirt pocket.

Mikel pointed toward the dome, and then let his finger wander down the road.

"Where ya gonna sleep? Have ya thought about that?"

He hadn't. He'd mostly pictured Anna's surprise at seeing him.

The man nodded toward the container gripped in Mikel's arms. "Ya gonna share whatever's in there with me?"

Mikel shook his head.

"Ha!"

Mikel returned a flickering smile. "It's a present for someone."

"But not for me."

"For Anna."

"She your girlfriend?"

Mikel frowned and shook his head.

"Your girlfriend. She live near here?"

Mikel shrugged.

"You don't say much, do ya?"

"Don't have nothing to say."

The man unfolded another piece of paper. "Dear Mom. Blah, blah, blah. Broke up. Boo hoo." He looked at Mikel and gave another snort. "Too bad everyone don't talk when they got nothin' to say. Shouldn't you be getting on home?"

"I dunno."

"You dunno if ya should get, or ya don't know how to get there?"

"Both I guess."

"Why ya runnin' away? Your parents mean to ya? Jackpot!" The man kissed a green bill, and then carefully folded it twice over. He slipped it neatly into his pocket alongside the comb.

Mikel tried to think of something to say. The uncertainty in his voice gave his words a defiant tone. "My dad—he's an enforcer."

The man glowered at him. "A policeman ya mean."

Mikel glowered back. "An enforcer!"

"Cra'ap!"

The man said it so loud Mikel fell on his bottom.

"You're from that dag-blasted sphere, arnchya?"

Mikel thought it might be better if he weren't. "I live down that way. In a house."

"Your dad. He from AARC too? From that dome there?"

Mikel's legs wobbled sideways as he climbed to his feet. "He lives in a house too."

The man roared. "Before the house where'd ya live?"

Mikel pointed hesitantly toward the arch of the sphere.

"What am I supposed to do now?" growled the man, "With some dag-blasted kid from the sphere. Just tell me that!" He kicked a can, sending it clanking off the road.

## Chapter 42 - Missing

Kantz opened the screen door. "Hello Mark. Come on in." He led the way to the kitchen. "Make yourself comfortable." He pulled an extra coffee mug from the cupboard. "Sorry it's so messy in here. We're having a little rebellion among the inmates."

"That's okay. Reminds me of home."

"Here."

Mark cradled the mug in his hands and took a cautious sip. "Camryn around?"

"She and Dobie went walking around the lake. Should be back before long."

"Look Doc. I've been wanting to ask you something. I know Camryn and the others aren't supposed to go out in public."

"I think that's best."

"But I was thinking I'd take Camryn out. You know, show her the sights."

Kantz sighed. "Look Mark. Camryn's cute, but do you think you have anything in common? You're from totally different worlds."

"Might not work with anyone. But I'd like to try. She's practically all I think about."

"Imagine that. An attractive woman with an unusual background—in a town where new faces are scarce. I can see your being infatuated—"

"It could be more than infatuation," said Mark, "but I won't know unless we spend some time together."

"You're welcome to stay for dinner."

"I can't talk to her when they're all yacking and squabbling like they do. Besides, then Dobie'll be there."

"You realize she and Dobie are pretty tight."

Mark nodded.

"Tell you what I'll do. Next time I catch her alone, I'll see how she feels. Maybe I can arrange some time for the two of you. But it'll have to be here."

"Golly gee, Dad. Thanks."

"Maybe I'm overprotective, but it's my job to keep her safe."

"From what? I don't see any torch-bearing villagers surrounding the place."

"Because no one knows they're here."

"Just like nobody knows there's more of 'em in AARC. That's been bothering me Doc. What happens if the electrical cable deteriorates? What if the water supply ruptures?"

"You've been talking to Dobie."

"With John actually. But still—"

Kantz smirked. "By all rights, they should have starved long ago. Instead they found a way to make food."

"From corpses and feces!"

"The point is, adaptability is the human condition."

Mark jumped out of his chair. "Hi Camryn!"

She looked over her shoulder at Dobie, and then back at Mark. "Nobody in AARC makes water?" she said. "I thought it was reconstructed. Like food."

"It's pumped in from outside," said Mark. "Same as it is into this house."

"So it's like the lights?" said Dobie.

"That's right."

"See!" said Dobie. "All of their life-sustaining systems originate from out here."

"And they don't even know it," said Camryn. "I didn't know."

"This again?" said Kantz. "Look. Everyone in AARC is fine. You know that! Until recently you lived there."

"But they won't be fine forever," said Dobie.

Kantz sighed. "I can assure you that the government isn't going to let an entire city of people dwindle away without water or power."

"And they'd never let them starve," Mark sneered.

"That was ages ago."

"We have to help them," said Camryn.

Mark nodded. "You said you came through some sort of emergency exit. There has to be more than one. Heck, a holotheater has two or three."

"We just have to find them," said Dobie.

"They're probably at regular intervals. If we can locate two, we can estimate where others might be."

Kantz frowned. "Mark, leave. Right now."

"What if I don't?"

"Then I insist."

"I'm not leaving."

"I'll have you bodily removed if I have to."

"Who are you going to call? The police?"

"Funny. I'll call the county sheriff if I have to. You're leaving me no choice."

Their eyes locked.

"There's always a choice Doc. Trick is, making the right one."

Nora stumbled into the doorway. "Mikel—" she panted. "Has anyone seen him? We can't find him anywhere! We practically ran around the lake. John's under the house right now."

"In the crawl space?" said Kantz.

She gasped for air. "You don't think the enforcers took him?"

"There are no enforcers here," Kantz assured.

"I think they must have followed us."

"We've been through this before."

"We'll find him," said Mark. "My truck's just outside. We'll drive down the road and have a look."

John stepped through the doorway. His face was smeared with dirt.

"Find him?" said Kantz.

"No. Found this though."

Nora snatched the paper from his hand and scanned the words. "He's gone. He's left."

Camryn took it from her and read aloud.

*To Anna*

*from Mikel*

*I wish you were here to play with. I hope you don't like Zeke. I am still your best frend. I wish you and your Mom and your Dad wood come here and live with me and my Dad and my Mom. If you come you can stay over nite.*

~~*Love.*~~

*Mikel*

"He's gone back for Anna," cried Nora.

"It doesn't say that," said Dobie.

"But we know what he's thinking."

"He could still turn up for supper," said John.

Nora's jaw dropped. "You wait if you want! I'm going to the sphere!"

"And then what? Go back in? Be questioned? Go to detainment? You'll end up right back here. And he may not even be there."

She grabbed the paper from Camryn and shook it at her husband. "How can you say that!"

"I'm trying to keep my wits about me."

"We need to go get him!"

"Maybe we should," said Dobie. "Go get Mikel. At the same time, we can bring everyone out who's willing."

"Now is not the time!" shouted Nora. "I'm going to get my son! Mark, will you drive me?"

"Please hear me out," said Dobie.

"Mark, will you drive me please?"

"In a moment," said Mark. "Promise."

Nora folded her arms and stared at the floor.

John looked at Dobie. "What do you have in mind?"

Dobie foundered as he watched Nora fume. "Hypothetically—"

Nora began to growl.

"If Mikel did go back, and if he's discovered, what happens to him then?"

John rubbed his chin. "He's too young to be considered a criminal. They might question him about us though."

"Which is irrelevant, since we're safely out of reach. But what will they do to *him*? To Mikel specifically?"

"Place him with a new set of parents, I guess. Whoever's next in line."

"But he'd be safe?"

"*We're* his parents!" screamed Nora.

John held up a hand to his wife as he looked at Dobie. "You want us to give him up?"

"No! Of course not. It's easy for me to say this because Mikel's not my son. But if he's safe, and just temporarily, we should leave him where he is."

Nora's heels clicked across the floorboards. "I'm not listening to any more of this! I'm going to get my son!" The storm door slammed behind her, and footsteps clomped down the veranda steps.

John's face reddened as he addressed Dobie. "How long does Mikel stay inside? In your hypothetical situation?"

"A few days—weeks. Until we can go around the perimeter of the sphere and find more openings."

"That could take months," argued Kantz.

Dobie shrugged. "Then we find a way to urge the people inside out. When everyone's safe, we reclaim Mikel."

"Now wait just a minute!" roared Kantz. "The government's not going to tolerate that kind of interference!"

"How will they know," said Mark, "unless you tell them?"

"What if I don't go along with all of this?"

Mark smirked. "Then I'll have to insist."

"Is that some kind of threat?"

John frowned at Mark in reprimand. "No one's threatening anyone." He looked at Kantz. "We're asking for your help."

"And if I refuse?"

"Nora will go after Mikel with or without me. It'll be with me if it comes to that."

"But I could lose my job over these shenanigans."

"And if you do lose your job," said Camryn. "Will you still be alive?"

"Of course I'll be—"

"Your only risk is this cubicle," said John.

"And you're always saying there aren't enough credits to take care it," reminded Dobie.

"And we do hate your sessions," said Camryn. "Really we do."

Kantz poured himself a cup of coffee, shaking out the last drop.

"Hypothetically," said Dobie, "if you were to help us, what would be the first thing you would do?"

"Besides have my head examined?" said Kantz.

"You can do that yourself," quipped Mark, heading for the door. "I better go help Nora."

"I'll go with you," said John. "When Nora's upset she's a handful."

"Good luck," grumbled Kantz. His hands pushed through the dishes on the counter. "Does anyone know where the coffee filters are?"

## Chapter 43 - The Search

The car ahead of them slowed amenably.

Inside the truck, Nora clung to John's arm.

"Stay here," said Mark, as he climbed out.

Voices squabbled inside the car as he approached. "Oh shit! Switch places with me! Told you I wasn't supposed to be driving!"

Mark regarded the redheaded driver. "Okay Brick. Out of the vehicle." He looked across him toward a slightly older, dark-haired boy. “You too Digger."

Another teenager climbed out of the back seat, and Mark furrowed his brows at him. “And you—what's your name?"

"Everyone calls me Weed."

Mark considered the green blades spiking from his head. "Appropriate."

We weren't speeding," said Brick. "Honest."

"Did I say you were speeding?"

"You want my license?"

"Have it in my office, remember?"

Digger swung himself onto the car hood, and dangled his legs over the tire well. Weed leaned against the car next to him.

"You takin' me in?" said Brick.

"Would it do any good?"

"Prob'ly not."

"Brick's in trouble," gibed Digger, swinging his legs.

"You boys drive up and down this road a lot?" said Mark.

"Ain't no law against it," snarled Digger.

"Unless you don't have a license."

"I do have a license. Does that mean I can go?"

Mark's attention returned to Brick. "How many times have you been up and down this road today?"

Brick shrugged.

"Have you seen any kids? Little boy. About so high? Dark hair?"

"Don't remember seeing anyone." His face glowed pink beneath his red tousles.

"Sure you do," laughed Digger. "Remember? You threw a bag of garbage at him."

"I think you remember wrong," said Brick.

"Was he hurt?" said Mark. "Did you even stop to check?"

"Did someone say Mikel was hurt?" Nora swept the water from her eyes as she came up behind him. "Where is he?"

Brick straightened. "He ain't hurt Ma'am. Honest."

"Where is he?" said Nora.

"This is his mom," said Mark. "You want to explain to her what happened?"

"She's gonna whoop your butt!" said Digger.

"If I don't first," said John, joining his wife.

"Nothing happened!" said Brick. "Honest! We just drove by. Some kid I've never seen before."

"Do you remember where?" said Mark.

"Yeah," laughed Digger. "Just look for the garbage."

"Digger, you drive. Take us to where you saw him. We'll follow."

"I have to get home," said Brick. "I'm grounded—have a three o'clock curfew."

"I'll explain it to your folks if you like."

"Never mind."

***

The car slowed to a stop. Digger pointed from the driver's-side window.

Mark climbed out of his truck and tapped the car roof. "You boys want to get out and help?"

"Not really," said Digger.

Mark looked into the back seat. "How about you Brick? You want to help?"

"Guess so."

"You gonna drive him home?" growled Digger.

"No," said Mark. "*You are,* when we're done."

Weed climbed quietly from the front passenger seat.

Nora and John climbed an embankment. Mi-kel!" they called. "Mi-kel!"

Mark watched them a moment, and then looked at Brick. "You make all this litter?"

Brick shrugged. "The bag fell out of the trunk."

"The trunk was open while you were driving?"

"Oh, that's right. It was on the back seat. The door came open."

"Did it ever occur to you to stop and pick up this mess?"

"How? It's all over the place."

"You have hands don't you? Legs?"

"Guess so."

"So all this trash will be gone by morning, right?"

"You're the one who dumped it!" Digger shouted, joining his friends. "You can pick it up yourself!"

"Mi-kel!" called John, walking along the tree line. "Mi-kel!"

"Why don't you boys spread out. His name's Mikel."

"Kind of guessed that," grumbled Brick.

Mark ignored their complaints and jumped a drainage ditch. He scrambled up an embankment, touching the slope with his fingertips for balance. He disappeared among the trees. "Mi-kel!" he shouted. "Mi-kel!"

"Sir." The voice behind him was barely audible.

"Mi-kel!"

"Sir."

Mark turned to find Weed trailing behind him. "Why don't you go in that direction? We'll cover more ground that way."

"I didn't want to say anything in front of the mom, but that kid? The one we saw? Well the bum might have got him. I just thought you should know."

"What bum?"

"There's this guy who picks through the trash. That's why Brick tossed the bag. We were playing 'Feed the Bum.'"

Mark slipped his fingertips into his pants pockets. "Explain this game to me."

A red flush climbed Weed's neck. "We drive out here and throw some garbage out of the car. Sometimes we park a ways down the road and watch this guy pick through it."

"That's what you boys do for fun?"

"Not me! It's Brick. He does it."

"But you don't protest."

"I did the first time!"

"How often does this go on? Did it ever occur to you to leave the man something to eat—besides garbage?"

The flush crept toward his jaw and ears.

"So this poor guy with no home—"

Weed averted his eyes.

"Is he mean? Nice? Have you ever spoken with him? Of course not. Then you might discover he's a better man than you are."

"I never threw anything!"

"You saw him with the boy? The one we're looking for?"

"No." Weed adjusted his crackling voice. "But he's out here a lot."

"Know where his campsite is?"

"No."

"You going to keep throwing trash at those less fortunate than you?"

"I didn't—" He looked at the ground and hissed. "No sir."

Mark turned and resumed his trek. Weed followed a few steps behind, mindful of the man's stiffened shoulders.

"Thought I told you to go the other way," said Mark, not bothering to look back.

"Mostly I've seen that guy here."

"Where we are now?"

"Yeah. Sometimes he sits up there in a lawn chair, just watching the road."

"You live around here? I don't think I've seen you before."

"My dad and me, we moved here a few months ago."

"Mi-kel!" Mark called.

"Mi-kel!" shouted Weed. "Mi-kel!"

"Know much about AARC?" said Mark.

Weed stammered. "Sure. I did a report on it for school. I couldn't wait to see it when we moved here."

"How close have you been?"

"To the megasphere?"

"Have you been in the parking lot?"

Weed hesitated before answering. "We couldn't pull up. There's a cement barricade. And some gates."

"But you tried?"

"We didn't bother anything!"

"That close, huh?"

"I just wanted to touch it. Once me and Digger, we sat outside and had a few beers—I mean pop. Digger wanted beer, but I thought we should have pop instead."

Mark looked over his shoulder and regarded him skeptically.

"Store wouldn't give us any anyway."

"Glad to hear that at least."

The more distant voices were growing louder. "Mi-kel! Mi-kel!"

Weed caught up to Mark and walked beside him. "Hey, my dad gave me a book about AARC. Read a little of it."

"Talk about clones did it?"

"Yeah, but I know there's no such thing."

"How are you at keeping secrets?"

Weed stopped abruptly. "I'm not a kid you know. And Brick and Weed already pulled that clone scam on me."

Mark turned and studied the boy's slumping form. "You're the one who mentioned AARC. I just thought you might be interested in something I'm working on. It involves the megasphere and I could use some help. But if not, that's okay."

"What do you want me to do?"

"Come by my office and we'll talk about it. How about your friend Digger? Think he can stay mum?"

"Digger? Sure. He hardly talks to anyone."

"Sure it isn't the other way around?"

Weed lowered his voice. "I think we're his only friends."

"That's a plus for what I need. What I'm working on is confidential. No one else can know about it."

"He has kind of an attitude though."

"I realize that, but I also know he's smart. What about Brick?"

A grimace crossed Weed's face. "I don't know about him. He *can be* a great guy."

"When he's not throwing trash at someone?"

"Yeah."

"But would you trust him with a secret?"

Weed shrugged. "Maybe."

"Why don't you come by the office tomorrow after school? Bring Digger if he'll come."

"Tomorrow's Sunday. There is no school."

"How about ten then?"

"I'm not in some kind of trouble am I?"

"If you were in trouble I wouldn't be asking you in. I'd be hauling you. It's like I said. I need some help with a project involving AARC. And I don't want it broadcast all over town."

"I don't know if the other guys will come."

"That's okay. Bring yourself. And on second thought, let's leave Brick out of it. I'm just not sure about him. And do me a favor."

"What?"

"Don't mention the transient to the kid's parents, okay? We don't know anything for sure, and it'll just upset them."

***

The three of them were silent on the return trip. Nora leaned her face into the wind, turning it a bit to hide her tears. John kneaded her fingers gently.

Mark watched the road ahead. He wondered whether he should tell Nora and John about the transient. He worried whether the man might harm Mikel, or that they'd never met and the boy was wandering alone in the woods. He worried over confiding in Weed. He really didn't know the boy and, now that he thought about it, his choice of friends was questionable. He worried about the clones inside the sphere, and what his mother would say when he brought them out.

They pulled into the drive. The sun streaked the sky orange. The house lights glowed yellow. The gravel pinged against the undercarriage as the truck slowed to park.

Nora opened the door and sprang out as the vehicle stopped. She walked toward the house, and then broke into a trot.

"It's going to be a long night," said John.

"Look," said Mark. "I didn't want to say anything—and I don't know anything for sure—but there's a chance Mikel might not be in the sphere after all. One of the kids said there's a man who lives where we just searched. Mikel could be with him."

"That's good, isn't it?"

"Hope so. I've never met the man. And Mikel might not be with him at all. Thought I'd go back in the morning. See what I can find. I'll leave it to your discretion whether to tell Nora."

"Let's not get her hopes up," said John. "Not until we know something definite."

"I'll let you know right away—whatever I find."

"Even if it's good news, don't tell her, all right? It worries me that Mikel's lost, and that she's so upset. But if you find him before we do, take him to your Mom's house, okay?"

"Why? She's in a pretty bad way John. If the news is good, why not?"

"I want my son back, but I also want to help those still inside. Nora won't want me involved unless we have a personal stake in the matter. She's been at me to slip away in the night. I've stalled, but she's more determined every day."

"I'll drive you wherever you want," said Mark. "Help any way I can. Kantz has no real authority over any of you. I hope you realize that."

"You're a good friend Mark. Like a partner. But if we all strike out on our own, who's going to help them—the others? Not Kantz. Not his precious government. No one! We're they're only hope, and I'm not letting them down."

## Chapter 44 - Deputy Brick

Weed sat on the edge of Mark's desk, his legs swinging to a song he'd heard earlier in the day.

Brick leaned back in a wooden swivel chair, his feet propped on the desktop. "Why are we here anyway? You sure we're not in trouble?"

"I told you, said Weed. “He said he needs help with the megasphere."

"I don't care nothin' about the sphere."

"Then you leave. I'm staying."

"If I leave," said Brick, "how you going to get home?"

"Walk."

Brick wadded a paper lying on the desk and tossed it onto Weed's green barbs. "When you going to get rid of the retro 'do, man?"

Weed shook the paper from his head. "Told you. I'm honoring The Clash. Do you realize that, without them, today's music wouldn't even be here?"

"I'm going down the street and get a soda. You want anything?"

"Depends," said Weed, "You buying?"

"Nope."

"Guess not then. Don't have any credits."

"Then I guess I don't want nothing either," said Brick.

"Loser."

"Brown-noser."

Brick pushed a stapler and some papers aside on the desk and stretched out. "It's too early!"

"It's ten-thirty."

"Like I said—too early!"

"You better just hope he doesn't check on that garbage," said Weed.

"If I'd have picked it up, he couldn't find the location again."

"Lame."

"You want anything?" said Brick.

"You already asked that. Told you. I don't have any credits."

"Maybe old man Peterson would take an I-O-U."

"And what if he doesn't?" said Weed. "You going to swipe it?"

"Stop being such a smart aleck, and maybe I'll swipe one for you too."

"I don't want no stolen pop."

"Pop!" moaned Brick. "Who calls soda pop? Look, I'm going. And if he isn't here by the time I get back, I'm leaving." He shuffled out of the office.

Weed stared at the ceiling. He got up and flipped through a calendar on the wall, and then peeked through the little window. Behind him the office door squeaked.

"Sorry I'm late," said Mark. "I went back to look for Mikel."

"Any luck?"

Mark shook his head. "And I wanted to get this." He held up an overstuffed, loose-leaf notebook. "There's a bunch of clippings in here about AARC. If you read them from start to finish, you get the whole story. Thought you might be interested." Mark laid the book on his desk. "What happened here?" he said, regarding the displaced stapler and papers.

Weed shrugged and reached for the notebook. "Where'd you get all this stuff? You must have been collecting it a long time."

"It was my dad's. His dad's before him."

Weed flipped through the first few pages.

Mark watched the boy's eyes as he scanned the columns. "I can give you the abbreviated version if you don't want to read it."

"I *do* want to read it," said Weed. "Honest." He continued to turn pages as Mark summarized a few of the articles.

"Can I borrow it?" said Weed.

"Sure."

The street door bumped open. "About time you got here!" said Brick.

"I didn't know *you* were coming," growled Mark.

"I needed a ride," said Weed.

Mark frowned. He reached into a desk drawer and retrieved Brick's license.

"You get your soda?" said Weed.

"You mean my p-pop? Nah. He wouldn't give me one."

"Maybe you could go outside for a while," said Mark. He handed Brick the plastic card. "I'd like to discuss something with Weed here."

Brick grinned at the photo smiling back at him, and then smirked at his friend. "You're in for it now."

"Actually, I'm enlisting his help," said Mark.

"Ooh!" snickered Brick. "Deputy Weed."

"Shut up."

"Deputy Weed," chuckled Mark. "I like that. And how about you Red? Any designs on becoming Deputy Brick?"

"Yeah. Right."

Mark shrugged. "I can drive him home later if you need to head out."

Brick folded his arms and shifted his weight to one leg. "Nah. I'm staying."

Mark looked at him uncertainly. "Okay then. Pull up a seat."

Chairs screeched across the floor as the boys got comfortable.

"What I'm going to tell you is in strictest confidence. I'm reasonably certain that Weed here can keep a secret." He glanced toward Brick and smirked. "Or at least I thought so. But you Brick—your track record isn't so great. If you're uncomfortable with all of this—"

"I finished my probation!"

"I realize that," said Mark.

"Got done early too! Good behavior."

"Or you got better at hiding things."

"I don't have to take this!" His chair jumped back, but he made no move to go.

"I just don't know if I can trust you," said Mark.

"I've already been punished. Sometimes I think no one wants me to do better." His lip quivered. "Everyone says 'straighten up'. But then when I do, they say it don't make up for what I did before. Where's the sense in that? Saying do better to make up for what you did, but no matter what, you can't make up for it."

"You were in jail?" said Weed.

"See!" said Brick. "No I wasn't in jail. Probation—that's all." His eyes grew bloodshot and his cheeks grew blotchy.

"I'm sorry," said Mark. "I didn't mean—"

"What's the point?" said Brick, sucking back a snuffle.

"From your recent behavior, I didn't know you wanted a second chance."

"Heck yeah! I might as well be bad 'cause no one believes it when I'm good. They just think it's a fluke or something."

"You're right," said Mark. "It isn't fair."

"Damned straight." A tear moistened the side of his nose and his hand moved to wipe it.

"I could use all the help I can get," said Mark. He stood up and walked to the door. "But if you want to leave—either of you—now would be the time, because what I'm about to tell you cannot leave this room."

Weed shifted uneasily.

Legs outstretched and hands folded on stomach, Brick stared straight ahead and drew up his bottom lip.

"Okay," said Mark. He turned the sign on the door to "Out on Call." He slid the latch and closed the slatted blinds on the windows.

Brick snickered. "Top secret."

"Shut up."

Mark swung a leg over the corner of the desktop. "Bottom line is, the kid we're looking for? Mikel? He lives inside the megasphere, or used to anyway."

Brick rolled his eyes. "Okay. I'm outa here."

"Now see," said Mark, "that's the very attitude I'm talking about."

"Okay, okay. I'm listening."

"I know it's hard to believe," said Mark. "Trust me—I know. I grew up thinking AARC was a fairy tale. My friends and me, we used to tell clone tales at Halloween. It doesn't help that the government's been saying AARC is all a hoax, but if you read the articles in that, you'll see they've only been saying that the past couple of decades or so. The fact is, there *are* clones. Lots of them."

"How many?" said Weed. "Have you gone inside?"

"No, but I've met some who've escaped."

"Excuse my *attitude*," said Brick, "but what makes you so sure these clones *are* clones. How do you know they're just not crazy in the head or something?"

"I wasn't so convinced when I met my first one, or even the second. But over the past few months, I've talked to half a dozen. They can't all be nuts."

"Can we see them?" said Weed.

"Best if you don't. We're trying to keep this whole thing under wraps."

"Who's 'we'?" said Brick.

"Me, the clones, and a doctor who's helping them."

"So you, the crazy people, and a psychiatrist?"

"Okay, I get your point. But the fact is, there appears to be an entire city of clones living inside the sphere. We want to go in and get them out."

"So we get to go inside?" said Weed.

"No. Well, maybe. I haven't thought that far ahead. We've just started working on a plan."

Weed leaned forward, elbows on knees. "You don't want us to meet the clones, and you don't want us to go inside. So why do you need us?"

"We know some of the clones came out through a small door, about so high. It was some sort of emergency exit. There are probably more doors—lots of them. Question is, where? That's where you come in."

"We're supposed to find doors?" said Brick.

"Right."

"Doesn't sound too exciting."

"Probably won't be," said Mark. "The sphere is roughly a hundred kilometers around. A lot of it's overgrown with weeds and brush. We need someone to walk the edge of the building and locate the exits—clear them so they're useable.

And we can't attract too much attention doing it. AARC's a government facility. Officially anyone on it is trespassing."

"You want us to break the law?" said Brick.

"If you get caught, it's a misdemeanor. At your age, they'll probably just run you off."

"No way!" said Brick. "Besides. Do you know how long it would take to walk a hundred kilometers?"

"Figuring a couple kilometers a day— You're right. It's probably too big a job for two boys."

"We're not *boys*," said Brick.

"I can do it by myself," said Weed.

"No. That wouldn't be right. You could get hurt—need help. I don't know what I was thinking."

"I'll take a phone with me."

"I don't think so."

"It might not take *that* long," Brick conceded.

"A month or two," said Mark. "Maybe less. Depends on how much of the perimeter is visible without cutting down brush, and how hard you work."

"Two months?" considered Weed.

"Or less. But I'd have to be able to trust you, because under no circumstances—even if you find a door standing wide open—are you to go inside. Rescuing the clones has to be a coordinated effort. We don't want strangers walking through and causing a commotion."

Weed looked at his friend. "Come on. We can do it."

Brick smirked. "Is this to get even for the trash on the road?"

"No," laughed Mark. "Believe it or not Brick, I could really use your help."

"Why don't you go chop weeds yourself?"

"As a police officer, I'd have a hard time explaining why I'm trespassing on government property. You two they'd overlook. And if anyone asks, I never mentioned clones, and I never asked you to look for doors. I have no idea why you're out there. You're just a couple of curious kids."

"Again," said Brick, "why aren't *you* taking the risk? And besides—what's in it for us?"

"Shut up."

"That's all right," said Mark. "If you have concerns, now's the time to voice them. I know I'm asking a lot of you. To spend most your free time working on this project. And to be perfectly honest, there's nothing in it for you, except that you might be helping someone. Hopefully lots of people. Do you know the people in there ran out of food years ago?"

"Then it's a little late to help them," said Brick.

"Oh they're still alive, but do you know what they're eating? Poop. Crap. Shit. And dead people."

"Jesus!" said Brick.

"Jeez," said Weed.

"Eventually they'll run out of other resources as well. And the thing is, they don't even know we exist—that anything outside the sphere exists. They've never watched TV. They've never gone swimming. They've never walked in sunshine."

The boys were silent, thinking of other things the clones had probably never done.

"Okay," said Brick. "I'm in."

Weed toyed with the ring in his ear, and then straightened in his chair. "I want to help. I really do. Maybe. But everything I've heard says clones don't exist. How do I know if what you're saying is true? I can see *you* believe it—"

"But what if I'm crazy in the head?"

He leaned back in his chair. "I just don't want to spend all my time chopping down weeds to clear out an empty building."

"Yeah," said Brick. "How do we know you're not just losing it?"

"You don't," said Mark. "Look. I could use your help, but if you're afraid I certainly understand."

"I'm not 'afraid,'" protested Brick, "but why should I waste my time for nothing?"

"Yeah! When you could waste it so much better spraying 'F—' and 'Damn' all over the place and throwing bags of garbage at poor people."

Brick reddened along the ears.

"Anyway, take some time. Look through the scrapbook. Talk it over. Just let me know in the next couple of days."

"What if we make you a deal?" said Weed.

"I'm listening."

"Let's say we do all of this and a bunch of clones come out of AARC."

"You mean, turns out I'm not crazy."

"Right. Then that would be explosive! But what if we chop and mow, and don't find any doors. Or we find doors but no one comes out of them."

"Yeah," said Brick. "What if there aren't any clones."

"Then we should get something for our trouble."

"Like what?" said Mark.

"Pay," said Weed.

Mark shook his head. "No deal."

"Okay. No deal," shrugged Brick.

"Do you know what I earn? Come to a town council meeting sometime. I can't afford to pay you."

"Not even ten credits an hour?" said Weed. "Heck, that's not even minimum wage."

"Besides," said Brick, "if there are clones like you say, you won't have to pay us anything."

"There *are* clones."

Weed gathered the notebook from the desk. "Then you don't have anything to lose."

"Okay, okay. No clones you get paid. A thousand credits flat."

"For each of us," said Weed.

Mark shook his head in disbelief, and then sighed. "Okay. When the job is done. And I'll be checking your progress."

"Explosive!" grinned Weed.

"Explosive!" Brick leaped from the chair and unlatched the door. "Come on. Let's get my machete!"

## Chapter 45 - Lost and Found

"Ow!" Dobie shifted off a splinter and rubbed the back of his leg. The desk had been moved and the chest was under a different tree. Nothing was quite in place. He hoped Freeman was still living here, and that he wasn't in town wading through dumpsters and visiting benefactors.

He lifted a pillowcase from the desktop. Camryn had suggested it for traveling. He pressed it to his nose, enjoying the scent of her hair; imagined his hand cupped gently around her breast.

He slipped a hand into the pillowcase and removed a small black box. Numbers flashed across it. "It's been hours," he thought. "Guess I can stay the night if I have to."

His mind went back to Camryn. Mark was dropping by later. He'd probably linger with Dobie gone.

"Kantz is going to be *P.O.'d*!" He chuckled at the expression. "*Royally* P.O.'d, when he realizes I'm gone. He'll probably encourage Mark just to get even."

Another hour passed with thoughts of Camryn and worries of Mark, when he heard footsteps among the trees. Freeman's voice was intermixed with a softer, almost feminine one.

"Dobie!" Mikel squealed. The boy ran to him, his face and arms smeared with mud. "Look!" he said, holding up a large fish by a bit of string. "I got one!"

Freeman stood a few steps away, evaluating Dobie. "Get tired of livin' in town did ya?"

"Never got to town. Been staying at Aarcania."

"T'ain't never heard of it."

"A house. Down the road some distance. With Doctor Kantz."

"The halfway house?"

Mikel stood at Freeman's mound of belongings and yanked back the tarp. He grabbed up an old newspaper and rolled the fish in it. He held up an open pocketknife for Dobie to see.

"Don't run with that there knife!" roared Freeman, but Mikel didn't hear for his excitement.

"I can clean it myself!" the boy bragged to Dobie.

"Take it down to the crick," said Freeman. "Gut it here and the 'coons'll keep us up all night."

Mikel grinned at Dobie, and then sprang off.

"Don't run with—!"

Mikel stopped, put his catch on the ground, and conspicuously folded the knife blade.

"Smart boy!" Freeman called to him.

"We've been looking all over for him," said Dobie. "His parents have been worried sick."

"So you come to collect the boy, or ya come to stay here with me?"

"You've rearranged things," said Dobie.

"Was some cop poking around. Mikel and me, we skedaddled a while."

Dobie held up his pillowcase. "I brought you some food."

Freeman humphed.

"Aren't you going to see what I brought?"

"Food is food."

Dobie smirked. "Just thought you'd like a break from dog chow."

"The fish'll do for tonight."

"Has Mikel been here the whole time?"

"What time's the whole time? Couple of weeks."

"He looks great—like he's had lots of fun."

"I ain't no nanny. Couldn't just leave him on his own though. And wasn't gonna take him into the sphere. That's what he wanted ya know."

"He has a friend there he's been missing."

"Didn't wanna leave him with the law, him bein' a clone and all. Figured someone would claim him sooner or later. Gonna miss him though. He's a good little man."

"There's a bunch of us from the sphere now. My dad came out. And the girl I told you about."

"Which gal would that be?"

"The one we cloned."

"Oh, that one. Workin' out fer ya is it?"

Dobie's face burned red. "Actually it kind of is."

"So ya here to announce the big news? That you're gettin' hitched?"

"Married? Not yet. Someday maybe. Hope so."

"Ya here lookin' fer the kid then?"

Dobie nodded. "John and Nora will be relieved. That's not why I came though. Just a happy coincidence."

Freeman snapped a branch in two, and added it to a pile in a blackened fire pit.

"I need your help," said Dobie. "We all do."

"Who's 'we'?"

"Me. The others."

"Might help you. Don't care about no others."

"Now how do you know that? You live out here all by yourself. You say you like it, but when I was here you seemed glad for the company."

"Tolerated ya." He tossed more sticks into the pit.

"Mikel obviously adores you. You seem to like him. There's probably a whole lot of people you'd get along with."

"You sayin' I'm disagreeable?"

"No. I didn't mean—"

"Told ya before. I don't need no one. I ain't livin' by someone else's rules. Had enough of that in the sphere."

"You know what you are? You're just a stubborn asshole!"

"Ha!" Freeman drew in his chin and considered Dobie. "Told ya you'd start talkin' like 'em."

Dobie stripped the leaves off a thin twig and added it to the stack. "Look," he said. "Maybe you *don't* need us."

"Finally we're seein' eye to eye."

"But we still need you."

Freeman pulled a few twigs from his collection. "At this rate we're gonna have a bon fire."

"Can I just tell you what we have in mind?"

"It's against my better judgment."

Mikel came running back. His arms were wrapped around a blood- and oil-spattered bundle.

"Did ya fillet it like I taught ya?"

Mikel beamed and unrolled his work.

"Good boy," said Freeman. He leaned toward the boy and wrinkled his nose. "And to the crick with ya after supper, ya hear?"

Mikel's smile disappeared.

"Less ya prefer to go now?"

Mikel shook his head. "After supper."

"And where's my pan?"

"I cleaned it! I'll go get it."

"Good kid," said Freeman.

"Lots more like him," said Dobie, watching the boy run off. "Inside the sphere."

"They're happy enough where they are."

"Maybe, but were you happy? When you were inside?"

"Never thought about it while I was there—and definitely not when I was a kid."

"We want to bring them out," said Dobie. "All of them."

"What fer? That'll just mess everything up!"

"Don't *you* like it better out here? You could have gone back, but you didn't."

Freeman searched the desk drawer for matches. "How do ya know everyone wants to come out anyway?"

"I don't, but I have to believe—"

"And this rescue of yers. How exactly do ya plan to carry it out?"

A trace of a smile crossed Dobie's lips.

"Here's the pan!" said Mikel.

"Good job," said Freeman. "Why it's almost shiny!"

Mikel spread the fillets across the pan, and then held them up to Dobie. "Smell," he said.

Dobie sniffed the pan's contents and scrunched his nose.

Mikel laughed. "It tastes good when it's cooked."

"Gotta be careful with fish, though," said Freeman. "Get it too hot and burnt and it falls apart."

"Just worm foddle then!" said Mikel.

"And ain't nothin' more worthless than worm fodder."

"Unless you're a worm," giggled Mikel.

## Chapter 46 - A Way In

After supper, Dobie retrieved a package of chocolates from the pillowcase. The candies were misshapen with the heat, but Mikel savored the remnants, licking the creamy smears from his fingers.

"Go on to the crick now," said Freeman. "Rinse those clothes and swim til ya don't stink no more."

Mikel rolled his eyes at Dobie.

"Better go," said Dobie. "Before it gets dark."

"So this help ya need," said Freeman. "What exactly did ya have in mind?"

"You're in?" said Dobie.

"Let's hear your plan first."

"Well, you and me, we left the sphere through the detainment corridor. But Camryn, she came through some sort of emergency door. Mark—he's an enforcer friend of Camryn's—"

"Your girlfriend?" Freeman frowned disapprovingly. "Sounds like she gets around. Might want to hold off on that marriage idear."

"It was your *idear*," thought Dobie. "Now I forget where I was."

"Got ya all flustered, does she?"

"You're the one asking me all the questions," said Dobie.

"Takin' her side. Yup. That's whut happens."

"I ain't takin'— I'm not taking anyone's side. I'm just trying to explain our plan."

"So what's stoppin' ya?"

Dobie held his breath a moment before continuing. "We thought we'd shut off the air conditioning inside the sphere—and the water. Sort of push everyone towards leaving. Then go through the emergency doors and guide everyone out."

"Told ya already," growled Freeman. "I ain't goin' back in there! Not fer nothin'!"

"We need you for something more involved. Something we can't do ourselves."

"Like what?"

"We thought people inside the sphere might be more willing to leave if we could generate some kind of notice—let everyone know what's going on. It might reduce confusion when the rest of us go in."

Freeman humphed.

"But we don't want to send the alert until we're practically inside. Otherwise enforcement might eliminate it and explain it off."

"How do ya expect me to do that without goin' back in?"

"There's a terminal you can use in detainment."

"That ol' thing! Prob'ly don't even work no more."

"It does. When I came out I sent a message to Dad. He says he got it."

"So I have a terminal. Big deal. What's that gonna do?"

"Mark said that years ago, people gained control over computerized networks by sending out a contaminated message. The message would contain hidden instructions for the receiving computer. Part of the instructions ordered the receiving computer to distribute the message to other systems. They called it a virus. *Catchy*, huh?"

"Hmm. Could work, 'cept fer one thing. Enforcement receives communications from detainment, but no one's allowed to read 'em—at least when I left.

"We wouldn't want to alert Enforcement in any case," said Dobie.

Freeman scratched the side of his face. "Too bad ya sent that message to yer dad. His computer could of been our entry point. Your girlfriend—you said she didn't come through detainment?"

Dobie shook his head.

"What about the others ya mentioned?"

"They didn't come through detainment either. The only one who came through besides me—" Dobie broke into a grin. "Was Dad! I was sitting at the computer when he came out. He never sat down at it. He never sent his last communication!"

Freeman scratched his belly and nodded. "Well then, we have a way in."

## Chapter 47 - The General

The general's wife was on a garage sale kick. Each and every Saturday, she and the general drove from one sale to another, followed by brunch at the Pastry Palace. There were the usual items for sale—a handful of dishes that had escaped years of breakage, yellowed pictures with dusty frames, and children's clothes with only one or two juice stains.

The general amused himself by keeping an eye open for a particular sort of chair; large enough to accommodate a man, but small enough to make him uncomfortable. After innumerable Saturdays, he found one that suited him. The owner wanted twenty credits firm.

The general offered ten.

"Like I said. Twenty firm."

"Civvies!" The general tested the chair again. Shifting his weight, it squeaked loudly. He crossed his legs and it moaned. It was too perfect to pass up. With a shrug and nod, the deal was closed.

This is the chair his new assistant now sat in. The general twiddled his thumbs, amusing himself with the lieutenant's discomfort.

"There's one more item," said the lieutenant, talking over the chair's protests. "I found this report in a stack of loose papers. I was about to file it when I realized it hadn't been signed." The chair squealed. "I'm very sorry sir."

"Do I make you uncomfortable Lieutenant?"

"No sir. It's just this chair. I'll take care of it sir."

"Good. I'll see you Monday then."

"Not the report sir, the chair. I'll order a new one if you don't mind."

"That chair not good enough for you?" The general jutted his jaw out to keep from laughing. "That was my grandpappy's chair. Had it with him on the U.S.S. Brigadier. He was in that *other* branch."

"I'm honored that you'd allow me to use it." The chair creaked as the lieutenant climbed out. "But it's not right. Here. You should sit in it."

The general swallowed a surprised chuckle. "Nonsense. Please. Sit back down."

"Oh no sir. I'll just stand. What if it breaks? I'd feel just awful."

"At least sit until we're done."

"I don't mind standing—at least for now. I'll order myself a new one from stores. Maybe we could put this one over there. Set up a whole corner in memory of your grandfather. If you have any other memorabilia—"

The general smirked, wondering how many garage sales that would take. "The report Lieutenant."

"As I said, it was buried under some papers. Apparently it's been there several months."

"Damned civvies! Never know when they'll quit. Leave all kinds of untended business."

The lieutenant hesitated. "I believe Mister Adams had a heart attack sir."

"Unreliable in any case. Go on. I'd like to get home sometime today."

"According to the report, Aarcania—that's a facility that houses clones leaving the AARC megasphere—"

"I'm fully aware of AARC and its accouterments," said the general. "It's been under my command for the past fifteen years."

"Yes sir. Well according to this report, submitted by a Dr. Smathers of the Bioengineering Council, there are currently six clones living at the facility."

The general snickered. "I think Kantz is trying to extend his funding again."

"Which is due to expire in December."

"And just how would you know that?" said the general.

"I looked through the files. I thought I should have some idea as to what I was talking about."

"So you were snooping!"

"No sir. The files are my responsibility now. It's my job to know what's in them."

"So I suppose Kantz is claiming these residents are clones?"

"Yes sir, except for two. An eight-year-old boy and a geneticist. He says they were born naturally—inside the sphere."

"Continue."

"According to Kantz, the clones are reproducing naturally inside the facility—a percentage of them anyway. He says the residents at Aarcania are claiming Union rights for these particular individuals."

"Clones don't have rights!"

"They're saying not all Aarcanians are clones. Some are born like anyone else."

"They're the result of cloning, aren't they? They only exist because we permitted AARC to continue without interference."

"According to the records, we did interfere. We made sure they ran out of food, and when they didn't die out, we told them the facility's an ark. That it's surrounded by water and that they'll drown if they leave. Considering the history, I think we owe it to them—"

"Where did you transfer from?" scowled the general.

"General Arnod's office."

"And when you served with Oddnuts, what was your view of clones then?"

"I thought they were a hoax, like everyone else."

"Do you know why clones don't exist? Because that's what's best for the public to believe. You're too young to remember, but whenever there's been the slightest inkling that clones exist—and that the government's commissioned them—there's been tremendous public outcry. We tried to eliminate the problem by allowing resources at AARC to run out. No clones; no problem."

"We denied them food sir."

"That's right," said the general coolly. "Just as we do when we blockade a hostile country." He studied his assistant's face. "And what would you have us do now Lieutenant? Let the public know we've deceived them for years? Wouldn't that hurt our credibility? The president's? He's your commander in chief, son. Think about that."

The lieutenant was silent.

"The clones in the megasphere are government property. Nothing more. To dispose of as we please."

"But they're people sir."

"Who created them?"

The lieutenant shrugged. "We did I guess."

"And who created us?"

"God."

"And do we belong to God? Does he dispose of us as he pleases?"

"Yes sir."

"And the clones belong to us. You tell Kantz the clones at his facility will stay put. They are not to leave the premises under any circumstance. Any of them!"

He thought a moment. "Once we take care of the ones inside, we'll let Kantz's clones go about their business. A handful won't be noticed. They'll be classified as loonies or AARC fanatics."

"Cloners you mean."

"Now we're on the same wavelength. But it'll be harder to explain things if hoards of them suddenly appear. Hell! I thought they were all dead. No clones have come out of AARC since I can remember."

"How many do you think there are sir? Inside?"

"Does it matter? To the world out here, they don't exist. And that's the way it's going to stay. Damned clones! Should be dead by now!" He got up and marched for the door. "And those files you read on AARC?"

"Sir?"

"Make sure they disappear. Today!"

## Chapter 48 - The Tin Can

The door to the metal building stood ajar.

"Mark said not to go in!" said Weed.

"He didn't tell me," said Digger.

"Because you weren't at the meeting."

"He said not to go into the megasphere," said Brick. "This isn't the megasphere."

"It's on the same property."

"Wasn't a few days ago," said Digger. "It's a tin can, a ready-made storage building. Army uses 'em."

"We're going to get caught."

"Nobody's even here," said Brick.

"And we shouldn't be either," Weed argued.

Digger wandered in and disappeared behind some boxes. His voice echoed. "I saw some Army trucks drive through a couple days ago."

Brick scowled at Weed as he pushed through the doorway. "Yeah," he called out, "I saw one yesterday parked at the diner."

"Hey look!" Digger shouted.

Brick came up beside him. Oblong plastic crates, each with a skull and crossbones above the center latch, were double-stacked on wooden pallets.

"What do you think's inside?" said Brick.

Weed came up behind them and Digger regarded him with a sneer. "How about it Brains? What do you think?"

"Would you stop calling me that!"

"Sure Brains, but how about it?"

"Some kind of poison?"

"Figured that much." He intoned a bit of mystery to his voice. "Should we open it?"

Weed shook his head. "I'm not messing with it."

"Look. If it was all that dangerous it would be sealed. It's not. Just latched." Digger flipped it up to make his point, and then opened the crate lid. Inside was a tubular container.

"Okay," said Brick, "that thing is sealed. I think we should just leave it, like Weed said."

"Pro-tor-porin," read Digger, running his hand over the canister.

Weed mouthed the word. "Pro- means start. Torpor means unresponsive. Some type of knock-out gas?"

Digger and Brick raised their brows at one another.

"Let's leave it," said Brick. "If I get dead, I can't spend my credits."

"What's that sound?" said Weed.

In the distance was rumbling.

"Just thunder," said Digger.

The boys separated to explore the rows of shelves and boxes.

Weed called to the others. "Those credits we're hoping to earn? Don't think we'll be seeing them."

Brick and Digger zigzagged through the rows, trying to locate his reverberating voice.

"Whoa!" said Digger.

Brick gazed up at a stack of huge black cubes. Each was wrapped in clear plastic. "So."

"They're body bags," said Weed. "Lots of 'em."

"Body bags," Brick scoffed.

Digger tapped on the enwrapping plastic, jiggling a foggy zipper pull. "He's right. When my dad shot himself, that's what they carried him out in."

"Jesus!"

"Must be planning on using 'em for something," said Digger.

Weed grimaced. "I'm thinking for clones."

The boys fell silent as they gaped.

Muffled voices echoed from across the building.

"Come on," whispered Digger. He crouched low to the ground and scrambled behind some boxes.

The voices grew louder. "I don't know why we had to put this thing up in the first place."

"Try to get to the door," Digger hissed.

"I mean, you have this whole megasphere thing that's supposed to be empty. Why couldn't we just put the stuff in there?"

"That's why we're the privates and they're the brass."

"It's air conditioned in there I bet. And another thing. I'm sick of hauling all this crap!"

The boys moved forward a few rows.

There was a loud bang as the men dropped their cargo. "Before you know it, they'll be needing it somewhere else. Then we'll be hauling it over there."

The boys could see the sunlight filtering through the door.

"Hey!" yelled one of the men. "Is someone in here?"

Digger scooted outside, and then back in. "There's more of them out there," he whispered.

Weed reached over and pounded his fist on the door.

Brick grabbed at his arm. "What the—?"

Weed yanked his arm free and banged again. "Hello? Is anybody here?" he shouted.

There were hurried footsteps.

Brick stood stupefied. Digger folded his arms and leaned into the doorframe.

"What are you boys doing here?"

"Have you seen a yellow dog?" said Weed. "A yellow lab? Kind of fat?"

"Drools a lot," said Digger.

Brick began to blink.

"This is a government facility," said a no-neck man in green fatigues.

"Sorry," said Weed, "but he jumped out of our car. Ran up this way."

"We haven't seen him," said the other man. "And you boys shouldn't be here."

"Sorry," Weed reiterated.

"Look," said No-neck. "Why don't you leave your number. We'll give you a call if we see him."

Weed fumbled through his pockets. "I don't have anything to write with."

"Here. Use this." No-neck handed him a marker.

"And nothing to write on."

"Just use the side of a box."

Brick and Digger watched their friend scribble a series of numbers.

"Thanks," waved Weed

"Thanks," called Digger, patting Weed's back as they passed through the door.

No-neck called out behind them. "Some sentries you guys! You let these kids get past you. Any of you seen a yellow dog?"

The soldiers shook their heads and mumbled as they pulled cartons and containers from truck beds.

The boys passed through them. "If you see a yellow lab," said Brick, "he answers to *Loser*."

As they neared the roadway, they passed the last truck in the convoy. In the back of the truck was a row of boxes. Inside one box leaned a collection of long, narrow tubes.

Digger climbed in and retrieved one. He jumped from the truck, and then held the container in front of him as he walked.

"What are you doing?" said Weed, looking back nervously.

Brick imitated Digger and came up beside him. They shouldered one another and stepped briskly through the open gates.

"I can't believe you guys!"

They rounded a bend and the trucks disappeared, replaced by a wall of evergreens.

## Chapter 49 - Protorporin

Dobie and Camryn shared a plate of waffles and scrambled eggs.

John passed Mikel the syrup.

Kantz topped off his coffee mug.

Freeman nodded a good morning to his fellow Aarcanians as he entered the room. He scratched at his vanished whiskers.

"The room we use for sessions will be unavailable over the next several weeks," said Kantz.

There was anticipatory silence.

"I've set up a small computer network in there so Freeman can test his programs."

"Let's hear it for Freeman!" Nora cheered.

They broke into applause.

"Our sessions," said Kantz, raising his voice above the fracas, "will now be held in the basement."

Slowly, as each registered his words, the laughter and chatter faded.

"Just kidding," said Kantz. He raised the coffee pot into the air. "As Director of Aarcania, I officially declare, *No more sessions!*"

"Let's hear it for Kantz!" shouted the professor.

They lifted their mugs in a toast.

Kantz joined the others at the table. "I have a friend who'll turn off the air conditioning in the sphere by killing the power. He said AARC's primary electrical link is on the outskirts of the property. Believe it or not, it's protected by an old padlock. So much for high security."

He took a sip from his mug. "Normally shutting off the power would mean losing the lights—the computers as well."

"We'll need the computers," said Dobie.

"Exactly. But my friend says there's a new converter that allows old, plug-in appliances to operate through electromagnetic generation. The way I understand it, a series of waves are generated to locate and identify every appliance and gadget within a specified area. The converter analyzes and logs the various responses and assumes control. Since heating and cooling systems generate distinctive post-pulse waves, it'll allow him to detect and control those systems without disrupting anything else. He said he just installed one in an old high-rise and it worked pretty well."

"What I find hard to believe," said the professor, "is that you have a friend."

"Hard to fathom I know," smiled Kantz. "Now may I continue?"

"Have we ever been able to stop you?"

"Anyway, my friend's son is a plumber. He'll shut off the taps."

They gazed at him blankly.

"The water. He'll shut off the water. But I have a question. Right now, the only open door is the one Camryn came out of. Won't you need more?"

John tossed a bit of metal onto the table. "Pass key. I can go in and unlock any door I find—make as many exits available as possible."

Nora glared at her husband. Her face turned crimson. "Your first responsibility is to us John. Me and Mikel."

"I'm an enforcer Nora. I have two families. One's inside the sphere."

"Fine. I'll be taking care of Mikel—our son." She rose abruptly, and then waited for him to follow. When he didn't, she stormed out of the room.

John frowned, but kept his seat.

"The sphere is over ninety kilometers around," said Kantz. "It's too much for one person to cover."

"Two," said Camryn. "I have a pass key too."

"And we still don't know where most of the exits are," Kantz reminded.

"Oh yes we do!" An out-of-breath Mark rushed into the room. He moved about the table removing dishes and coffee mugs.

"Hey!" shouted Freeman, retrieving his cup from Mark's grasp.

"We know exactly where the exits are, because we now have blueprints." He unrolled a yellowed document across the table.

Kantz tapped his finger on the map key. "Property of the U.S. Army? Where did you get this?"

"The boys who were looking for the exits? They swiped it."

"From whom?" fumed Kantz.

"From soldiers setting up outside the megasphere. Here." He placed a finger on the north parking lot.

"What would the Army be doing—?"

"The boys said they have body bags. Lots of them."

"I think your boys have vivid imaginations," said Kantz. "I haven't seen any soldiers."

"You don't live in town," said Mark.

"This changes everything. I'm a government employee. I can't be involved in this!"

"You've been a government employee through weeks of planning. How does it change anything now?"

"The Army's here. They're handling things. I just don't see the point."

"Do what you want," said Mark. "We'll do the same. Look guys, timetable's moved up. Instead of months we have days. Maybe."

"I think we should trust the Army to do its job," argued Kantz.

"And what do you think they plan to do with body bags?"

"Maybe the Army's on its own rescue mission. Perhaps something happened inside AARC that we don't know about. An illness maybe. One that's devastating the population."

"How likely do you think that is? Something is about to happen and soon."

"I think that's a very presumptuous statement," said Kantz. "You know nothing of what's inside the sphere. Our guests don't even know. They've been out for a while now. Anything could be happening."

"The boys spotted something else," said Mark. "Cases and cases of Protorporin."

Kantz's eyes grew glassy.

"Ring a bell Doc?"

"Ya gonna fill us in?" rumbled Freeman.

"It's an anesthetic gas," said Kantz, "developed for microbiokinetic procedures. Fast-acting. Allows the patient to understand and follow orders, but remain unconscious of pain or trauma. Unpredictable though. Even at low doses the patient often fails to resuscitate."

"They die," said Mark. "That's why Protorporin isn't used any more. Yet the Army's brought tons of it." He looked around the table at the others. "Time frame's changed everyone. If we don't move soon there'll be no one to rescue."

## Chapter 50 - The Key Maker

At the antique store, Mark turned over a plastic figurine to see where it was made. "Figures," he mumbled to himself.

Another customer walked around him, eyeing the object in his hands. Mark acknowledged her with a nod.

Lou called out from the cash register. "Hey Mark. Need any help?"

"Just looking. Need to find a gift for Mom."

"She's been collecting music boxes lately. Next aisle over."

"Thanks."

"There's a nice box with some birds painted on it. She loves song birds."

"Everyone knows more about my mom than I do," he thought. Locating the box, he slowly lifted the lid. A melody tinkled sharply and he quickly closed it.

A bell clanked loudly as the other customer left. Mark wandered to the front door and quietly turned the sign to read "Closed." He approached the register. "Hey Lou."

Lou looked up from his magazine. "Find anything? I might have something in the back."

"Actually I need your expertise." Mark held up a metal key. "What do you make of this?"

"Old, but fairly common. Not worth much if you're looking to sell it."

"What if I want to copy it? Is there a way to do that?"

Lou took the metal slip in his fingers. "In the old days, a person could get in trouble copying this. It's a security key. The originals were the only ones held."

"What about now?"

"Not illegal now. No one uses 'em any more. Everything's facial identification and key pads."

"Let's say I want some copies made. How exactly do I go about it?"

"How many are we talking?" said Lou.

"Dozen maybe."

"That could be expensive. See, you need a specialized piece of equipment to duplicate these things. Then you need someone who knows how to work it. Not to mention some blank keys that haven't been shaped to fit yet."

"With your connections, you think you can find someone to do it?"

"It'll cost you."

"How much are we talking?" said Mark. "Remember I'm a public servant here."

"Depends on why you're duplicating them. If you're planning to market them, figure a fee plus a cut of the profits."

"I'm not looking to sell them."

"Too bad," said Lou. "On something like this, the dupes are worth more than the original—if you market them to kids or at gift shops."

Mark glanced toward the security monitor behind Lou's stool. Another customer approached the door, glanced at the sign, and then marched away shaking her head.

"But you're in luck," said Lou, passing the key back to him. "I happen to have the equipment here. And there's an old instruction book on how to work it. But the book's missing a few pages. It might take me a while to figure it out."

"How long exactly?"

"How soon do you need them?"

"Actually now. Tomorrow at the latest."

"I can try."

"What if I told you it had something to do with AARC? Would that make a difference?"

Lou's jaw dropped. "This is an AARC key?"

Mark glanced over his shoulder, reassuring himself no one was there. "One of the clones you asked about? The ones who passed through? One of them gave it to me."

"How much you want for it?" His tone calmed; deepened. "Keep in mind that old metal keys don't go for much."

"I'm not looking to sell it. Just copy it."

"Will it let you inside AARC? Are you going inside?"

"I just want copies. Let's leave it at that."

"Let me go with you!

"I need to get going," said Mark.

"Look. I'll do it! I'll make the copies. I'll close the store today and just work on this. But clue me in as to what's going on."

"Never mind."

"But I might be able to help. It's between you and me if that's what you're worried about."

"Thanks anyway Lou." He headed for the door.

"If it makes a difference, my key-maker's the only one in sixteen-hundred kilometers. Know that for sure."

Mark stood at the plate glass window. A camouflaged van rumbled by. "Okay," he sighed. "At this point what do we have to lose?"

## Chapter 51 - Cloners

Lou locked the shop. In the storage room behind the register, he pulled several large boxes from teetering stacks. He spilled the boxes' contents across the floor, and then rooted through the debris. He picked up an old knob and key set, still encased in molded plastic. With a grimace, he sliced the clear encasing with a box cutter. "There goes its value."

Lou turned the key in the lock a few times, and then set up his duplicator. He read and reread the instructions, programmed the settings, and then looked for a box of blanks. A yellowed cardboard box read "Quantity 200." By the time he was done practicing the duplicating process, forty-three were spent.

Feeling confident in his new ability, he made thirty copies of the AARC key. He rubbed his face and looked at the mess around him. "I'll do more in the morning."

He took a meal at the diner, gulping down cup after cup of coffee. "Hope you plan to leave a big tip," said Tammy, pouring him yet another.

At home, Lou leaned back in his easy chair with his computer in his lap. A bug-eyed dog smiled up at him. Lou reached over and patted its head. "Too few people for such a large rescue. Mark might argue, but he'll thank me later."

He tapped at his keyboard, contacting AARC chat rooms and Cloner groups.

> *They're alive! Confirmed clones living within the sphere. Plans to bring them out. Can someone supply sunscreen? How about hats? tents? sleeping bags? bottled water? extra clothing? Anyone a doctor or nurse? Anyone have a camper or trailer to serve as a medical station? Does anyone own a motel, or have extra rooms where the clones can stay? Duration of stay indeterminate. Anyone have access to a bus?*

Word spread rapidly. Cloners called Cloners in the middle of the night.

"Did you hear—?"

"Are you going?"

"Do you want to—?"

"Why not?"

The Blue Sky Motel, the only one in fifty kilometers, filled to capacity that very night, the first time in nearly a decade.

Motels and camping resorts filled two-hundred kilometers away. Sledge hammers destroyed barricades blocking the east, south, and west lots, which rapidly filled with tents and trailers.

In the sphere's north parking lot, incoming campers passed outgoing convoys. Soldiers paced nervously in front of the tin can, scratching their heads. "Some kind of Cloners convention?"

As a precaution, the captain in charge added locks to the storage building and a loose collection of guards, armed with impressive but empty machine guns. Teenage girls giggled at the soldiers. They offered the men cold soda and the occasional coy peck on the cheek.

Mark followed the stream of vehicles. He wandered through the crowds, speaking with anyone who didn't smirk at the uniform. "What's going on?"

He drove to the open emergency exit and, with Dobie's help, covered it with brush.

At the west entrance, they chased children from the detainment corridor, and then hanged the leaning glass door.

Cloners watched them work. Many huddled nearby, hoping to glimpse an actual Aarcanian. Some staked out the best vantage points with blankets and folding chairs.

The doors were chained and a notice posted. "Authorized personnel only. Entry beyond this point may contaminate facility and residents."

When so many visitors filled the north parking lot that trucks could no longer pass, word leaked back to the general.

> *No additional supplies able to reach target. Unexpected Cloners convention delaying project. Crowds in tens of thousands. Advise postponement.*

The general fumed before replying.

> *Request civilians cease and desist north parking lot only. Diplomacy vital. Continue storage detail as before.*

Reluctantly the soldiers cleared the north lot of fans. Huge metal frames were transported in, and a tarp-covered tunnel constructed. It ran from the tin can to a hydraulic door on the north side of the megasphere.

The general called in a select group of soldiers to assure his mission's success, and then issued a new edict.

*Equipment will be transported from the storage building to the north entrance in covered vehicles only. No vehicle is to be loaded or unloaded outside of the tunnel's confines. There is no need to excite convention-goers. Let them enjoy their festivities. You do your duty.*

In town, businessmen recruited their own reinforcements. Relatives drove in from surrounding counties to help with the free-spending crowds.

A line trailed from the diner, down the sidewalk, and around a corner. Inside, Cloners and soldiers regarded one another curiously. Erv, exhausted by long hours in a steam-filled kitchen, gave up making the world's best fried chicken for making the world's most adequate. He tossed wings, backs, and thighs onto thick white plates lined in a row.

Lou asked his brother to take over sales at the antique shop. AARC memorabilia was selling particularly well, although Lou was more reluctant than ever to part with it. In the back of the store, he managed to make seventy more usable duplicates. Mark hadn't requested them, but if they weren't needed, they'd make great souvenirs for the tourists.

Just outside of town, a temporary human corral was equipped with tents, fold-out cots, and portable commodes. It offered a place for over-enthusiastic revelers to sleep it off.

The bartender at Smitty's was amassing a collection of useful and potentially lucrative articles left behind by customers—wallets, knapsacks, handheld computers, and even a yo-yo. Donnelson played with it after hours, sitting atop a barstool with a sweating bottle of beer.

Vendors lined the road leading to AARC. They sold everything from reproductions of antique cigarettes—which were developing a cult following—to fast food, toilet tissue, and boxed sets of twin clone dolls.

Here and there along the road were pockets of reporters. Some reported from the yellow line in the center of the street, sound men and cameramen waving passersby around. Others gave up reporting among the throng and teetered atop their vans, the dome of AARC creating a backdrop.

Weed, Brick, and Digger, fearing they'd never see the two thousand credits, found other ways to earn money. They dashed through the ocean of visitors, running errands for those not wishing to wade through crowds or lose prime camp sites.

Chunks of the AARC walls were being chiseled away and pocketed as souvenirs, or sold to those less daring. "At this rate," grumbled Mark, "the clones inside won't need to come out."

John discreetly recruited a team of twenty from among the crowd. The goal of the team was to enter the sphere disguised as technicians, and then open all doors impeding freedom. Each volunteer was armed with a pass key and a data pad containing the blueprints. Each was warned of the deadly risk posed by the Protorporin. Some fed on the danger; others on curiosity; a few on their hatred of government.

The team members filtered into the complex over several nights, using the open emergency exit. Freeman gave them pointers on how to behave. A Cloner with a mail-order uniform business had khakis expressed in, slightly modified to Aarcanian dress code.

In Nora's mind, her husband had deserted her. The veins pulsed in her neck and she glared at anyone daring to address her. "It was his idea to leave AARC in the first place. He'd rather die in a gas chamber than live out here with his family—in Kantz's damned prison!"

Mark's mother moved out of her house until "all of this AARC nonsense dies down." A visit to her sister in Macon was long overdue. She left Mark in charge of the house, who in turn passed the keys to Nora. With her angry outbursts, wide-eyed stare, and never-slowing breath, Kantz agreed it might be best.

Mikel of course went with her. Each day he imagined his father at the door, bedraggled in his technicians' uniform, holding the hand of a smiling Anna. "My dad's a hero," he thought, but he kept it to himself. The very words *Dad* or

*John* sent his mother into a tirade of curses. He avoided her wrath, and tried to ignore the cauldron when it frothed over. He crayoned policemen and firefighters in a coloring book Mark gave him.

## Chapter 52 - The Plan

Kantz and the professor stood at the stove, each with a frying pan in hand. They debated ownership of the carton's last eggs.

Heavy footsteps trudged up behind them. "We have a problem," said Mark.

There was clatter on the stairs as Camryn and Dobie made their way down.

"Do I smell bacon?" said Dobie.

"It's on the table," said Kantz.

"We have a problem," Mark repeated.

"Which problem would that be?" said Kantz, pressing his thumb into an egg shell. "The circus that's surrounding AARC? The fact that Freeman's still testing programs?"

"Hey!" Freeman protested from the table. "I'm doin' the best I can, considerin' I have to dumb down this new-fangled equipment."

"Or the fact that half of John's team has already been detected *and* ejected? They should have taken phones. Then at least we'd know what was happening."

"They'd attract attention," said Dobie. "Phones don't exist in the sphere."

The professor frowned at Kantz's sizzling eggs. "Just tell us what's wrong now," he said.

"The convoys," said Mark. "There haven't been any going or coming for twenty-four hours."

"That's good news," said Kantz.

"Except it might mean they've completed step one. With step two being the obvious. I think we should go in tonight."

"I'm not sure the program is ready," said Freeman.

"We'll go with what we have then."

"I still have to test it."

"Look," said Mark, scattering duplicate keys across the table. "Lou went ahead and made these."

"So," said Kantz, scrambling his eggs with a spatula.

"The rest of us can go in and distribute them to as many people as possible, along with copies of the blueprints. It'll be me, Dobie—you're fine here Professor."

"I'm going!" he said indignantly. "Granted I'm a little slower than you are—"

"You can go with me," said Dobie.

"Us," said Camryn taking Dobie's arm.

Mark shook his head. "Too dangerous. There's the Protorporin. And we don't know what the reaction will be inside."

"Stay," urged Dobie.

"Who do you have without me?" Camryn argued. "Kantz is coordinating things out here. There's Tom—"

"I wouldn't count on him," said Kantz, slipping his eggs onto a plate. "He says he's not sure it's any better out here than it is in there."

"Okay," said Camryn, "so you have Mark, the professor—"

"And me," said Freeman sheepishly. "I'll go in once I run the program. Added a few commands that should open all the hydraulic doors."

"So four definites and one maybe?" said Camryn. "I think you need me."

"Some of John's crew is still inside," said Mark. That makes fourteen definites."

Camryn hissed a sigh.

"Stay," said Dobie. He gazed into her eyes. "If not for me, for the future."

"Okay," said Mark, halting the conversation with Camryn safely put. "We go in tonight then. Freeman can take the west side; go in through detainment. Dobie; Professor—you go in from the south, through the emergency exit already open. Lou and I will try the east side. Lou's got an old laser saw that might cut an opening. If not, we'll come around and join the two of you."

Camryn squeezed Dobie's arm. "What if you don't come back? What if—?"

"I'll be all right," said Dobie. He pulled her close and placed a hand on her belly. "*We'll* be all right."

## Chapter 53 - Life or Death

The general planned the assault for midday, when the Cloners would be up and moving about, their activities masking the Army's own.

Notices were posted and distributed to the crowds.

*Soldiers are practicing with live rounds. The north section is restricted until further notice.*

Small explosives and artillery were prepared for effect, and to mask screams inside should they grow too loud.

***

It was still dark when Freeman marched down the detainment corridor, a map tucked under his arm. He turned at the echo of footsteps.

"I'm going with you," said Camryn.

"Dobie'll have a fit!"

"Dobie's responsible for giving them free thought. I'm just as responsible for denying them. I'm not denying them any more."

"No time to argue about it now," Freeman huffed.

They entered the little computer room. Freeman sat at the keyboard and executed a long series of commands. Throughout the sphere, hydraulic doors squealed, hissed, and moaned apart.

Inside the sphere, people awakened to find the doors of their cubicles standing wide open. "What the—?"

Couples scrambled for clothing or covered themselves with bed sheets. Children skipped up and down the halls in birthday suits or gray pajamas. "Get back in here! Right now!" scolded their parents.

Computers were booted in unison as people searched for explanations. The combined pull generated a wave not recognized by the electromagnetic converter. For the first time in Aarcanian history, the entire sphere went black. Petrified screams reverberated throughout the building, and then fell away as some lights flickered on.

In the north parking lot, a sentry awoke from nodding slumber. He listened, and then shrugged it off as a dream. He climbed to his feet and patrolled the north lot, making sure no one else was awake to report his dozing.

Inside the sphere, families huddled on beds or in corridors with neighbors. Some clicked away at keyboards, trying to make sense of it all. A message appeared on their screens.

*Ventilation and water systems not functioning. Please download the attached maps to your data pads. Proceed in an orderly fashion to the emergency compounds indicated. When the systems are repaired, you will be permitted to return to your quarters and assigned duties.*

*By Order of the Chief Enforcement Officers*

Following the downloaded maps as best they could, scattered bands of Aarcanians navigated unknown corridors. They rode elevators and climbed down stairs to unfamiliar levels. Others stood in their cubicle doorways, watching their neighbors pass.

Pockets of blackness were scattered throughout the sphere, wherever the electromagnetic wave had failed to penetrate. The unusually well-prepared, who kept their emergency spotlights charged, carried them into corridors. Long shadows climbed the walls and stretched onto ceilings. Where people gathered, the mouths on the shadows moved. The hands waved and gestured.

Where doors to emergency exits remained locked, evacuees milled about in confusion, eventually moving on to the next destination.

Hours passed and the air inside grew hotter; stuffier. The reaction to locked doors intensified. "Where do we go now? How far is the next one?" Panic ensued and people ran.

Where one group merged with another, the atmosphere grew aggressive—competitive. People prodded and pushed, elbowed and punched. Older and slower individuals were left behind or trampled in their attempt to keep up. Parents dragged their children over bodies, some still twitching with fragmented life.

Dobie and the professor meandered through corridors, up and down levels, referring to their maps but never quite sure where they were. They guided passing throngs as best they could. "I never realized how many—" said Dobie.

The professor stared at a mangled victim, and his lip quivered. The white hair reminded him of himself. "It's not a humane death."

Dobie stood blinking, transfixed by the body himself. He felt dizzy as they staggered away; dizzier still as they rounded a corner. More bodies. Lots of them.

The bloodied corpse of a man covered that of his wife. Dobie turned away. He pressed his palms to a wall, and then leaned into it. His face blanched and vomit dribbled from his mouth. He slid to the floor.

"We should go," the professor quavered. "Before we're trampled too."

"They're panicking." Dobie pulled himself up and leaned over the body of a young woman. Reaching down, he took her cold, limp wrists in his hands. He pulled. "They'll stay calmer if they don't see this."

Together they pulled several victims into vacant modules. One moaned softly as Dobie pushed it against a wall.

The professor took his son by the elbow. "Come on Dobie. There are too many. And there are others we can save." He jingled the keys in his pockets. "We still have some to distribute."

Where doors to exits were open, things went more smoothly. The Aarcanians crawled into fresh air and breathed deeply, glad to escape the staleness within.

Crowds of Cloners cheered as they emerged. Some took Aarcanians by the arm, guiding them through the throngs to awaiting cars, trucks, and vans. Horns honked in celebration.

The noise leaked over and around the sphere to the north parking lot. The captain in charge ordered his lieutenant to investigate, and then called the general.

"It's o-three-hundred hours Captain! It better be important!"

"Clones are leaving the sphere sir. Cloners are helping them."

"Go in now!"

Soldiers geared up in gas masks and protective suits. Trucks, filled with empty body bags, awaited deployment in the canvas-covered tunnel.

"There's just one problem, General. Power isn't reaching the ventilation system. It isn't working."

"How can that be? That system is fourth generation. It never malfunctions!"

"Apparently it does sir."

"Then make it work, damn it! This mission must be completed. Now! Understand?"

Where emergency exits stood open, a handful of Cloners filtered into the sphere between exiting Aarcanians. They pressed along corridor walls, gawking at the "real live clones" passing by. Now and again a camera flashed.

Some of the interlopers entered cubicles, pocketing anything readily portable as a souvenir. In some cubicles, they found Aarcanians hiding in closets and under beds. They laughed as the residents darted past them for the door.

Freeman and Camryn continued their brisk march through look-alike corridors.

"Where the hell are we?" growled Freeman. He stretched a map between his arms. "Keep goin' this way it'll be forever before we reach our first compound!" They stood in front of a closed door. "Says this here's an elevator."

Before the button could be pressed, the door opened. People poured out, nearly knocking them down in the process. Freeman motioned the drove toward the exit, but they were already on their way.

"Looks like they don't need our help. What do ya say we getchya outa here?"

Camryn's lips drew tight. She stepped onto the elevator. "Coming?"

Freeman followed with a protesting growl.

It felt as tough they were floating. The door to the elevator opened and they stepped forward, only to be swept backward by an engulfing mass. They found themselves plastered to the back of the box.

Freeman grumbled, and then roared. "Get the F— outa my way!"

The stunned crowd grew silent.

"Get outa my way you goddamn F—in' assholes!"

The crowd slowly parted for them to squeeze through.

"There," said Freeman, pulling Camryn out with him. "Ain't no reason fer ya to panic!" he yelled. "There's plenty of time for everyone to leave."

The elevator door closed as he spoke. The light on the button darkened.

More people stood in the hallway, waiting in a jagged line for the next available ride.

"Everyone here will get out safely," yelled Freeman. "*If* ya don't act crazy."

"Look who's calling whom crazy," someone yelled.

Camryn gazed at the faces around her. "He's right," she shouted. "Everyone here will be safe. Is there anybody willing to assist others? To help guide them out?"

A few men and women stepped hesitantly forward. "What do we do?"

Freeman called to the line of people. "Anyone here got data pads? The downloaded maps?"

A handful of data pads was passed forward.

Freeman addressed the recruits. "Some of the exits on there will be open. Some won't. There'll be a door blockin' 'em. If ya find one of those, this'll open it." He handed out keys while Camryn explained how they worked. With nods and chatter, the volunteers dispersed.

"Our job's done," said Freeman. "You should head home."

Camryn shook her head. "We'll go inside cubicles. Make sure everyone's out. You go that way. I'll go this. If I don't meet up with you again, I'll see you at the house."

On the east side of the megasphere, Lou was cutting through an exposed exit door, albeit slowly, with his antique laser saw. As he and Mark worked, Cloners collected around them and watched.

An arm-sized hole was finally achieved. Mark reached through and pushed down the door latch. The door opened to reveal a pair of smaller doors. He pushed, and they swung apart. "We're going in through a cabinet," he laughed.

In the corridor beyond, people milled about looking for the indicated exit.

"Hey!" Lou beckoned, "Over here!"

The Aarcanians spilled toward them.

"Through the cabinet," Mark directed.

Cheers resounded from outside.

Mark and Lou ran down the hallway, heading for the next exit on their map. Lou peeked into a cubicle and frowned.

"What's wrong?"

"It's just so—primitive," said Lou.

"What did you expect?"

"Something more advanced than us I guess."

Throughout the sphere, there was a deep, reverberating hum, and then loud echoing clicks.

Cool air swept across Camryn's face. The ventilation system was working.

From somewhere far away, arose the screams of a panicked horde.

"The gas!" thought Camryn. She ran through the corridors, directing families and coaxing people out of hiding.

"Hurry. Stay calm. You have plenty of time." She hoped they did.

She went up a level. An enforcer blocked her way.

"Return to your cubicle," he commanded.

"It's imperative that everyone proceed to the emergency compounds," said Camryn.

"That directive is invalid—the product of a saboteur. Please return to your cubicle. By order of the authorities."

Camryn straightened herself. Her eyes glowered. She looked directly into his. "I'm a Chief Enforcement Officer. As such my authority overrides yours."

He snickered. "Please proceed to your cubicle miss."

"I'm hereby directing you to assist in this evacuation."

"And you are hereby notified that you are under arrest. Please come with me."

"I'll do no such thing! You're breaching the direct order of a CEO!"

Another round of screams arose from someplace distant.

"Those are your people," said Camryn. "The ones you vow to protect. My people! I am ordering you to assist in this evacuation now!"

"If you won't come with me willingly—" He reached for her arm, but she jerked it away.

"I'll need your number Enforcer. Your actions will not go unnoticed—or unpunished."

He hesitated. "Its ten-forty-seven miss—ma'am."

"I depend on you to enforce my directives. Obviously there's a flaw in your engineering. One that will be corrected in the future."

He squinted at her. "You don't look like a CEO to me."

"Tell me Enforcer Ten-forty-seven, what does a CEO look like?"

"I—"

"We don't go parading ourselves about now, do we?"

"No ma'am."

"I hope you've downloaded the maps as I've instructed."

He touched a satchel strapped to his waist. "I have them right here sir—ma'am."

"Then get these people out of here!"

"Yes ma'am." He walked briskly down the corridor, looking back anxiously.

She watched him go, her legs shaking beneath her. Another round of screams sent her scrambling through the corridors.

How long had she been in? Hours? A day? The screams were getting louder—nearer. She found a stairwell and descended to another level.

She didn't know where she was. She found a module with a data pad and computer. Camryn shoved the back of the data pad into a port, and downloaded the maps.

In the corridor a pregnant woman waddled toward her. Camryn met her halfway.

"How do we get out of here?" said the woman.

Camryn handed her the pad. "The maps are there. Take it with you."

"But what about you?"

"I'll be fine." She hoped so anyway.

Camryn zigzagged from one cubicle and module to the next. As the screams grew louder she found fewer people hiding.

"Hey! Hold up there!"

She turned to find Freeman swaggering toward her.

"I think we should get outa here," he said. "One floor up they're droppin' in the halls. Ain't gettin' back up either."

"But there could be others—"

"Maybe, but Dobie'd be mighty disappointed if I let you—"

"Dobie!" She ran short-breathed to greet him.

He staggered toward her. "Come on," he panted, taking her arm. "It's coming this way."

"Where's your dad?"

"He's right behind me."

They stopped abruptly and looked down the corridor. At the end of it, the professor waved to them. He clutched at his chest and his smile vanished. He dropped.

Dobie stood dazed, and then bolted toward him. Camryn gripped his arm, pulling back with all her strength.

"I have to—"

But Freeman was at the old man's side. With the professor draped over his shoulders, he took a few steps, and collapsed.

"No Dobie! You can't go!" said Camryn, tears streaming down her face. "I love them too, but it's too late." She yanked on him as he gaped. "Please Dobie! For the sake of your child. *His* grandchild!"

Dobie looked at her and blinked. "You shouldn't be here," he mumbled. He grabbed her arm and they ran.

"Where do we go now?" she gasped.

A group of people funneled out of a stairwell.

"Let's follow them," said Dobie.

"I don't think we have a choice."

They were swept along by the channeling throng. They could no longer see the walls for the people around them. They locked arms to steady themselves and stay on their feet. Arms and heads stirred beneath the soles of their shoes. The shifting crush of people seemed never ending; ever moving. It suddenly jammed, pushed them back, pressed them down and forward. They were on their knees, Camryn grasping for Dobie's legs. Hands reached through the mash of people, pulling them up. Flashlights blinded them, but they were out!

"Here come some more!" someone yelled.

"Is my son there?" a woman cried. "Kenny? Kenny?"

There was no reply.

"Has anyone seen my son? I told him not to go in!"

A man barreled through the crowd. "The army trucks! They're filled with bodies! What's going on in there?"

The woman searching for Kenny elbowed her way through. She headed for the roadway.

Camryn and Dobie stumbled through the mob. People gaped at them as they passed, wondering if they were Aarcanians or simply Cloners like themselves. They passed vendors and walked around reporters blocking body-laden trucks. Cloners climbed onto the vans and tore off the tarps.

A woman climbed into a truck bed; unzipped bag after bag. A camera zoomed in. "Oh God! Kenny!"

Camryn and Dobie walked for hours in a hazy morning light, intermittently resting in the dew-laden grass. As noon approached, they walked slowly up the gravel drive and into the house. The door smack behind them was comforting.

From the kitchen came the aroma of coffee. "You're back!" said Kantz. "Where's the profess—"

Dobie's eyes reddened.

Camryn shook her head. "Freeman too."

"I'm sorry. I'm very sorry."

"The others," said Camryn. "Have you seen them?"

"Lou came by. Said Mark and John are safe. John was detected right away. Spent most of his time in a holding cell."

Dobie's legs trembled as he took a seat. "A lot of people died in there."

Kantz studied his face and slid into the chair next to him. "But because you risked your life, a lot of people lived."

Dobie gripped the sides of his head with his hands.

Kantz's voice hoarsened, as he put a hand on Dobie's shoulder. "I wish I'd done more. I wish—" He swallowed dryly, gulping guilt and regret.

***

Mark stopped the pickup in front of his mother's house. "You going to be okay?"

John nodded as he climbed out. "I'll be fine."

"When things settle down, we'll see what's what."

"Thanks," said John. He stood on the stoop, watching the truck pull away.

Behind him, the screen door flew open. Mikel beamed and glowed; then seemed suddenly disheartened. "Where's Anna?"

"She and her family are safe. They're sheltered at a school just a few minutes away." He looked into his son's glimmering eyes. "No hello for your dad?"

Mikel hugged his father as hard as he could. "You're a hero! Just like a fireman!"

They stepped into the living room. The television blared. "It's estimated that two-hundred thousand people may have inhabited the megasphere. At this time the number of survivors is unknown."

"John?"

He turned toward the familiar voice.

"I thought— I was afraid— I saw on the news—"

He stepped toward her uncertainly, the corners of his mouth trembling. They embraced, and his eyes closed. She was hugging him back.

Thank you for reading *The Clones of Langston.*

If you enjoyed the book, please stop by

http://ClonesofLangston.com

to tell others.

You can also leave reviews at Amazon.com

and BarnesandNoble.com.

LaVergne, TN USA
07 March 2011
219173LV00002B/8/P